TURTLE POINT PRESS

BOOKS & CO.

𝓜

HELEN MARX BOOKS

THE

DEPOSITION

OF

FATHER

McGREEVY

THE
DEPOSITION
OF
FATHER
McGREEVY

BRIAN O'DOHERTY

TURTLE POINT PRESS

BOOKS & CO.

HELEN MARX BOOKS

NEW YORK

Design and composition by
Wilsted & Taylor Publishing Services

Library of Congress
Cataloging-in-Publication Data

O'Doherty, Brian.
The deposition of Father McGreevy /
Brian O'Doherty.—1st ed.
p.   cm.
ISBN: 1-885983-39-5
Library of Congress Number:
98-61034
1. Ireland—Fiction.
2. Priests—Fiction.
I. Title.
PS3565.D46D47   1999
813'.54
QBI98-1301

CONTENTS

FOR LYN CHASE

AND

FOR RUDOLF BARANIK

PROLOGUE

I t's a mystery why a pub draws a set of people and gets a name for itself. Suddenly, it's the place to be—until some other pub replaces it. The Antelope in London has had a bit of a shine to it for several years now. The beer, apart from the Guinness, was as good as you'll find, and the owner decent enough, though he wasn't too keen to see me after he'd had to call a taxi a few times to bring me home.

I was well on that day when Augustus John came in. He always came in as if Lear had found a door on the heath. He had some Polish fellow with him by the name of Felix. It was Felix this and Felix that and by the end of the night we were all drinking toasts to Felix, who was as convenient an excuse as any. John, a large, shaggy animal, presided as he always did, always the center of attention. He's a fine looking man, and if I looked like him, I'd think the world owed me its attention too.

"Oh my God, I don't believe it, is that Augustus John himself?" said Séamus when John came in. Séamus is my wife's cousin from Listowel. He'd been a medical student at University College, Dublin, for ten years, a dark, thin fellow with a pale face and a taste for painting. I always looked him up for a drink when I went back to Dublin, even after my wife got tired of picking me up and bringing me home. When she left me for good, he never held it against me. Séamus had peculiar drinking habits, pale sherry after pale sherry. He drank in that determined and careful way that some Irishmen do, including myself, I suppose. The story he was telling me was beyond belief.

He'd been down in Kerry on his holidays with another medical student from Dingle, who'd picked up this story about a dead village up in the mountains. "There's more than a few of those," I said.

"This is different," he said. "There was a trial that shamed the town. They still won't talk about it."

Once he'd got my interest, neither would he. He sat there leaning forward, surrounding his drink, cuddling the details he wouldn't share with me.

"When did this happen?"

PROLOGUE

"Years ago," he said, "at the start of the War."

"But that's only fifteen years ago," I said.

"So?" he said with a shrug. He waited for me to order another drink.

"This priest was defrocked," he said. "A lot of women died. They never got to the bottom of it."

He wouldn't utter another word, only nursing his damned sherry and nodding sagely and mutely at my questions. Well, as sure as my name is William Maginn an editor is an editor and closer to his magazine than to his wife. I was taking the night train the next day to Hollyhead and the boat to Dún Laoghaire, so I thought there would be no harm in looking into it. I meant to go over for a week but as it turned out I spent a month traipsing around. I was born near Dingle—Irish was the first language I spoke—but I've no great love for it. When I got the whole story it wasn't right for the magazine, and I'm not sure who or what it's right for. But everyone can make of it what they will. You can tell the same story to five people and if you asked them to tell it back, you'd have five different stories.

I hadn't been back in Kerry for years—the family moved to Wicklow when I was sixteen, and I was never happy at the thought of going back to it. As they say, home isn't where the heart is, it's where you understand the sons of bitches. I made my life, such as it is, here in London, and I'm lucky to be doing what I want to do, editing a "literary" magazine, pushing young poets uphill, squeezing novelists for a part of their next opus, and soliciting occasional political and social commentary from those addicted to it, while making a show that the very epicenter of the world was located precisely where my desk met the floor. I had no notion who this mysterious priest was until I got to Dingle, where many genealogical inquiries—everyone in Ireland is related to everyone else—converged in the photograph on my mother's side-table. She used to dust that frame lovingly, hug it to her bosom, and say what a lovely man he was, so handsome and a near saint. Never a word out of my father, of course. Fr. Hugh was a second cousin of my mother's once removed, but he lived vividly in my mother's emotional past.

"I hope he's happy down in Kerry," she'd say. "Wouldn't I love to see him again!"

A necessarily sublimated passion, I imagine. Sometimes the dark passions of Irish housewives come right up against the white circlet of the Roman collar, and stay there. My mother, now that I can think of her from the ruins of my own untidy passions, was man-crazy and a devout Catholic. In another culture she'd have afforded a great deal of pleasure—as well as mischief—to many. I'm glad she's not alive to hear the story of Fr. Hugh's fall from grace.

The answers were mainly voiced from the shards and fragments of my mother's family scattered in the vicinity of Dingle and North Kerry. The family wasn't very forthcoming with details, and those outside the family met my questions with a variety of stares, with—from the more sociable—mumbles that "some things are best left alone." The pub is a great place for unlocking a few secrets. With my desire for real draught Guinness, it was no hardship to take my place at the same stool in the same Dingle pub every night. I was anxious to find Fr. Hugh, but no one knew a thing about him. "He's somewhere up north" was the closest I got. He was up north sure enough when I found him. He was also down under six feet of earth, his name on a small marker let into the ground. No headstone.

Putting facts together out of rumor and silence isn't easy. I found out where two of the mountain people—Muiris and Old Biddy—had been put away. I was giving up when I got my hands on Fr. Hugh's deposition, if that's what you'd call it. It was lost and I found it by

accident. I'd been long enough in the town to have
made no friends. Questions are never welcome down in
the country. I'd made a sort of a friend in the local doctor, a Dr. McKenna, and after I met him we took our
drinks into the snug every night for a week. A powerful
force seems to propel some men away from their wives
and towards the warm proximities of the pub. We
walked back together each night after the pub closed.
There was still light in the sky well after ten. Once he
stopped and pointed up towards the mountains.

"That's where it happened," he said. "That's where
the village was. Don't you see it?" he said, irritated,
when all I could see was a whale of a mountain with
other ones shouldering into it. "See the ridge there," he
said, "and the purple rocks?"

"Oh, yes," I said to satisfy him, "the very place."

Next night we were back at the old stand. The doctor
drank with a deliberation which slowed as he pro-
gressed. It was after completion of a slow-motion cir-
cuit from hand to glass to lip to draught to return of
glass to table, accompanied by a discreet inversion and
savouring of the lips, that I got the goods.

"There was a whole thing of Fr. Hugh's, poor man,"
he said, "a deposition a mile long. He gave it to the local
policeman without a solicitor or anyone else around. It

wasn't allowed in court. I don't know what happened to it."

Of course I was down at the court house and into the records office the next day, where I didn't get much of a welcome. There were two people there, a man in double-breasted blue serge and tie, as thin and bent as a question mark with glasses, and his assistant, a young girl also with glasses over bright eyes with a figure of definite pneumatic possibilities. I got nowhere with the court clerk or keeper of records (I never knew his exact title) and before he left at twelve on the dot and saw me lingering, he informed the young woman that he had done all that could be done for me. I changed my story for her. I said I was searching for title to a house my mother had left my oldest brother, and that I wished to contest his ownership.

"But then it isn't here you should be at all," she said.

We got on so well I asked her if she'd have a drink with me that night. She said her boyfriend would kill her. So we laughed and chatted and I suggested she let me have a peek at the old records downstairs for just a minute before his lordship came back.

"It's a mess down there," she said. "We haven't got round to straightening it up yet. Anyway, if I let you down there, he'll kill me."

"God above," I said, "there's a lot a people want to kill you around here. It's away with me to London you should come."

"Now wouldn't that be wonderful," she said, "but that'll never happen."

"Ah, you'd never know," I said, and before a minute was gone I was down in the old records room, which was a chaos of unfiled folders, half-open drawers, and sealed boxes. My heart sank. The young one stayed at the top of the stairs looking down at me, then over her shoulder to make sure her boss wasn't on his way.

"I told you it was a mess," she said. The phone rang and she disappeared.

I found Fr. Hugh's deposition by closing my eyes. It was so hopeless that I did a sampling at each of eight points turning clockwise from the center of the room, eyes closed. When I opened my eyes at the fourth sampling I had the records of one Peter O'Mahoney, who got six months hard labor for assault while under the influence. Next to it was a thick bent stuffed yellow envelope which I knew was it before I put my hand on it, if you can explain that. I put it under my shirt next to my skin and closed my coat over it and was up those stairs light as a feather. I had a grin a mile wide on my face.

"Nothing doing," I said, "but maybe I'll see you to-night."

"Maybe you will and maybe you won't," she said.

I ran into her boss on the main street coming out of a shop painted an eye-splitting orange, and gave him a big hallo. No response. I was on the train to Dublin within the hour.

Fr. Hugh's long soliloquy is clear enough to me. He was talking to a policeman, who obviously had no experience in taking depositions. Fr. Hugh seems to forget his listener more often than he remembers him. He tells his story in his own way, which might be hard for some to understand, so I will assist the reader with comments on Fr. McGreevy's narrative when I deem it appropriate. I leave it to the careful reader to tolerate, perhaps welcome my intrusions which are designed to be useful, thereby avoiding the sententiousness with which footnotes tend to fondle themselves in the page's basement. I shall not ascend "above the line" until my meetings with two of the protagonists in the final stages of this book. Slothful and careless readers should ignore these footnotes and stay with the good Father, above the line.

I'm not sure what it all tells us beyond the fact that there are some good people, some bad people, and a lot of people who are one or the other depending on the circumstances. And the day that that becomes news, there will be a blue moon. After all this, I should tell you again who I am. My name is William Maginn, editor of *Fraser's Magazine*, and a distant relative of the good Father.

THE PRIEST'S STORY

You'll have to let me tell it in my own way, or I won't talk to you at all. I'll be as honest as I can in this deposition, and the word can't help but bring to mind the Deposition of Our Lord Himself from the Cross. For with every word out of my mouth, it's putting me up on the cross you are, make no mistake about that.

Here I am suspended from saying Mass by the Church to which I gave my life as my mother's only son. And think not of my agony but of my mother's pain, a pain she shares with Mary herself for her only Son. If it's penance you're talking about, penance speaks of a guilt that before God I do not feel in my heart. For the circumstances were such that I do more than forgive myself. I take humble pride in the fact that I kept a Christian community together in its extremity, and prevented it, through the grace of God as conveyed by his sacraments, from falling into barbarity. That should not be forgotten.

Paddy MacArdle's son, when he was here at the police station the other day, made reference to "my role in this degraded nightmare." I wouldn't have expected that from the son of a man who is a distant cousin of my mother's and a decent man from the day he was born. But I can expect little understanding from lawyers of every stripe, including Paddy's son, now that he has come back from Dublin to enlighten us. Justice wears a blindfold so that she can't see lies and falsehood overcome truth on her scales. The scales drop from my own eyes when I see the hatred offered me from this town, let alone the great world outside where the newspapers say that I've disgraced the cloth, giving comfort to every enemy this country ever had by proving that we are a degraded people. Truly, this breaks my heart. For if young MacArdle spoke about a nightmare, the nightmare was not up in the mountains. It is here, around me at every turn. That village up there was as decent a community of God-fearing people as you would find on a long day's march.

How did it start, you ask me, as many have, but never a moment does anyone believe my answer, or if they do,

THE PRIEST'S STORY

I can tell from their faces that no explanation of mine will ever change their opinion of what went on. When Bishop O'Farrell, God rest him, sent me up there thirty years ago, I swear he forgot me the instant I passed out of his sight. Nor did he or anyone else pay much heed to the souls in my charge, only when they came down for hurling matches and fairs and the like. And never a great welcome for them either, so dark were they in face and feature. There was talk about how they wouldn't return a greeting. But how can you give back what was never offered, when all they met were suspicious looks? Only one shop in the whole town would give them credit. On fair day, everyone turned up their noses at their few sheep and cattle. Maybe they weren't fattened up like others, but there's little grazing up on the mountain. I remember those young fellows lounging outside Moriarty's pub who never did an honest day's work, jeering at old Paddy, God rest him, when he tried to sell his cow in Irish. They hadn't had their ears boxed enough at National School.

It was the terrible winter of '39—only two years ago but it seems an age—that began it, as you well know. We were so cut off we didn't see the face of a stranger until May. Maybe there were some attempts at relief,

I'll grant you. When the men came down to the town that summer, I'll guarantee that it wasn't for love of you. And you know the welcome they got.

Why did we stay up there? Why does anyone stay where they are? Because their fathers were there before them, and their fathers before that. Do I have to explain that to anyone who makes a living from a bit of ground, if living you can call it? Do you ask that of the people on the Blaskets? Oh, indeed there would have been a great welcome for us if we moved down here! There are times when I find it hard to live by my vows of charity when I have been offered none, even by the ministers of God Himself, in Whose charity and grace I will trust until the day I die, and may that not be far distant.

It was that first winter that laid the groundwork for it, make no mistake about that. The wind was cruel that winter. Buried in snow we were. We never saw another soul but ourselves from dawn till dusk. But the calamity the Lord visited upon us passes understanding. It was Máire Rua who went first, the only fiery head among all those dark ones. We put her by the hob for the heat and she died there, where she'd spent most of her waking hours. The cold was such you could hear your own bones clicking against each other. We kept the fire burning as best we could. The turf was sodden so it gave out more smoke than heat. Not a one of us could tell what was wrong with her, except that she couldn't breathe right. I'll never forget the terrible look of concentration on her face trying to keep the spark of life going. Near the end, she didn't know Muiris—her husband—at all, though he never left her. The women gave her inhalations of honey and spirits, though where they got the honey is a mystery. You'd never suspect what comes out of hiding when matters are desperate. It's easy to say now they stayed too close to her.

Both she and the fire died in the night, and no sooner was she stiff and cold than one of the other women complained of a pain in her side that wouldn't leave her. The next night another of the women—Josie Mahon—was laboring away with her breath. There was no way to get help. The snow was up to your shoulders, and you couldn't see the trace of a path. The whole mountain-side looked so different under the snow. You couldn't tell where one man's patch of ground ended and another's began. When the wind wasn't blowing there was a silence like I've never heard. Not a sound, only when a cow or a sheep stirred.

We couldn't break a bit of ground to bury the poor

woman. We cleared a patch where we always buried our dead, but the spade struck the ice beneath the snow as if it were made of iron. The earth didn't want our dead, no more than the sky above gave a welcome to the living. As we stood there, the sky over us was the color of lead and it seemed heavy enough to press on our shoulders. It's the right of everyone to bury their dead, and to take consolation from it. But there was no dignity in that attempt at all, no way of setting the poor woman in her grave. Little did we know what we had was a luxury compared to what followed.

I said the prayers for the dead, the body lying there on the side of the hill in that makeshift coffin. We took the boards from old Matt's barn, old Matt O'Connor who died ten years ago this winter and well out of it he is. There we were, with the dark sky above us, the earth white as a ghost, as if it were giving out the light. The only dark spots were ourselves and the coffin lying on the snow, with the poor woman inside doubly stiff from death and the cold. The shame of leaving her out in wind and weather made us attack the ice and make a kind of ledge for the coffin. Then we half-covered it with snow, hoping to freeze it in, and with a few branches we had broken from the trees. What trees, you may well ask, since you could count them on the

16

THE PRIEST'S STORY

fingers of your hand, so scarce and scalded are they by the wind, which bends them to the East. Sure enough, the wind had whipped the branches away the next morning. But at least we did have the wake, if you want to call it a wake.

The women prepared the body and laid it out with her scapulars on her chest and her rosary beads in her hands. And there were enough spirits to warm us, though I left before the spirits moved them to gossip and singing. Of course, you could never stop Old Biddy talking. They weren't great talkers, except when they had a drop in or a story to tell. As for Muiris, he said not a word. What his thoughts were then, only he himself knows. But before the whiskey and the porter got going, the women set up a keening that seemed to have no end. The sound went out over the darkness outside, a darkness that pinched those short days into no more than a blink. If you blinked yourself, the day would be half over and another night upon us, so dark you couldn't even see a glimmer of snow.

I never cared much for the keening. It always unsettled me. You rarely hear it nowadays. The sound would frighten a scarecrow. It has madness and pain in it and exaltation too, as if its agony was a hurtful pleasure, like that of John of the Cross and Saint Teresa and

17

other saints you could mention. If you've never heard it, you've no cause to seek it out. It opens a void in me that prayer can't fill, a void through which the spirit drops endlessly. That sound, rising and falling, those throat spasms putting a hitch in it before the breath urges it forward again, makes you question your beliefs, as if Christ never died on the Cross and all we have is a wilderness beyond reason. It brings back a wildness that the Holy Mother in her wisdom was always eager to moderate but not chastise, for it speaks to a part of our souls that precedes even the birth of Christ. I take my lesson from the Church itself, which acknowledges that what is deep in the people's minds is dangerous to displace. But it can be joined with the true teaching and adapted to God's plan.

The keening did not console me as it consoled them. It always made me a little uneasy, and I felt far from the Diocesean seminary where all those farmers' youngest sons were preparing to give their lives to the Lord. My mother made a bigger sacrifice with her only son— working herself to the bone to ordain me, selling her little farm and taking on work in the town she should never have looked at twice. What must she think now, close to ninety, to see me without the right to say Mass? When I said the words of the burial service at

THE PRIEST'S STORY

Máire Rua's grave, earth to earth, ashes to ashes, *de profundus ad te clamavi*, it seemed to me that the Lord was mocking us, for the earth wouldn't yield a scrap of soil, burnished by the winter with a shield of ice and the snow over that. It wasn't too long before there were four more coffins out there beside her, and the last of them you could hardly call a coffin at all.

· · ·

That sickness was like a plague and we prayed to the Lord to have mercy. It would begin with a weariness that the cold didn't help, and then the breathing would labor, like a bellows that had to be pushed in and out, when normally you don't give a thought to breathing. Then the throat would hurt so that swallowing was like swallowing a knife. Then you could see them take on a shade of blue that was the shadow of death. We all got a touch of those throats, except for the children, mark you. Strange indeed.

Sometimes it started with the throat, and sometimes with the breathing. Whatever way it started, it went the same way. Breath is life to us all, and that life was slowly squeezed out of them. Some had trouble breathing in and others had trouble breathing out, and some, most painful of all, could find no ease either way. It was a torture to witness. Sometimes, I tried to match my breath with theirs and had to give up. But they had to go on, and go on they did, according to their natures. Each of us finds our own way to the next life. They were women of great faith and an example to the living. The Lord received them with open arms, you can be sure of that. For there was not a stain on them, who had never done anything but honor their Savior and keep His commandments, minding their children and waiting on their husbands hand and foot, dragging themselves from one task to the next from dawn till dusk, year after year. It was the children that caused them the most grief, for they didn't want to leave them, and they told me a hundred times between breaths to take care of them and make sure their fathers took care of them. What could I do but promise on my solemn oath? And you will see how that turned out.

I had trouble with the confessions when some of them were far gone, for they hadn't enough breath to spare for a whisper. Their eyes would fix on me with a stare I can see to this day, and they made their penance with the eyes and a nod as best they could. It was because of sin that death came into the world, and yet having heard their confessions over the years, I knew how sinless they were, apart from the usual gossip and

white lies. It was a comfort to me as well as to the dying
to give them the last sacraments, to anoint each separate sense. "Through this Holy Unction and His most
tender mercy, may the Lord pardon thee for whatever
faults thou hast committed by sight," and then anointing the other senses, "by hearing, taste, touch, and
smell." Though what sins are available through taste
and smell is a mystery to me. But when I anoint each
avenue of sense with the Holy Oils, God's sanctifying
Grace flows along them almost visibly to the spirit
within. It seems to calm and soothe them, no matter
how harsh their torment. If unbelievers should ever
doubt the power of grace, all they need do is to come
with me on my rounds to the sick and dying and they
will see for themselves. For the oils of Extreme Unction—I had trouble warming them in the bitter cold—
heal as much as they reconcile those on the edge of
eternity to God's will.

When I anoint those suffering eyes and lips and ears
with the oils, I can often tell what God has in store.
Sometimes I learn their fate from the eyes, when they
look at me with a new peace, but from a distance as if
their spirits had moved through an invisible door. I
know then that they will die as surely as if God has
whispered it in my ear. It's after that they begin the

long hard work of climbing to heaven as they slide downhill, a paradox surely, for the body is returning to the earth, while the spirit ascends to its Maker, to be reunited on Judgment Day. When the Lord wants them for Himself, nothing will change His mind.

But sometimes I see in their eyes a peace that reaches out towards me and the living, and they sleep and sleep as their spirit fastens on to their bodies again, as if putting on a new garment, as indeed they are. For the body is the temple of the Holy Ghost and no matter how ravaged with disease or accident, it should always be treated with the dignity due to it. The hands seem to be a station on the way to eternity. And sometimes on the way back, if that's the way it's to be. Either way, getting better or worse, they look at the backs of their hands as if they belonged to a stranger, one examining and rubbing the other. Some say the hands pluck at the bedclothes when they're going to die, but I've never seen that. I've seen them limp as two geese at times. And I've seen them lift themselves to the eyes for a close look, dangling as if the wrists were broken. But there wasn't any coming back for these poor women. The pillows got bigger as their faces shrunk to nothing, with noses like beaks. The rest of them melted away like a candle. Their arms were sticks and when we lifted them, they didn't weigh more than a child. I was almost demented running from place to place without a soul to help. That housekeeper of mine, Old Biddy McGurk, was in her element. You'd almost think she enjoyed the dying.

The hardest thing of all is at the end, when they lie still as a waxwork, then draw a breath that startles you out of your wits, especially in the dead of night with the candles casting shadows. Then the long delay until the next gasp, and you say to yourself—there's life there yet. The body won't let the tired spirit go. So you wait for the next gasp. It comes, as unbidden as a hiccup, and then everything is still as if time had stopped. That's when you fancy you can feel eternity. And sometimes as time stretches out, you feel you could take it in your hands and pull back the past, recover the healthy woman previous to the poor soul giving her last gasp.

So there I was, in the long nights of November and December, measuring the length of time until the arrival of the next breath, or next to last, or last. The interval becomes longer and longer, until you don't breathe yourself for fear you might disturb the passage of the spirit to the next world as it rises off the body and appears before the throne of God. Some say they can see it leave, see a shudder in the air or a glow gone so quickly you think it's inside your own eye. Then the body is left behind to become as solid as the table or the chair, and the worn face, no matter how old, has a memory of its youth. Then all the pain seems justified, and the anguish of witnessing it eased, I don't know why. That's the moment of relief before the pain of loss.

Five women died that way, except, would you believe me if I tell you, the oldest one of all, that Old Biddy. I've had her for the past five years. She was the only one who'd come up and housekeep for me. I was never that happy with her. But I suppressed my irritation with charitable thoughts. Who else would take her? She was always a great one for the herbs and cures. More than once I had to put a stop to her mischief. When all was well, there was no great harm in it. But when the plague was upon us, the men would as soon turn to her as to me. Inscrutable indeed are the ways of the Lord, who took to Him five women who couldn't be spared, and left one old woman who could. Then one of the men died, old Paddy Meagher, who was always ailing and short of breath with his heart. We thought our time had come. We put him out with the others.

I missed the moment of Sarah Donoghue's passing— Jamesy's mother. Can you imagine this village—if you call a few houses placed every which way a village—in the arctic heart of a terrible winter, with men here and there sitting beside their sick wives, and in Jamesy's case, by his mother's bed, all dying at different rates of departure? I was tramping through the snow on a path of my own making, for I recognised my own footsteps made that morning, when I heard a shout out of Jamesy Donoghue (he was a strong young fellow whose voice would wake the dead).

In I ran and he was holding his mother in his arms and weeping like a child. All the more shocking to me, since these men appeared to have so few passions— they were deep within and never a sign of them except when they were well on. I went down on my knees to start a rosary but Jamesy did nothing but rock her back and forth. It took two of us to release his grip and sit him down. He covered his face with his hands and sometimes looked at his empty hands as if a part of him had been removed, as indeed it was. His mother had kept a tight rein on him. He paid no attention to his young brother who kept pulling on him, a young boy of eight, Tomás, his name was, a bright young fellow and manly enough. Not a tear out of the boy, but he had a face on him between fright and wonder. I haven't spoken of the children at all, but that's another story and a sadder story was never told.

The fathers had a rough way with them so as not to spoil them for the hard life ahead. Apart from Thady's sickly lad, they were the hardy children of mountain people who don't complain even when the earth turns against them, and the earth was never as unforgiving and cruel as it was that winter. There were only seven children left. For when they reached the age of fourteen or fifteen, they got restless and many's the quarrel that would stop when I came in with my *God save all here*. They didn't want to stay up the mountain, though some did, those whose parents had a better hold on them. Once they got to be young men and women they were off down the mountain on Sundays to the dances at Cahirciveen and as far off as Tralee. You wouldn't see sight nor light of some of the young men for three days, which I can tell you didn't please their fathers, who had to mind the animals themselves. On a farm every day is a work day.

Some wouldn't come back at all and the next thing we'd hear from them would be a letter from England. I'd read the letter to the family, though they could just as well have read it themselves, but my presence seemed to make it more solemn. Simple letters they were too: *I'm in London. It's a big place. There's a lad from Listowel I'm working with. He got me a job helping him laying bricks. I'm learning the trade. I'm all right. Hope you're all well. I'll write soon.* Sometimes they'd add: *I'll send some money when I get it.* And send money some of them would. Sometimes I didn't have the heart to read word for word, for some would say: *I have no desire to go back to the hard ways. I met this girl from Clare and she seems very nice. There's always work to do here and well-paid too.* They'd listen to these letters without a word, though the wife might say *God help us all* or *It's a strong young lad he always was* or *He doesn't give much thought to us here.* The father would say nothing. A silent lot they all were. And more silent after the six coffins were laid out on the snow, covered every morning with a fresh snowfall.

· · ·

There was an endless supply of snow. On quiet days it would fall so gently that if you fixed your eyes on it, it would look as if the earth were rising up to meet it. More often it was whipped hither and tither by the wind, one scarf of snow going crossways to another, so that if you tried to follow the weave you'd get dizzy with the sudden switches and changes. The wind would come in the night and drift the snow up against anything in its way. All you could see of the few trees were the top branches and we were on a level with them, living six feet and more above the ground. Our feet never touched it all winter. The only black thing to see was the underside of the branches. We had to dig down to get into our houses, and dark it was inside with the smell from the paraffin lamps and candles and wet turf, and the snow pressing against the small windows. The snow was always covering our tracks, so when you went out in the morning you didn't know right from left. If you've ever had a familiar place turn strange on you, then you know what I'm talking about. It's easy to lose your direction when the things you hardly notice that guide your way are gone. One time I was sure I was in Jamesy's kitchen, and there was Thady, sitting down comfortable as you please. So I said *Why are you visiting Jamesy so early, and where is he?* Thady said *In his own place as I am in mine.* You can see how distracted we were with the weather alone, and when you add to that the tragedies that befell us, you'll have a notion of our distress.

You've heard enough about the weather? It's doing you all a favor I am to be talking to you at all. The only reason is to help that poor man over in the jail that you've all turned against. If you can't keep up with me, go get someone who can. I'm telling you what happened and you can't begin to understand what hap-

pened until you hear all of it, not the bits and pieces that
have people laughing behind their hands and showing
a pious face in public. The Lord Himself will make His
judgment on them. That will come as sure as night follows day. Then we'll see what real justice and mercy
are, not justice according to the perjurers and liars in
that courtroom over in Listowel.

Keep your pen moving there without any more guff
out of you or they can find someone else to set down my
story. Where were the animals? Where they always
are. The cattle were in the big barn we built when we
thought we'd be getting ten more, and we managed to
get them all together, ten of them and two calves. The
calves died early on. The cattle kept together for heat,
and thanks be to God, it turned out that we had enough
hay to carry them through that terrible winter. They
even gave milk, God bless the beasts, right through to
the end, and nothing ever tasted better than that hot
milk, especially for the children. Many's the time you'd
hear those cattle mooing and moaning with full udders
and it was a torment to get to them through the snow,
slipping and sliding and maybe falling into a drift.
Their heads were sticking out over the wall of the byre,
as you stood on the snow looking down at them. Cattle
can't take their eyes off you, as anyone knows. When

you got close enough you could see their big eyeballs, and two plumes of steam forking out of their nostrils every few seconds.

The sheep? There were fifteen sheep and one ram. The sheep were black-faced mountain sheep so they had their winter coats on. The dogs? Three or four, though we had a wicked tinker's dog at the end. They lived in or out of the house, depending on the weather. That winter you were glad to have a dog lying across your bed. One morning we found young Jamesy Donoghue's ewe stiff as a board with her four feet in the air and the others a distance away all huddled together for the warmth. It was a great loss to Jamesy, though he wasn't as good with the livestock after his mother died. Thady was always a great one to skin a beast, starting at the front legs as always. You'd think he was taking off a coat. Biddy stood by to fill a bucket with the blood to make black pudding. But the blood was frozen and it wouldn't stir. She had cleaned a length of gut but she never got to use it. It's bad luck to get the blood of a sheep on your hands, but Biddy never worried about that, though she was so full of other superstitions she must have been born under a whitethorn bush. It wasn't without its good side for we all benefited from that sheep. Nothing ever tasted better, even though we had a hard time getting a good flame out of the damp turf.

We made a kind of enclosure for the sheep by laying some poles across the walls of an open barn, covering them with straw, and putting stones on top of that. It didn't help at all. The wind snatched the covering away in the night and it was open to the sky the next morning. The coats of those sheep were thick with snow and ice. Some of them got out. A few were up to their heads in the snow. All you could see were the black snouts sticking up, snuffling and trying to breathe. I helped out as best I could, tugging them out of the drifts. We searched for one lamb and never found it until the thaw. I remember Muiris coming in with a sheep like a collar around his neck, holding two legs in each hand like the lapels of a coat.

Sheep are like sheep, that's the truth. What one does the rest will do as if they had one mind. They go into a panic at the sight of a dog. When a dog looks at you, you know what it's thinking. It wants to find out what you're thinking. But when a sheep looks at you, you might as well be looking through plate glass into an empty shop—there's nothing there at all. Why they say young lads look at girls with sheep's eyes, I never could tell, unless it's because they haven't an iota of sense left.

By the end of March there were no women left at all, only that Old Biddy in my house, that no germ would touch. Why she was preserved made no sense to me then and it makes no sense to me now. She's still alive, over in the county asylum and mad as a hatter. I went to visit her and she emptied a pail of slops over me from the top of a fire escape. You'd think they'd keep her where she couldn't do that to people walking below. But that's enough about her. It's only when the women are gone that you realise all the things they do in a house. A man doesn't ever notice anything until there's no woman to do it. A house becomes strange without a woman, even a daft one. You can't find anything. Everything soon gets out of its place.

Without the women we all seemed out of place. I've seen the village go through hard times before. But nothing remotely like that winter. The men had great patience. But this was beyond patience. There we were, cut off from everything and everyone, alone on the side of that mountain and no way of getting out or anyone getting in. Just the children, the men, the livestock and that earth like iron under the packed snow. Why these

poor men were the ones to witness this disaster was a
mystery to me and a mystery to them. They responded
in their different ways. Muiris, who had a great store
of stories, was silent after the death of Máire Rua. You
couldn't get a word out of him. He still went about his
business, but he looked smaller to me.

Jamesy cursed the winter—everyone heard him—
and confessed his sins to me. I explained that God was
singling him and all of us out to redeem the sins of the
world by joining our suffering with the suffering of
Christ on the cross, with whom his mother and the
dead wives were now united in paradise. If you lose the
Faith, then you have nothing at all. If faith could move
mountains, it could melt the snow. And I prayed that it
would. I did the nine Fridays and offered every kind of
penance if the Lord would lighten our load.

I said masses for each of those poor souls on the side
of the mountain in their coffins, if you could call them
coffins. And I never failed to offer the Holy Eucharist
so that no one would be cut off from God's grace as we
were cut off from supplies and provisions. The church
—you've been up there—is hardly a church at all, and
it doesn't fit what comes to your mind when you say
"church." It's just a cabin, larger than the others, with
a slate roof, the altar at one end and benches for seats

and small colored pictures for the stations. But it served us and those before us well enough. It looked like one of those penal churches you see in illustrations, when worship was forbidden. Very bare, with an earthen floor. But it was cozy in the summer and not too bad in the winter, with the fire burning in the hearth half-way down the aisle. There used to be forty and more grown-ups and children when I came thirty years ago this Easter. There wasn't much privacy. I put on my vestments in full view of the congregation. But that made them part of the ceremony. We had two kneelers and a curtain for confessions opposite the fire. These people were naturally polite and left a good distance between the penitent and themselves as they waited for their turn. Like every priest I had trouble whenever there was a touch of deafness. Old Paddy Meagher used to share his sins with everyone because he thought I couldn't hear him unless he raised his voice enough to hear himself. Once I found the children playing Confession, one pretending to be me and the other poor Paddy, the others around laughing at his small sins, exposed out there on the side of the mountain for all to hear, if there had been anyone around. You can be sure I boxed their ears for them.

THE PRIEST'S STORY

The children were on my mind all through that winter. Seven of them—did I say that? From six years to twelve. They couldn't go to school. What was I to do with them? Before, they always whisked down the mountain with their *málas* [schoolbags] on their backs, down to the road far below to wait for the bus. Coming back in the evening, you'd hear them a mile away—the lads shouting and fighting and throwing stones, sometimes at each other, the three girls walking along talking and paying no attention to them at all. Muiris's young boy, Éamonn, walked with the girls. He wasn't one for fighting. They were stuck up there with the rest of us that winter. There isn't a bishop in the whole of Ireland that doesn't think his priests are the best teachers in the world. I'd gather the children in the church from ten till twelve every weekday morning, and at twelve I'd let them ring the bell and we'd say the Angelus. Their mothers would bring them, until the sickness destroyed them. When the snow got too high, the children found it hard to get out of their homes. Sometimes only a few would straggle in. It was a real hardship trying to keep some sort of learning in their heads. After the mothers went, I kept it up. The fathers were good about bringing them around. Some of the fathers were slow to read and write since they had no need of it. They knew well enough how to sell a calf or a sheep and get the best price they could.

I'd give the children a bit of religious doctrine, reading and writing and sums, though I was never a one for sums. There we'd be, some of the young ones with the pencil in their fists trying to make pothooks and hangers, not a bit of chalk or a blackboard to our name, and only a few used copybooks. The copybooks were the same as in my day—model letters and sentences in perfect writing with a ruled second space underneath to copy them. There was the right width of space for every letter, and lines above and below you couldn't go beyond unless it was a capital or "t" or a "p" or a "g" or an "l." There were plenty of pencils and would you believe it, not one pen apart from mine in the village.

The children had a few books, Carthy's *History of Ireland*, an *English Reader*, and a book of tables. I had Saint Augustine, Canon Sheehan's *Apologetics and Religious Doctrine* and a *Life of Cardinal Newman*.[1] Any man that

---

1. John Henry, Cardinal Newman (1801–1880). His conversion from the Church of England to Roman Catholicism is one of the great spiritual dramas of the 19th century. Coming gratefully to the rumored sanctity of the Irish Church, he founded, and was the first rector of, the Cath-

could write a poem like "Lead Kindly Light" was a man after my own heart. I believe there wasn't much affection for him among the bishops, Englishman that he was, but none the worse for it to my way of thinking. The Cardinal founded the university up in Dublin, you know, and it made me smile—one of the few things that did that winter—to think of my tiny university up there under the snow, not far removed from the hedge schools of long ago.

The only other thing I had—apart from the Old and New Testaments and my breviary—was a book about the four Kerry Poets, in Irish. Piaras Ferriter[2] was al-

---

olic University of Ireland, the predecessor to University College, Dublin, of the National University of Ireland. Fastidious, brilliant and aristocratic, he patiently suffered the enmity of his Irish peers. Eventually he returned, sadder and wiser, to England.

2. Piaras Ferriter (c. 1660–1753) was a gifted poet and gentleman, much honored in the Dingle peninsula in north Kerry. His poems construct a space in which metrical elegance and quick wit comport themselves with themes of love and generous friendship. One of his best poems favors the conceit of the young woman, armed to the teeth with lethal beauty, under siege by male desire. One verse (probably not the good Father's favourite) could be freely translated: "Conceal your sweet bosom / let not your soft side be seen / For the love of Christ let not anyone see / your shining breast, a flowering bud." After Ferriter's unsuccessful rebellion against the English colonists, he was hunted down and hanged in Killarney.

37

ways a favourite of mine, though poets are always trouble and at their best when they're dead, like that rascal Donnchadh Rua[3] who caused grief in any place he stopped long enough to recite a poem or get a girl in trouble. There's no way you can make English out of that poetry. It's like dragging a cat through a hedge backwards. What's sleek and smooth gets all ruffled up. The words won't lie down on the page, or worse, they lie down without a geeks or meeks out of them.

I found out what it was they were learning down in the National School. For their own language they had

3. Donnchadh Rua MacConmara (Red Donagh McNamara, ca. 1715–1810) was one of the great wanderers of Irish poetry, and of the bardic tradition. Expelled from the seminary in Rome, he thereby won the indispensable Irish qualification of "spoiled priest" (one who studies for the priesthood but loses his vocation, thus detained in a curious penumbra of quasi-spirituality no matter how many children he may legitimately father after the fall from the uppercase "F"). He returned to the famous Latin school at Slieve Gua in County Waterford, from which he departed following some satires their subjects found unwelcome. On his way to Newfoundland, he eloped with a young woman, Mary Hogan. He soon left her. Following at least two visits to the continent, he returned to the nomadic life, seeking patrons and ale at weddings, christenings, and feasts, where he was much sought after. He finally achieved the destitution to which his habits led him. He abandoned his religion, was rumored to be an informer, and would apply his gifts to any immediate poetic task. Old and blind, he managed to retrieve his soul with a late conversion.

THE PRIEST'S STORY

Séadna by an tAthair Peadar,[4] and Pádraic Ó Conaire.
That wasn't too bad. They had a *St. Columba Reader*
with stories about "The First Etain" and "The Magic
Well" and "The Treasures of the Lake People" in
which King Conn loses a game of chess to the Queen,
who sends her step-son to get the apples of gold, the
black horse and the great hound—which of course
would send him to his death and put her own son first
in line. Fair enough. They'd left most of their books
down at school. Why? For fear we might lose them, Fr.
How did you do your homework then? Not a word out
of them. I tried to teach by rote to put some learning
into their heads. The memory needs to exercise itself
or it'll forget everything entirely. The best times were
when I got them doing multiplication tables, all of
them sing-songing it out together—*two times two is*

---

4. An tAthair Peadar Ó Laoghaire (Fr. Peter O'Leary) was a benign
cleric possessed of a transparent prose style in which he told charming
stories of some wit, tributaries to the pure well of the Irish language as
construed by the new nationalists—particularly the President, Éamon
de Valera, who believed that the language served, among other utilitar-
ian functions, as a prophylactic against sexual immorality. Ó Conaire,
whose statue sits, knees pressed together, book in lap, in a story-telling
posture in Eyre Square in Galway, was a quirky writer of some genius
whose nimble prose stretched itself over dark patches in the national
character.

four, two times three is six, two times four is eight—and the rhythm of it gave me reassurance there was some sanity left in the world. When I had them going like that, I'd as often as not step outside in the snow and overhear their voices coming from within. I still had a bit of tobacco and I'd take a few pulls of the pipe before putting it out and saving what little I had left. When I cast my eye around, it looked like the Arctic Circle.

They weren't bad children at all, poor mites. I tried to give them some sense of their past and pride in their country. All I had to offer was what remained in my own head, and my memory wasn't the best, though it wasn't the worst either. I had a bit of a feel for poetry, and we had a teacher at the Diocesan College who was mad about Shakespeare. Every second word out of his mouth was about how it was as true to human nature now as when it was written. He used to quote what he called Shakespeare's *seanfhocals:*[5] sayings that everyone thought were common language. *Neither a borrower nor a lender be,* he'd say, wagging his finger at us. I had a taste, as I say, for Piaras Ferriter. I also made them

---

5. Literally "old words," i.e., proverbs sanctioned by time and usage to achieve a vernacular wisdom. *Aithníonn ciaróg ciaróg eile* is one of the most famous of these. The Irish version translates to "One earwig recognises another earwig," or in English, "It takes one to know one."

learn a bit of *Bán-Chnoic Éireann Ó*.[6] Maybe as some say the language is going to disappear, with only a few scholars in Dublin able to speak it. But until that day comes, they should keep it as long as they can. Some of them had to learn English when they went down to the National School and the other children jeered at them for not knowing it.

The life of a language is in its poetry and there's great poetry in Irish. There are first lines that still set my heart beating—Tadhg Gaelach's *Gile mo chroí do Chroíse, a Shlánaitheoir* and Ó Rathaille's *Gile na gile do choraic ar slí in uaigneas*.[7] There's no end to the joy of a

---

6. This is from one of the most famous of Irish poems, redolent with exile's homesickness. The line quoted is the refrain. It is usually translated "The Fair Hills of Holy Ireland"—a sentiment (suitably capitalized) consistent with the conflation of religious purity and nationalism, which served to get the oppressed through many a bad day.

7. The good Father is quoting (accurately) some of the most famous first lines in Irish poetry. The divisions of Irish poetry are thematic (religious, visionary, cradle poems, drinking poems, laments) rather than prosodic (ode, ballad, lyric, epic, etc.). The Father's two lines are from the first (religious) category. Translated, they read, "Your heart is my heart's brightness, O Savior" and "Brightness most bright I beheld on my lonely way." Tadhg Gaelach Ó Súilleabháin (1715–1795), after a fast secular start, fell into the ways of the Lord and thereafter devoted himself to His praise.

Aogán Ó Rathaille (c. 1675–1729) was the disillusioned poet of the great decline—the loss of native patronage and of the old social order.

great poem, scamps though some of their writers were.
That Merriman[8] is a blight on the language and I
never want to hear a word of his from anyone's mouth.

Born near Killarney, growing up in the depressed aftermath of the Williamite wars, he remained, like his countrymen, haunted by the elusive phantom of the return of the Stuarts. By this time, the Stuarts were themselves phantoms and Bonnie Prince Charlie would soon be a drunk in Paris. Ó Rathaille's first line is from an *aisling*, a traditional verse form that allowed the poet to express his radical political sentiments in a dream-vision of a beautiful woman (a *spéirbhean*, literally, "a sky woman") who would expel the foreigner and restore the lost civilization. The praise of this visionary lady—a nationalist personification— allows the release of intense if futile patriotic feelings. Ó Rathaille's work is powerful, passionate, and suffers its disappointments and regret with considerable force. Like most of the poets of the old order, he is a superb technician, measuring out his spleen in impeccable meters, assonances and internal rhythms. The most negative sentiments are delivered with a stylistic breeding that is an echo of the high bardic tradition. When ill-treated, however, many of these poets became masters of vituperation.

8. The reference is to the laureate of randy profligacy, Brian Merriman (1749–1805), whose long masterpiece, *Cúirt an Mheán-Oíche* ("The Midnight Court"), describes a night of drinking, sex, and merriment in County Clare. It begins in the usual *aisling* manner: the poet falls asleep on "lush grass" in a "convenient hollow." As it happens, in this burlesque on the *aisling* form the woman who initially appears is the fiercesome bailiff of the court. But the body of the poem is a satiric attack on the continence of Irish bachelors who remain unaroused, even though a woman was "snatching the blanket and quilt from his loins / to fiddle and play with the juiceless lump." It stands as a vigorous earthy counter to the nostalgias and anguishes of the fading—and virtuoso—bardic tradition, which lasted into the eighteenth century.

THE PRIEST'S STORY

I taught them English and Irish. The youngest ones
had begun to forget the English after the winter closed
us in. Sometimes after teaching them English, when
they'd be making tracks for home, black as crows
against the snow, I'd notice a strange thing. The words
that come into your mind when you look at something
shape it. After teaching English, English would be in
my mind. When I looked at the mountains in "English"—if you can follow me—they looked less fright-
ening and bare. What do I mean? Is it that there's a
difference between a mountain and a *sliabh*? Yes, there
is. In English, those giant rocks and snow seemed less
threatening, as if everything would work out in time
and that time wasn't too far away. A mountain was a
mountain and snow was snow and nothing was more
than itself. But when I was thinking in Irish, the whole
place looked wilder and suspenseful, as if you were
waiting for a stone to hit the bottom of a well. You felt
that the snow would fall forever to the last silence of
the world when there wasn't a living thing to be found.
Then I'd have the notion that the landscape would
shake itself like a wet dog—and that if I took my eyes
off it, it might. That's something that English never
puts you in mind of.

There's a strangeness in the language that always

43

opened up the world in ways that would frighten you if you thought about it. As a priest of God, I know the superstitions that have been banished and the stories that call them back. That Old Biddy McGurk is full of them. She's full of fairy hostings and dances and hares that turn into beautiful women. Humps jump from back to back, the King of Spain's daughter is a reward for every simple lad, lost folk turn their coats inside out, *arplucas*[9] leap out of parched mouths, and the *Pooka*[10] is at hand for every mischief. Muiris's stories aren't like hers. He tells of the Queen and the Bull, of the meeting of Oisin and Patrick, pagan and Christian, as if he were there himself. They say his uncle was a great *seanchaí* [a traditional storyteller]. He always tells his stories the same way. It's not easy to get him started. She's off if you give her half a chance.

There was little to do in the long nights with the wireless out—all it gave out were whistles and crackles—but listen to the two of them. Saturday night was

9. An *arpluca* is a small, hairy demon who sets itself up in the stomach and consumes all its host's food, inducing a wasting-sickness. If the host is deprived of water and a bowl of water placed near the mouth, the *arpluca*, dying of thirst, will come up to the throat and, after suspenseful equivocation, eventually leap out.

10. The *Pooka*, which takes many shapes, is sometimes a phantom white horse, rarely seen, and is usually a harbinger of bad news.

44

always a night for singing and telling stories, though there was little cause for singing after all we had lost. The auld wan had no manners at all. One thing you never do is interrupt a *seanchaí*. But Muiris paid her no heed and just went on. He never corrected her, just looked into the fire without a word out of him. He gave respect where he didn't receive it. These old stories are all very well, and the *Béaloideas*[11] people love them. So do the *gaeilgeoirs*[12] who come up every summer. But up there listening to the two of them in a dark kitchen with the oil lamp turned low in the window, I missed the news of the world.

When I left the church one Sunday morning when things were at their worst and looked down on the village, what did I see but Old Biddy, wrapped up like a tinker woman, going from house to house. I knew what she was up to. She fancied herself as a healer, that one. She was a throwback to those times when the auld

---

11. *Béaloideas* (literally, "mouth learning") is the definitive magazine of folklore gathered from every part of the country.

12. A *gaeilgeoir* is a semi-contemptuous term for city people visiting the rural areas to learn from "native speakers" the proper accent ("*blas*") that would certify their genuine possession of the language, thereby drinking from the pure, idealised well of the ancient tongue. In their earnestness, *gaeilgeoirs* were the unconscious butt of rural ironies, deadpan responses and ribald jokes.

wans were thought to have some of the world's secrets under their oxters. No child was born in the village without her. She kept things going until the doctor came up over moor and mountain from the town below. There hadn't been a child born in the village for a while—Éamonn, the youngest, was six years old, the son of Muiris's old age. Máire Rua was no spring chicken when she gave birth to him. As often as not the doctor would be late and she'd have the baby out and screaming. The way she was always *plamawsing*[13] the doctor, you'd think he was a saint come down from heaven. "Poor man," I heard her say many a time, "coming up the mountain in the blackest of night or the crack of dawn. It's a saint you are, your reward will be in heaven. Aren't we the lucky people to have a man like yourself? May the Lord increase you and give you the greatest of good fortune, for no man deserves it more. We don't deserve you at all." He seemed to like it. A bawdy old thing she was. I heard her greet him once at the door—"God bless you, but there's nothing better than a man doctor—" Then she said in Irish, *"Fear a chuir isteach é, tógadh fear amach é"* and you know what that means ["A man put it in, let a man take it out"].

13. Flattering in a mode obvious to a third party but not to its recipient.

He got a great laugh out of that. A right old rip she was and is, making mischief over in the asylum.

I was coming home one twilight. Darkness fell at four o'clock. I was doing my rounds to the cottages to console the fathers and raise the spirits of the children, who were lost and idle and didn't seem to know how to pass the time. Idleness is bad after a loss. When I got in, I lit the paraffin lamp. Old Biddy came in soon after and leaned over the lamp at me. Her face looked like a field after harvest. There wasn't a particle of her face that didn't have a wrinkle or a bit of stubble on it.

"Oh, Saints of Jesus!" says she. "I just saw the dead women passing in front of their houses!" She put the heart across me.

I said as stern as I could, "Bad cess to your imagination!"

"It's as true as I'm standing here!" says she. "I saw them as I was coming around the cattle barn, plain as day."

"As plain as day in the half-light?" says I. "Woman, get a hold of yourself and stop your nonsense."

"May the Lord strike me dead before morning if I'm telling a lie," says she.

"Go to the kitchen and put on the kettle and let me hear no more out of you," says I. But my flesh was

47

crawling. She had that effect on you. She went off invoking Jesus, Mary and Joseph and all the saints to witness the truth of her story. I shouted after her, "I'll believe you when they come trooping through that door, and leave the Holy Family out of it." She had my head *tréna chéile* [literally "through itself," i.e., confused].

She fancied she had second sight. We all know that's superstition and nonsense, but in the black of night when you can't see your hand in front of your face, and a cow breathing in a ditch could be a madman ten feet tall, you can understand how some might come to that belief. I heard her mumbling from the kitchen as they do when they have a grievance. You can't hear what she's saying then, only the sound of her sulk. She was always talking to herself. Sometimes I'd hear her arguing with herself and if you didn't know any better you'd think there'd be two people in the kitchen. She was always talking to the hens and the dogs. You could say it was never lonely with her around, but she was like a wireless you couldn't turn off that was stuck on one station instead of the three I could get when the wireless was working. A Telefunken it was, like a beehive with a golden cloth in front, covered by diagonal lozenges of brown bakelite, with two knobs below and a third in the middle on a circular gadget you could turn to the numbers that showed in a half-crescent of light. When the number fit in a little wire rectangle at the nine-o'clock position, then you had a lot of howling and shrieking like a great wind before you got a voice or a bit of music from Radio Éireann or the BBC. I don't know how the thing works at all, it was as temperamental as Old Biddy herself. It had been out since the winter came down on us like a lion. I could get an odd shriek out of it, but nothing more. Maybe the weather was killing it like it was killing the rest of us.

I got a shock one day that made me understand better what she was talking about when she said she saw ghosts. I was doing my rounds, making tracks in the snow. Coming near Muiris's cottage, who did I see bending over emptying some slops but Máire Rua herself. It put the heart across me, since I knew she was lying stiff and cold in her coffin. It didn't last but a heartbeat until I saw it was only young Éamonn wearing her coat and looking nothing like her at all. But though I wouldn't admit it, I began to see the dead women around the village, glimpses out of the corner of my eye that would vanish into a tree branch or nothing at all when I turned my head. Habit and expectation were deceiving me. How many years had I come across them going about their business? Each time I thought I saw one of them, for a second my heart would jump out of the dull pain of their loss.

Old Biddy was right. She was seeing the same thing I was, but she didn't have the education to tell her the tricks her eyes were playing on her. And if I was seeing the dead, what must the poor widowers and children be seeing and feeling? I told Old Biddy not to say a word to anyone about what she called her "visions." She had a hold on some of the men that is a mystery to me, an ignorant old woman like her. That she hadn't been carried away by the plague of sickness was a cause for wonder and superstition. I came across her talking to a few of the men in Séamus Mór's kitchen and when they saw me they went silent, as they often do when a priest enters. But I knew right well what they were talking about and what mischief they were up to. The darkness of superstition is in every soul until it is lit by divine grace.

I tried to cast out that darkness in my sermons. I spoke about the dangers of superstition to faith, a faith we needed more than ever now. God had chosen us to test our faith in Him, and our sacrifices, the sacrifices of their wives and women, were a sign of God's infinite love for us. But we couldn't see that now, with our eyes darkened by the original sin of our first parents. But in the next world, where their wives were waiting for them, the scales would drop from our eyes.

. . .

There is no torment, I told them one Sunday, that does not have its ending. It was now March and the thaw was not far away. Just yesterday I had seen the beginnings of a bud, a small knuckle on the branch of the tree-top near the big barn. What's that you say? Of course there were trees on the mountain. Not great trees as you have down here, I'll allow you, stunted as they were by the wind that never stopped blowing in from the sea. Every tree and bush leaned away from the wind, and pointed after it. Another wind was blowing through our village too. A wind of desolation was bending our spirits towards superstition and fear. But our spirits, if we kept our faith strong, would flourish and flower as surely as the spring followed the winter. God has a reason for everything.

I'd finished my sermon when a strange thing happened. We kept the door of the church closed against the cold. It opened—softly, without a bang—and there were half a dozen sheep or so, with a dog behind them, crowding into the church. In the country you live with animals and you pay them little heed. A few donkeys, hens and a cock, a few cattle, the ram and fourteen sheep—they were our company. And the dogs of course. The sheep pressed into the aisle. The dog looked in and was gone. The church is not the place for the beasts of the field, even if they're sometimes sheltered in the lower level of a cottage built against a hill. But there they were and what was I to do? Thank God it was after the *Sanctus*. I had my back to the congregation. The sound of the door and the rustle of the sheep coming in made me turn around. Now the sacred miracle of the Mass must continue without interruption. I wouldn't profane the Body and Blood of Christ with an angry word. I pointed to the door. Would you believe one of the boys got up and *shut* the door?

I tried to show no sign of anger. There should be no anger in a priest during the sacrifice of the Mass. When I turned around again to give the *ite missa est* I stood for a long moment, with my hands apart, looking at them. If I stared at them, maybe they would know what was in my mind. Why didn't I say what was on my mind? I just told you.

They just looked back at me. If a lot of countrymen have ever looked at you in silence, you know it's a powerful thing. The sheep were standing there at the back. Had this happened before? The sheep, you mean? Well, maybe a sheep or two would wander in in the summer. But never like this. The men were looking at me and it came to me that they were at the end of their patience— and the patience of country folk is surely patience. They had been through so much, you see. And they were to go through much more—more than anyone should be asked to bear. Then something else happened.

Did I tell you about Muiris's son, Tadhg Óg? I didn't. Well, a fine young fellow he was, always out in the fields, a great worker. He'd do a day's work in half a day. Ten years ago, one of the boys pegged a stone that hit him on the side of the head. He fell down without a word and was unconscious for three days and three nights. The doctor said he'd come out of it or he wouldn't. He wanted to take him down to the county hospital, but his mother—Máire Rua—wouldn't hear a word of it. She said, if you take him there, he'll never come back. So we kept him, and come back he did, but not as himself. He never did a day's work after. You wouldn't credit the change in him. He was always sloping around with a kind of sideways look to him. You'd come across him behind a hedge or a bush. He made noises that were next door to speaking, but most of the time you couldn't get a good word out of him. He always had a streak of dribble on his chin, no matter how often he wiped it away. It's a consolation to me the way country people deal with this affliction. When someone is touched like Tadhg, God's hand is on him and he deserves our special care. That's the nicest thing I have to say about country people. You're born and bred yourself in the country, so you know this as well as I. There was never a hard word to the lad that threw the stone, though which one did would be hard to tell for each blamed the other.

Well, there was the poor lad himself, sitting down in the second row with his father as he did every Sunday. Every now and then, he'd say an odd word to himself which we all learned to ignore. Sometimes he'd say, "Rain tonight" or "Give it a puck" or "I'll tan your arse." There's no blame to him for he didn't know what he was saying. Most of the time it was just noise that came out of him. This time up he rises and says clear as day: "Lamb of God! Lamb of God!"

Agnus Dei, qui tollis peccata mundi. Lamb of God who takest away the sins of the world. There were the sheep with the steam rising off them. And the men looking at me. And this poor *amadán*[14] suddenly uttering the sacred words. What's worse, he stood up—he often stood up and sat down for no reason at all—he stood up and stretched his left hand out pointing to one of the sheep. Which sheep? How do I know. They're all the same. There was a silence you could hear. I can hear it still. I looked at his father, but Muiris just looked back at me. They all kept looking at me. At least he didn't say it in Latin. He could have. For Tadhg—before he went soft —was one of my altar-boys and had served Mass like many another.

Why, of all times, did this pop out of his mouth? When his poor brain couldn't support a single sentence that made sense? Why am I telling you this? Isn't it as plain as the nose on your face? The time that was in it, of course. In the middle of Mass, in come the sheep. Then the men pay no heed when I show my displeasure. And then "Lamb of God, Lamb of God" out of this fool. And me provoked and confused. What else could they think, because of the strange times that were in it, their wives out there in the cold, their children motherless, but that someone or something had

---

14. An *amadán* is a male fool, as opposed to an *óinseach*, or female fool. The gender distinction premises that men and women are witless in different ways.

spoken through young Tadhg? Daft and all as he was. Indeed because he was daft and God's hand was on him, his words at that moment could be a message. I saw Old Biddy's face grinning at me from the back of the Church.

Only the Sunday before I had given a sermon about Christ's exhortation to "Feed My Lambs, Feed My Sheep." I spoke about the difficulties of feeding the sheep with the earth covered with snow. But we always found a way. And the Lord, our Shepherd, will find a way to feed us, through Divine Providence, if we have faith. Then the following Sunday, there we were, looking at each other, sheep and all, Tadhg Óg with a run of spit down his mouth. It made a mockery of what I'd said. And it seemed to offer a meaning, as things out of the ordinary do. And that frightened me, because there's no end to superstition and ignorance. The Devil is always ready to pounce, and he has infinite ways of making himself known. However much I tried afterwards, I had trouble joining future and past over that moment. It always stuck out in my mind. To this day I don't know what to make of it.

When I blessed them, off they went, the sheep running out before them. One or two of the men looked at me in that cautious way of theirs, giving a quick twitch to the forehead with a finger, and settling their caps on their heads—old Muiris always wore a hat pulled down on every side like a saucer. They went through the door taking little steps on each other's heels. I gave the young server a penny, though there was no place to spend it on sweets until the thaw. I folded my surplice and soutane and kissed my stole, washed out the chalice and the patten and put them back in the tabernacle. Or I must have done all that, for I don't remember a bit of it. But doing what I had done thousands of times in the same order calmed me down. And as I calmed down, I began to understand how upset I was at what had happened. To tell you the truth, I didn't quite know what had happened.

I went out the door and looked across the flank of the mountain. There were the six coffins, nudged out of line by the shifting and freezing of new snow, without a bush or a branch on them—swept away by the wind as it came around the next mountain. The men and the children stood among the coffins. The dogs sat on the snow looking at them. And there was the ram looking at all of them. All still as statues. With their hats and caps in their hands. No stranger group of mourners have I ever had occasion to witness.

I took a step in their direction before something

stopped me. The feeling came to me to leave them be. I
went to my house, and fell to my knees. With the picture of those coffins and men and children and beasts
fresh in my mind, I besieged God to grant us his favor,
for I felt a great mischief was about to befall us. The
whole thing was a strange experience entirely. It was
so close to nothing at all, you see. It depends on what
you make of it.

       . . .

We have a way of forgetting the worst of hardships.
Not that I've forgotten that first winter. I remember it
as well as my mother's face. But when it's past, it's past.
There are times now, even on the best of days, when I
think back on that winter and a shiver runs down my
back. And not just from remembering the cold. For my
faith in Our Father in Heaven was tested so severely
there were times when I was looking into the pit of un-
belief. There's a darkness inside us from original sin,
and you wouldn't want to spend too much time looking
at that aspect of yourself.

    It's the sharpness of the pain and suffering you for-
get. If we remembered that, we'd never be free of the
past. There are times when I think that first winter
must have happened to someone else. Then I can bear
the memory of it. But it's never that simple. When I try

to remember, I don't remember too well. When I don't try, it comes back to me unbidden in ways that tilt the world so that all my level thoughts, if I can put it that way, slide away from me.

Eager though we were for the thaw, when it came we weren't ready for it. When you wait and wait for something, and then it comes, it's not like you imagined it at all. So it was with the thaw. There we were stuck to the side of the mountain, the land paralysed under six feet of snow and ice, crouching over the turf fires, six coffins outside bare to the sky without a pinch of earth on top of them. All of us held in the fist of winter. Looking forward, looking forward to the thaw.

Its first signals were little beads on the tiny branches. The beads would run one into the other and force a drop out at the end. Imagine grown men standing around watching this? We had a view like we never had of the tree tops. It's as if we were ten feet tall standing on the shelf of snow. And these little drops seemed like the tears of the Blessed Virgin, taking pity on our plight. *To thee do we cry, mourning and weeping in this valley of tears.* And these tears turned into an avalanche of mud.

Yes, mud. It wasn't long before it seemed that the whole mountain was sliding down on itself. The thaw came so fast. The small stream—thank Heaven the houses were above it—turned into a raging river and, misfortune on misfortune—away went one of the sheep. Gone. Quick as you can snap your fingers. I saw it myself. Just the black muzzle raised out of the water, no expression on it at all, riding down the river as if on its way to a fair.

But I'm getting ahead of myself. Before the mud, waking up in the morning, you'd hear the crunch of men walking outside as the thaw softened the ice. It was a slippery, sliding world we woke up to from our long winter. The children loved it, mucking and messing around. The children that had just lost their mothers. They had laid up a winter's supply of energy that had to be let out. There was a burst of play out of them like you've never seen. I even saw them playing around the coffins as if they had forgotten what was inside them. We had a hard time keeping them away from that stream, and going the way of that sheep. Séamus Mór's sheep it was, and he was there when it was whipped away. He ran after it, and slipped and fell over, then got up and just watched it. There was nothing he could do. An innocent stream it was before it fed on the snow from higher up the mountain. At night, you could hear it smashing against the stones and gargling away as if a giant from one of Old Biddy's stories was out there clearing his chest. The mud was a terror. It lay like thick soup over the hard ground underneath, so that every step was treacherous. And in the middle of this, the lambs, four of them, born at the right time for them, but the wrong time for us. But more of them later. It's the coffins I want to talk of now.

As soon as the thaw came, we tried to bury them again, but it was too early. We didn't want the coffins to slide away—everything was sliding. One morning we came out and the six coffins were every which way, as if you'd thrown down a handful of matches. We had the trouble and pain, and pain it was, of sorting them out and finding which was Jamesy's mother and which was Máire Rua and which was Thady's quiet woman. Old Paddy's coffin was easy. It had broken open and we could see a bit of his sleeve. The last two we couldn't make out which was which—Josie Mahon or Peg O'Sullivan. Oweneen made a joke and said "It's a strange husband that doesn't know his wife's coffin." They laughed, but it was a bitter laughter. That poor half-wit, Tadhg Óg, started laughing too. There were times he'd imitate whatever he saw. He kept laughing until the humor went out of it. The men told him to hold his whist, and he did.

After the months exposed to wind and weather all the coffins looked much the same. The thought of opening the coffins never entered our heads. Who could stand that? You'd be frightened of what you might find. Even though the bodies must have been frozen ten times over. But with the thaw, it was urgent to put them in the ground. Oweneen made another joke. He said to the other husband, Séamus Mór O'Sullivan, "If we never find out, you and I will have two wives!" Not a smile out of Séamus at that. "We'll have to put flowers on both graves, both of us," said Oweneen. The others had enough of Oweneen at that point. There we stood in a silence thinking of what we'd lost.

Digging through that mud into the hard ground was like hitting the bottom of your plate through a thick soup. Even with a pick the ground wouldn't yield. The mud would still freeze a little at night. There would be a crust on it in the morning and of course the moment you put a foot on it, you'd go right through it to the hard ground. But the pick began to do the trick. It was something to see the fury of the men attacking the earth. As if they hated it for its harshness. There never was a harder week's work than it took to bury the dead. It was done, coffin by coffin. No sooner had you dug a hole than it would fill up with water. You'd think it was a boat, the way they had to bail out water. They made a bank of stones and earth above the graveyard to divert the water. You had to go down six feet or you'd regret it. Each time a coffin was let down, I'd say the prayers for the dead for the second time, as if each of them had died twice. The men would take off their caps and Muiris his hat. The prayers soothed us, and I hope soothed the dead watching us as we tried to give our respect to the bodies they had left behind.

Not another thing was done in the village while this was going on. What were the children doing? They watched the men working, as children do. One or two tried to help and were shooed off. Then it lost its fascination for them and off they drifted. We'd hear their shouts as they played yonder. It wasn't easy finding the right places to dig in our little graveyard. There were more dead people under the ground than there were in the village. Each grave had a headstone brought up from the town. The freezing and thaw and mud had tilted some of them, and one or two were knocked over. There wasn't much room betwixt and between. Once, we went down into the ground and, God preserve us, we opened the side of another coffin before we knew what we were doing. We stood there looking down on Oweneen and what he had uncovered—a hand and a bit of cloth sticking out from a coffin that must have rotted away. A hand black as a raven's claw and not un- like. Oweneen had no joke for that.

I learned something about digging graves and it's not something I ever had a desire to learn. As we dug each grave, one by one, we'd have a pyramid of earth beside it ready to go back in. And back it went, after I said the prayers and sprinkled the holy water. Letting down the coffins was a torment, because we were afraid they'd break open. When we lowered the last one, I spied a bit of forsythia down the mountain, the first bit of color I'd seen since Autumn. I had two of the chil- dren go down and fetch a sprig of it and cast it on the last coffin below. What did I learn about gravedig- ging? I learned that you can put back exactly the same amount you took out and it looks as if it's too much. And then it's never enough. For the grave sinks and sinks as if it were being sucked down from below. A strange thing indeed. So you have to find more earth to make it level.

We finished the burials on a cold blue day when there wasn't a cloud in the sky. We hadn't seen a sky like that for many a month. The swifts were flashing across the sky so that you could almost see their trails criss- crossing. The birds were back, and it was a comfort to hear their clamor morning and evening. That blue sky, and the swifts, and the sharp, clear sound of them, made that morning stick in my mind. All winter long you look up at a roof of clouds laden with snow—and when it lifts it's as if your eye could go on forever into the blue. As the clouds lifted, it took a weight off our minds too. We had buried our dead. And each man knew where his wife was, except the two that didn't. But at least they knew she was one of two, and I wouldn't want to make light of that.

How to find some grazing for the cattle and sheep and donkey in all that mud? There was some between the pools on the upland where a bit of pale grass was showing itself. And the houses and the barns had to be cleaned out as the snow level fell. The runoffs had to be guided to the stream that was draining the mountain. So there was digging and, yes, cursing when the water broke a bank and flooded a house again. A wave of clay had been washed down the mountain in the long slide and with it the gardens around every house. So the men tried to put back a bit of soil and make a garden again, gathering up the droppings for manure to grow the cabbages and peas and potatoes. They also tried to reclaim a bit of the fields, stony though they always were, for a crop or two. That was the first thing they

did. There was a terrible fear of the next winter in
them, even as the spring was breaking through the
earth under their feet. I think a bit of the darkness of
that winter stayed in everyone, no matter how bright
the sky or warm the sun that summer, and a wonderful
summer it turned out to be, a summer when the rest of
the world was in a terrible convulsion. We'd hardly
given a thought to that. But the dignity of surviving
that winter wasn't long left to us.

· · ·

The first to go down the mountain were Séamus and
Oweneen. You always saw them together, even though
Séamus sometimes took offence at Oweneen's jokes,
which always had an edge to them. The confusion
about their wives seemed to have drawn them closer.
We were to take the children down the following Sunday to the convent and the National School. No one
came up to find out how the winter had gone with us.
There's always a bit of suspicion between the mountain
people and the town. But that you know. As if any of
God's creatures should lord it over another. In His
eyes, we're all the same and the humblest shall be
raised in the end and pride will suffer a fall. You know
what happened. Séamus had a little too much to drink

66

and got into a fight and ended up in jail. Oweneen tried
to calm him and he fought Oweneen too. Far be it from
me to condemn either of them. The town must have
seemed strange after the best part of five months. Séamus was minding his own business when some of those
idle young fellows jeered at him, calling him "The *Bo-
dach*"[15] and making a joke about his coat.

That's what I heard from Oweneen and I believe him.
They asked if he was still running around on all fours
up in the mountain. After the winter we'd had, and
the terrible losses! Séamus just went straight at them.
There were three or four of them. He's a big man and
he gave a good account of himself, I'm told. Oweneen
was let out after a few hours, but they kept Séamus.
There's a queer notion of justice in some places. The
young rowdies told the police he was like an animal,
and away they walked, calm as you please.

Séamus gave out our story when he was ranting and
raving in the cell about the five women we'd lost, including his own wife, and not a doctor to be had, and if
the dispensary doctor knew, he wouldn't have come up
the mountain anyway because he was only half a man
and that the worser half. I can hear him say it. He had

15. Literally "The Beggar."

a temper that would scald a cat. After he left Séamus, Oweneen went to the post office to get all our letters— we hadn't seen a letter for over four months. He gave that nice woman who works there, Miss Regan—his second cousin, she is—some notion of our troubles. Then he went over to his cousin's house to tell of the disasters of the winter. No one had any idea of the terrible time we'd had. It's not that they're evil people. It's just they didn't have any thought of us.

So the story was told, once in the Garda station and once to Oweneen's cousin in the post office. You know as well as I that you can whisper at one end of a town in Kerry and it'll be heard at the other end before it's left your lips. By six o'clock the whole town was talking about nothing else. After he left his cousin's Oweneen said he must have met six people who told him how worried they'd been about us. And who do you think they were? The women of course. The men didn't want to lie to his face. It may be that such lies come easier to women. I don't know. Guilt is a great provoker of lies. You'd think from what they said to Oweneen that they were hanging on the edge of suspense worrying about us all winter. They even said to Oweneen, "The aeroplane went up to drop supplies for the children and fodder for the animals." It isn't as if we were romping around in the mountains and never noticed the plane. What they did—would you believe this?—was send the plane up to two villages farther away, and not a thought of us. Then they said the plane is the Department of Agriculture's plane and the decision on where to send it was made from Dublin. It was the five dead women that did it. Then they knew something terrible had happened.

When the story about those deaths got out I believe there was a question asked in the Dail about it by our T. D. [*Teachta Dála*, the member of the parliament ("Dáil") for the region]. Where was he when we needed him, I ask you? All through that summer—and a lovely summer it was—people were telling me what a tragedy had happened and how did we stand it at all? They said it was an act of God like a storm or a failure of the crops. Some spoke to me. Others turned their faces away. Ashamed they were, and ashamed they should have been. A disgrace it was to leave us up there with the children with never a thought of us. If the men weren't too welcome in the town before, you can imagine how welcome they were when the sight of us walking a street or sitting in a pub reminded the town of its own lack of charity. But I'm getting ahead of myself again.

When Oweneen got back, I went right down the mountain to the parish priest, Canon Moriarty, to get Séamus out of jail. When I got down here, the whole thing had been blown up entirely. I also wanted to talk to the Canon about getting the children down to school as quickly as I could even though it was the beginning of May and the holidays were only a few weeks away. A fine old man the Canon was, as everyone knows to this day. With a ring of white hair, curly at the back, and a red face shining like the sun. Like many another, he was fond of the drop. No shame in that. He always had a kindly, absent air about him, as if he were thinking of something else and couldn't give you his full attention. He'd had the same housekeeper for thirty years, a skinny one in black with a vinegar face and a good heart. He was always raising that wide-brimmed hat of his and half-bowing to the ladies of the town. "Canon," they'd say, "how are you?" Almost genuflecting, I'll swear. He was a decent man surely. He's dead six months now, God rest him. Buried up near Sligo. His mother was one of the Toomeys from Tubber. A big farm they had. The three boys all became priests. One was a Dominican and went to Rome. I believe he did very well. When the father died it went to the daughter. She married a waster from Loughrea and he ruined it.

You can see some of their children around the town on
market day, they must be close to forty now.

I wanted to talk to the Canon to see if I could get the
children in. Some would go to the convent and the
older ones to the National School. The principal of the
school—a Corkman with a heavy hand on the leather
but sweet as honey to the Canon—persuaded him that
it was better for the children if they didn't come back
for the last month. I said I'd been keeping them up with
their books myself as best I could. "It might upset the
learning of the other children, and it would be best
if they made up for the lost year over the Summer so
they'll be caught up by Autumn." And who's to teach
them? says I to myself. The only one he let in was Séamus's big lad, Brendan, twelve years old and six feet
already. I'm sure he just wanted him for football. The
nuns couldn't have been nicer. The fact that the young
ones were without their mothers opened their hearts.
They took in Muiris's son, Éamonn, a delicate lad aged
six, and little Bridget, Oweneen's daughter, aged
seven, and Séamus's youngest, Annie, who was six.
Thady Kelleher's little lad, him with the big eyes—I
can never remember his name—was taken in too.

I couldn't get Séamus Mór out of jail. The sergeant
wouldn't hear of it. I went after that to Judge Murna-

han. Everyone has a "drop in" from time to time, I said, and he has two young children without a mother and now they're without a father too. "He should have thought of that beforehand," he said. You could talk yourself hoarse to the Judge and you couldn't shake him. "It's a matter for the police," he said. "I've no official knowledge of it." I shouldn't have gone to him at all. Even the Canon couldn't shake him. I got Dr. McKenna to go over with me to the station and certify that Séamus had a bad pair of lungs—several in his family had died of TB. The doctor talked to the sergeant and did his best. Do you know what the sergeant said? "He'll be better off here safe and sound with three meals a day." The long and the short of it was there wasn't much sympathy for Séamus, who'd been in trouble before. But the doctor said, "I know Sergeant Mulally. He'll keep him for a day or two and if the fuss dies down you'll have him back as good as new." I had a feeling that if the town had its way, they'd lock up the rest of the men with Séamus so they could forget about the whole business. I got the impression that the town thought our misfortunes were our own fault. Can you beat that? Sometimes the cruel nature of people would break your heart. Without God's grace we're all in darkness.

The newspapers didn't spare the town. You can be sure that publicity didn't warm the town's hearts to us. *The Irish Press* put it in the back pages, but the *Independent*[16] had it on the front page. *The Kerryman* varied its story from one day to the next, because the editor was the cousin of Cornelius Murphy, the solicitor. His office is just a few doors down the street as you know. Of course he didn't want any bad reports on the town. Oweneen wanted to take an action against the town, but Mr. Murphy made sure none of the other lawyers in the town would touch it. That's the way of the world. Wouldn't you think there would be a helping hand to set things right? No one took up a collection even though the Canon mentioned it in his sermon. Five pounds came out of it, from the Canon himself and the curates. Five pounds. And all the help that was needed.

In the middle of this up came a young lad with a message from Dr. McKenna asking me to come down and see him. Little did I know this was the start of more trouble than I'd ever dreamed of. When I got to him, he started round-about enough.

"Father McGreevy," he says, "that was a terrible winter you all went through up there."

---

16. *The Irish Press* supported the Fianna Fail government. *The Irish Independent*, the opposition newspaper, was eager to embarrass it.

"That we did," I said, "as the whole town knows."

"They do indeed," he said. "It was a terrible affliction that destroyed the poor women. I never heard the like of it."

"Nor did I," says I. You could tell already something was coming.

"It's a mystery why the men and children were spared," said he.

"It's a wonder we weren't all found dead with the coming of Spring," says I. "Now that would have made a fine story in the papers."

"A great tragedy indeed," he says, nodding away. He was a man about my own age, with three children, two in Dublin at the College of Surgeons. It must have been costing him a power of money. He was a decent man. If there was a bad harvest he never pressed for his money. I remember he came up the mountain in the dark of night when Muiris's boy, Éamonn, had scarlet fever. He didn't send his assistant, a half-baked young fellow from Mallow. The old Doctor, as we called him, is well liked in the town to this day.

"A mystery indeed," says he.

"I can't make rhyme or reason out of it myself," said I. "As the whole world knows, we had a hard time burying the poor bodies. It makes me weep to think of what they went through."

The doctor took a few puffs on his pipe. "How did it ail them?" he said. "How did the sickness come on?"

I told him as best I could about the way the breath was squeezed out of them, with their faces pinched and blue, and the terrible anguish in their eyes. As I did I heard those slow gasps that I never want to hear again.

"The lungs," he said, "it sounds like a pneumonia. Did they cough at all or get up any spit?"

"A kind of white spit now and then," I said.

"Not yellow?" he said.

"Not that I saw," I said.

"It seems like a kind of pneumonia, but I've never heard of one so lethal. And only the women. I don't understand that. If only we'd got to them before things got too bad," says he. And then he said, very solemnly, "We must make sure this never happens again."

"There won't be much likelihood," says I, "since there isn't a woman up there now but my housekeeper and no germ would dare go near her."

"It's a strange business," he said, "very strange. I had a ring on the telephone from Dr. Aughney—the County Medical Officer—and she was worried, I'm afraid. It's a great worry to have five women die of a disease we know nothing about. So she's coming over to talk to you. We have to get death certificates for them. I'm not sure I know what to write for the cause of death. The old man is not a problem. I examined him a year ago and his heart was ready to give out at any moment. I was going to sign for the five women until she called. 'Acute pulmonary oedema due to viral pneumonia.' But I'm afraid it's out of my hands now."

"What in God's name are you talking about," I said.

"Only this," says he, leaning forward. "We may have a disaster that could strike again, here in the town, anywhere. And we haven't a notion what caused it. Why it should attack only the women is a mystery."

"Some of us were laid up for a few days with the same thing but it didn't strike us as hard," I said.

"There are women here in the town who are uneasy about the next winter. Do you know Dr. Aughney?"

"I never heard her name until this minute," I said.

"Henrietta Aughney," he said, "as County Medical Officer she's accountable for anything that threatens public health—epidemics and communicable diseases. She's a very careful woman and she takes her responsibilities very seriously."

"I'm glad to hear that," I said.

"She'll be coming over next week," he said. "She's over in Tralee now, where a man died last week of measles. He never had it as a child and when you get it late in life it can be a dangerous thing."

"What does she want with us?" I said. "We've enough grief and trouble to last us two lifetimes."

"She'll want to talk to you," he says. "We'll have to find a way to get those certificates signed."

"Why don't you sign them yourself now," I said, "and we'll have an end to all this?"

"The word has gone far and wide about what's happened," he said, "and Dr. Aughney has a report to make."

"To who?" said I.

"To the County Manager and to the Department of Health in Dublin."

"In Dublin!" I said, "What a great commotion there is now! Where was everyone when the poor women were drawing their last breath?"

"We'll do the best we can, Father," he said. "I know we can count on yourself to help us." It was as plain as the nose on your face that there was something he wasn't telling me.

I passed the graves on my way back to my house. The sun was shining and the world was so calm you couldn't imagine it being so cruel. There were sprigs and branches of flowers on all the new graves and crude crosses made of wood with the names on three of them. The bright yellow of the forsythia was a pleasure to see. There were a few blue-bells and bits of heather too. The men put them there, but they'd never let you see them doing it if they could help it. They were embarrassed to show their feelings. Usually they got the children to do it. Once I met Muiris with a bunch of flowers he'd just plucked on his way over to his wife's grave. We stood there talking about the lambing and the planting and the weather. I had enough sense not to mention the flowers.

The next thing was to get the headstones done down here in the town at Matty Clarke's. He had a whole gathering of them spilling out into his yard. Jamesy Donoghue must have been to Matty's already because Sarah Donoghue's grave had one of those glass domes with artificial flowers under it—like a transparent cake. Flowers that can never die. I couldn't see the pink and white flowers too well from the condensation clinging to the inside. Those waxy things always upset me for some reason. They make death more deathly.

I was hardly up the mountain before I was summoned down the next day. Dr. McKenna wanted to see me about something very important. That's what the young fellow said who brought the message. Down the two of us went, past the graves again, across the stream—it was a stream again—down the path to the road and then along that road with a fringe of grass down the middle and cart-tracks on either side lipping up the mud which was now baking in the sun, to where it met the main road into the town. A car was waiting there. I drove into town sitting beside the driver with the young lad in the back delighted with his ride. The driver I recognized as a man who did the gardens for the wives of the doctor and Mr. Murphy the solicitor. And for the Canon too, I seem to remember. You'd find all sorts helping out at the Canon's. A big heart he has surely.

When we got there, the doctor introduced me to a thin woman with a pale face, about forty-five or so. Dr. Aughney. Dressed county-style in tweeds. She had transparent lips and pale eyelashes. The Canon wasn't there, but one of his curates was, a Maynooth man named Staunton. His people were from Drogheda and he'd spent several years in Dublin. A good-looking man with his hair always done. I don't know why I didn't like him. Maybe it's because you could never get a scrap of news or a laugh out of him. Or maybe because

I had the feeling he didn't like me. Who knows these things anyway?

"I hear we have a bit of a problem, Father," said Dr. Aughney.

"And what problem might that be?" I said.

Dr. McKenna rushed in. "It's a great sorrow that has befallen your little community."

Befallen, says I to myself, what kind of language are we speaking now?

"Fr. McGreevy," said the curate, "the Canon regrets he can't be here today. He has a touch of the flu that's going around."

"Indeed a bad flu it is," said Dr. McKenna, "especially at his age. But he'll pull through. He always gets it at this time of year."

Dr. Aughney didn't hesitate. "We've a serious problem, Father. We have six deaths up there and no cause of death for five of them. We have to find out the cause of death. I've been in communication with the authorities in Dublin—the Department of Health and the secretary to the Minister. They're all very concerned. We'll have to bring the bodies over to the County Hospital to ascertain the cause of death."

"But they're all buried up there!" I said before I knew

the words had left my mouth. "They're all in their graves."

"Well, we'll have to get them down. We have the exhumation order here," said Dr. Aughney.

You could have knocked me over with a feather. "Are you telling me that you want to dig up the remains of those poor women? Take them up out of the earth where they're lying in peace? It's a desecration, Father," I said, turning to Fr. Staunton. "Do you hear what's being said here?"

"I do," he said.

"Are you agreeing with it?" I said.

"I'm afraid I do," he said. "It's out of our hands. Some good will come of it if the cause can be found."

"That's the truth," said Dr. Aughney, uncrossing her legs. "It's not a course of action that I relish myself, but it has to be done. There's no other solution."

"Fr. Hugh," said Dr. McKenna, "I hope this isn't too much of a surprise to you. I tried to indicate to you what was about to transpire."

"I hadn't a notion of what was on your mind," I said. My mind was running ahead. I hardly heard what Dr. Aughney said next.

"Fr. McGreevy," she said, standing up and looking

out the window. "I have to be in Tralee tomorrow, but the sooner this is done the better. I'll send the exhumation team up tomorrow. Now what's the best time? Usually early in the morning is best. Then we'll have the bodies down by the end of the day. We should be finished in a few days. The chief pathologist is coming down from Dublin. The Professor of Pathology from Cork is coming over also."

"They'll be back in their graves before Sunday," said Dr. McKenna.

It took my breath away. "You know this country and you know this town and you know that mountain and the men who live on it," I said to the doctor. "If someone comes up there and lays a finger on those graves, I won't answer for what will happen."

"We're depending on you, Fr. McGreevy," said Fr. Staunton. "The Canon expects you to offer every assistance."

"Assistance my foot," I said. "Do you know what you're talking about at all? Is it gone mad you all are? How would you like it if your own wife was buried and dug up a few months later? Can't you let those poor men alone after what they've gone through? Do you expect them to stand by while their nearest and dearest are exposed to wind and weather in what state of decay God only knows, their burial clothes stripped off and their bodies cut up in pieces? Do you know what you're asking of these men? If you expect the men to swallow this, God give you sense. We have one of them in jail already and his little girl is with the nuns. We have children up there without mothers. Do you want to leave them without fathers too? These men aren't like townspeople as you should know. They mind their own business until they're crossed, and when they let out their anger, there's no stopping it. Do you expect me to go up there and tell them you're going to dig up their wives' graves and they're going to say 'Oh, that's grand, Doctor, come up and dig up my wife any time you please and you're very welcome. And please cut her up to satisfy your curiosity.' I won't answer for what will happen. This very minute, Dr. Aughney, you should get in your motor car and go back to your health board or whatever it is and tell them leave us alone in the name of God. Leave us alone, for mercy's sake, leave us alone. I'm leaving you now. And if you want to pursue this madness, you can talk to the men yourself and tell them what it is you have in mind. For not a word will I say to them. Not a word. And not a finger will I raise to help. Not a finger."

There wasn't a word out of them. I stood up.

Fr. Staunton said, "I don't think the Canon will be too pleased to hear this."

"I've no doubt you'll be running off to tell him, Fr. Staunton," I said. "And I think you'll find he'll have a better way of dealing with this, for he knows these people better than you."

Dr. McKenna tried to smooth things over. "Fr. Hugh," he said, "your sentiments do you honour and I'm sure in your position, I'd think no differently. Your loyalty to your flock is admirable, and none is more aware of that than I—from what I've heard—of the way you kept things going this past winter. But these deaths are matters of concern to others than ourselves. What has to be done has to be done. Maybe it's all in the manner of doing it. That we can talk about, for there's every wish on the part of all of us here to spare their feelings. I just lost my youngest sister this past year and I know the kind of grief that this causes."

"Nobody dug her up," I said.

"No, they didn't," he said. "But the dead are past feeling anything."

"The men aren't," I said. "Their wives are sealed in their graves with the prayers for the dead said over them not once but twice. They're in the ground and there they will stay."

84

All this time, Dr. Aughney said nothing. She just looked at me out of those pale eyes. Every time I looked at her she was staring straight at me. I was tired of her looking at me like that.

"Father," she said at last, "I understand your feelings. But some things have to be done that don't please everyone. My job is to protect the health of the community. There may be a virus lurking up there that's new to us. You remember the terrible flu that killed millions after the Great War. We lost more than our share of children and old people in this county. Something that killed only the women is a danger to women all over this country. You wouldn't want to look forward to a country made up of men, now, would you?" She smiled but she made a poor job of it.

"The men were sick too," I said, "but they recovered. I was sick myself, coughing up that white spit. Why don't you cut me up instead?"

"Bitter as it is, Father," she said, "I'd be greatly obliged if you could use your good influence to help me do my job, not for myself, mind you, but for the health of the public."

"Dr. Aughney," I said, "I've no doubt you're a good woman and a good doctor and mindful of everyone's health. All I'm telling you is that raising these coffins,

85

THE DEPOSITION OF FATHER McGREEVY

if that's what your mind is set on, will be the cause of a great unpleasantness, and one that won't look nice in the papers when people read of it. I'm begging you to bury your virus or whatever it is along with the dead and leave them in peace."

"Would you take it on yourself," said Dr. McKenna, "to convey to the men what Dr. Aughney has said about the health of the county?"

"What's the health of the county to them?" said I. "Where was the county when we were dying and half-starving up there? There's more fuss now about the dead than about the living. With the time that's in it now—trying to start up again with their grief fresh in their minds—there won't be an ear eager to listen to you. I'll take my leave now, if you don't mind."

"Fr. Hugh," said Dr. McKenna, "can I have a word with you outside?"

Outside, I spoke before he did. "You're a decent man, Doctor. You did well by Muiris's young son, and God will give you your reward for that. But I'll tell you here and now, I'm not open to one word of persuasion. There's always a way to do things. And you know what I mean by that. And there's a way to do this thing."

"It's gone too far, Father," he said. "It's gone too far. But Father, that's not why I asked you out here. I wanted to tell you that I had tea not long ago with the Canon and Mr. Murphy the solicitor. Fr. Staunton and the other curate were there too. They were talking about your village and the Bishop. Apparently the Canon had dinner with him at the Palace and he mentioned—the Bishop did—that he was worried about the decline in your numbers. And that was before you lost these poor women. Now he probably feels even more so."

"Feels what?" said I.

"He feels there's little need for a separate church to serve less than ten people."

"He can't count then," I said, "for there's twelve of us."

"The Canon says he—the Bishop—was thinking it might be best to join your people with the town down here."

"What's he talking about?" I said, "Amn't I joined already, for I report to the Canon these past five years? I used to report to the Bishop directly when we had fifty people up there and fifty more from around."

"I'm not up on these things, Father. All I'm telling you is what he said to the Canon and what Fr. Staunton and myself heard the Canon say."

"Wouldn't it be nice if the Canon had told me this

himself rather than telling the whole world before he mentioned it to myself?"

"I'm sure it's in his mind to tell you, Father," said Dr. McKenna, "for he stood up for you, the Canon did. He said you were as good and decent a priest as could be found on a day's march. He said that."

"I'll thank him for that," I said. "He was always a gentleman, not like the young whippersnappers that are coming around these days. This is no great surprise to me. I've heard rumors that the Bishop wasn't happy with my little church. There was a time when half the congregation would be kneeling outside, because there wasn't room for them inside. But those days are gone."

"So it behooves you to take care that there's no more trouble," said the doctor. "I'm thinking of yourself now."

"Does the Bishop have any notion of the real world at all?" I said. "Doesn't he know that there's many a winter when we're snowbound and couldn't get down to the town on Sunday even if we wanted? What do you think kept us together over the terrible winter that's just gone by? If we hadn't had the church and the sacraments week after week, what do you think would have happened? Without God's grace, we'd have fallen into a state of nature."

THE PRIEST'S STORY

"Father," says the doctor, "I'm only telling you what I heard. I'm worried about you and your people up there. And to tell you the truth, I'm worried about this town. It wouldn't do to have more of this in the papers. We want to get things back to normal, just as you do yourself. And there's nothing you or I or anyone can do to stop what's going to happen."

I thanked him for his kindness and left without another word. He called something after me but I never looked back.

.   .   .

I was fast asleep when the shouts woke me. Angry shouts they were, like a pack of dogs fighting. I couldn't hear the words but it's a chorus you hear on many a fair day. Barks and snarls and strips of sound torn out of people. With no rhyme or reason to them. They go straight to the pit of your stomach. It's their disorder and madness that goes against your grain, putting you on edge. I listened for a moment before I knew what I was listening to. And that moment is like chaos itself, until you connect it to its cause. Then your legs jump you out of the bed and across to the window.

Down by the graves I could see a fight going on. One man was lying on the ground. Even from that distance I could see the blood on him. Half of them were strangers. A big fellow swung a shovel and knocked Oweneen over. I ran down in my combinations holding my collar around my neck. The children were running down from the houses. All the men were down there except Thady Kelleher. He was standing outside his door looking down. If there was any trouble, he was always sure to be far away from it. There were four or five of these strangers. One was well-dressed, sitting on a headstone holding his head. The fellow bleeding on the ground was well got out too. The three other strangers were getting the worst of it. Working men, they looked like. The soil of Máire Rua's grave was turned, and one of the men must have been thrown into a pile of it, because he looked as if he were made of dirt and clay. Muiris was standing in the half-open grave with a stick in his fist that would brain a bull. I shouted at the top of my lungs. For a moment I thought the strangers wouldn't know I was a priest. I didn't know I had as big a shout in me as I did. It stopped them long enough for me to ask what in the name of Jesus Christ and His Holy Mother was going on. Although well I knew.

The well-dressed fellow held out a sheet of paper to me. Séamus and Oweneen, who had blood running down his face, were talking all at once. "They're here to dig up the graves, Father, and take the bodies away.

Before they do that they'll have to kill the lot of us. No one is laying a finger on those graves. Will you talk to them, for God's sake?"

"Steady on, now," I said. "Steady on." I read the paper. It said EXHUMATION ORDER on top and it was signed by Dr. Kieran McKenna, Coroner, and Dr. Henrietta Aughney, County Medical Officer. If I felt sick before, I felt sicker then. I hadn't told them. My own anger had led me astray and brought them to this pass. I looked at Muiris standing on his wife's grave. The look in his eye frightened me. A wrong word from me would start them off again.

Three of the strangers looked like road workers or county council men. There's a difference between those farming for a living and road workers boiling tar and filling potholes with gravel. Two of them didn't have much stomach for their job—that I could see. The big one was in a towering rage. "They came at us like madmen, Father," he said. "We were just hired to do a job."

"Are you getting paid now to open up graves?" said Oweneen.

"The gravediggers from the cemetery wouldn't come up here because they know what madmen you are. Off your head, the lot of you," said the big man, who had his share of blood on him, his own or another's.

The one who'd given me the exhumation order took back a bit of authority now that I was there. "There'll be trouble about this, Father. This is assault and battery and good for six months hard labor at least. We're here according to the law."

"And where is the law?" I said.

"We stopped at the station, and one of them was to follow us up. We should have waited for him."

Oweneen stuck his head in. "How would you like to have your wife's grave dug up?" said Oweneen. "It's ashamed of yourselves you should be."

One of the road workers said, "You don't have to worry your head about that, for you won't see us up here again."

"If you show your face, there'll be a welcome for you, sure as I'm standing here," said Séamus Mór.

"We'll be back, have no doubt about it," said the well-dressed man sitting down again on the tombstone, holding a handkerchief to his head. The fellow on the ground was sitting up and looking around as if he didn't know where he was.

There was a cart close by—I suppose to lay the

corpses on. Muiris said to the man on the headstone, stepping off the grave, "If you have it in your mind to come back here, may the Lord strike you dead before morning." I asked the man on the headstone to leave before worse happened. They lifted the man on the ground and laid him flat on the cart. A cruel-looking cut on his forehead was pumping blood. We saw their backs go down the pathway and over the rise until they dropped out of sight.

Oweneen and I went down to the ridge. In the distance we could see a man in a uniform coming up to meet them. "It's the Sergeant, by Jesus," said Oweneen.

"Don't take the name of the Lord in vain," I said. We watched until he met the five of them coming down. The well-dressed man was waving his arms. The Sergeant turned and looked up towards us for a long moment. I thought he was coming up. Then he turned and they all started down. We went back up to the others, who were looking at the half-open grave. "Wash yourselves off," I said, "send the children back home and come to the church. I have to talk to all of you."

"I'm not leaving this graveyard," said Oweneen. "I wouldn't trust those fellows not to come back."

"After that welcome, I guarantee you they won't," I said, "but you can leave one of the young lads here to call us if they show their faces."

Séamus Mór called his son, Brendan, over, and gave him a big stick. "Stay here," he said.

We went slowly up to the church. I stopped at my house to dress. Old Biddy was at the door of course, watching everything. She was smiling, I don't know why.

"Take that look off your face," I said. "Where are my clothes?"

They were sitting at the back of the church when I went over. What is it in human nature that makes people always sit at the back? I asked them to come up to the front, and they did—slowly. "This is a terrible distress to us all," I said. "After the winter we've had, and the loss of your wives, it's the last straw. There isn't a person in the world would blame you for what you did. The Blessed Virgin is weeping in Heaven for you."

I was surprised when Muiris spoke.

"What madness is this, Father," said Muiris, "tearing up the graves of our nearest and dearest? All we know is we're up at six o'clock as usual and there are these strangers digging up our dead. It's a wonder we didn't kill them."

THE PRIEST'S STORY

"Let me tell you the true story—" I said. Before I could go on Oweneen spoke up. He was always quick.

"Did you know about this, Father?"

"I heard about it yesterday when I met with Fr. Staunton and a Dr. Aughney at Dr. McKenna's house. That was the first I heard of it."

"In God's name, why didn't you give us warning?" said Oweneen. "Look what you let us in for."

"I hadn't a notion they were coming up this morning," I said. "I asked them to wait until I had time to talk to you. I told them myself I wouldn't allow it. You could have knocked me over with a feather when they told me what they wanted to do. I pleaded with them. I was sure I'd given them enough cause to think twice about it."

"What in God's name are they going around digging up graves for? Are they doing it anywhere else?" said Séamus Mór.

"I have an answer to that," I said, "and it's not an answer that gives any comfort. They had this Dr. Aughney, the County Medical Officer, down there and she has orders to find out why the women died."

"They died because they had a terrible sickness in the chest," said Muiris. "Any fool could see that."

I saw Biddy at the door of the church.

95

"Go back to the house and stay there," I shouted at her.

"Is it putting me out of the church you are, Father?" she says, bold as brass.

"Sit down," I said, "and let me not hear a word out of you. It's a matter of death certificates for the women. Dr. McKenna would like to sign them, but the health authorities fear an epidemic."

"If it was an epidemic," said Muiris, "we'd all be dead."

"Well, it attacked some of us too. Séamus there had a dose that left him as weak as he's ever been. He still has a cough."

"It never weakened me at all," said Séamus.

"Unless they get a cause they won't sign the certificates," I said, "and to get a cause they say they need to examine the bodies."

"That they'll never do," said Séamus Mór. "Not as long as we can draw a breath."

"Are you in agreement with them down there?" said Oweneen.

"I'm in agreement with you," I said, "and I've made that plain. But you see what heed they paid me. Dr. McKenna said we might have stopped all this if it hadn't got into the papers and gone as far as Cork and Dublin.

But it's too late now. They'll be back with the police. And we won't be able to stop them. They said it would take a week and then they'd be back in their graves again."

"All cut up in bits and pieces," said Oweneen. "We're not going to have that."

"We'll take steps, Father, and you're better off not knowing what they are," said Séamus Mór.

"In the name of God," I said, "let's not have more trouble."

"Father," said Muiris, "you did your best and that didn't stop them. Had we known, they'd never have turned a sod on Máire Rua's grave. But now it's not your concern."

"It's my concern indeed," I said, "for I want no more disaster to befall us."

"You're wasting your breath, Father," said Séamus Mor. "Do you see us sitting quietly by while they trot five bodies down the hill? If that's the way you're thinking, Father, it's a dream you're in."

"Don't talk to the priest like that!" said Muiris. "He should have told us, but it comes to the same thing in the end. They're gone now and we have time to think what to do."

"There might be a way," I said, "if we talk to the solicitor and let him find a way to put a halt to it. Where there's one law, there's often another contrary to it. Murphy down there is a clever man."

"And what are we to pay him with?" said Oweneen.

"Enough talk of lawyers," said Séamus Mór. "We can get a shotgun or two from my cousins over in Brandon."

His words put the heart across me. "We need to calm down now," I said. "We need to calm down now and not give ourselves more hardship. Take it easy now."

"Father," said Muiris, "you did your best and that didn't stop them."

"I suppose it's our own fault we lost our wives," said Oweneen.

"There's no fault to anyone here," I said. "But we need to pray for guidance. You're all God-fearing men, with children who depend on you. What we'd best do now is calm our spirits. We'll say a rosary. I'm going to say the sorrowful mysteries, for whatever the day it is, it's full of sorrow for us. The prayers will give us peace and then we'll consider what course to take."

That night in bed I thought of something that happened twenty years ago during the war of independence. About five o'clock on an October evening Séamus Mór and Oweneen Mahon came to the door and asked for an envelope and pen and paper. I asked what they wanted them for.

"Just give them to us, Father, and don't ask any questions."

Then I noticed two others a distance away holding a man in a British uniform between them, his hands behind his back. A young man. An officer from the stripes on his arm. The two had leggins and bandoliers and I didn't need to ask who they were. There had been bad trouble the week before in West Cork. I noticed Oweneen was leaning on a spade.

"I will give you nothing of the sort," I said, "and if what's in your mind is what I think you're thinking, in the name of Jesus Christ who died for us, put it out of your mind at once."

"Give it to them, Father," said one of the two holding the officer.

"That I will not," I said.

Then the Englishman said in his accent, "I'd appreciate very much if you would be so kind." He must have been no more than twenty-one or two. I gave pen and paper to Séamus Mór. I shut the door in their faces and prayed all through that long night. From five o'clock on, I was straining my ears. I heard the shot at six o'clock, barely heard it, plucked by the wind. Oweneen was at my door a half an hour later with the envelope. It was addressed to a Mrs. Someone, someplace in Surrey, England, I remember. He was sweating and he had the spade over his shoulder. There was fresh clay on it.

"Take that down to the post-office, Father," he said, "and let no one know your business."

"May God forgive you," I said, "and Séamus too. You've done an evil thing."

"Stay out of it, Father," he said.

Séamus and Oweneen were gone for a year after that. God knows where they were or what they did. But I knew that when Séamus spoke about that shotgun, he wouldn't be shy to use it. All this came back to me, and just like twenty years ago, I didn't close an eye all night.

· · ·

What else could I do the next morning but traipse down the hill again and knock on the Canon's door? Who answered it at that hour but Fr. Staunton. He must have thought I was a sick call.

"It's the Canon I want to see," I said.

"The Canon is in his sick-bed and you can't see him," says he. "And I don't want you disturbing the poor man with the goings-on of yesterday."

That skinny housekeeper of the Canon's spied me as

she stuck her head out of the kitchen. "When you're finished, Fathers, there's a cup of tea in the kitchen. It's still cold early these mornings." People are always surprising us. To look at her you wouldn't think she had a heart at all.

Fr. Staunton went upstairs to put on his collar, but before he went up he said, "I think you should go see the two men from Cork that were supposed to supervise the disinterment. They're at Mrs. O'Shea's Bed & Breakfast, and one of them has ten stitches in his head. They went right over to the police station when they came down yesterday."

When I knocked at Mrs. O'Shea's door, I could see the two men having breakfast through the bay window. When she showed me in, the one with the sore head didn't even look at me. The other one said, "If you've come to try and smooth things over, Father, you've come to the wrong place."

"I'm not here to argue with you," I said. "I'm here to see what can be done."

"There's nothing to be done at all," says he, "but to get these buckos to stand back and let us do our job. We'll be up there tomorrow, with the Sergeant and two policemen and then we'll see how brave your fine lads will be."

"Mister," I said, for I didn't know his name, "don't you see there's going to be nothing but trouble this way?"

"There'll be more than trouble for that little fellow that hit me," said the other man, speaking for the first time. "Does he think he can go around whacking a man's head with a stick as if he were driving a cow through a hedge?"

"I'm not going into that," I said. "There are a few men up there with broken heads from the boys you brought up with you. I'm here to help you do your job, if you'll help me."

"We'll see how six months' hard labor helps that little runt," said broken-head.

"Have you sworn out a warrant?" I said.

"No," he said, "but I intend to."

"If I can keep them off you, and we get this done nice and quiet, will you forego that complaint? You know what a Kerryman is like when he's roused. I can't answer for it if you come back the same way as before. If I manage to keep things quiet will you—"

"A fine job of that you did before," says he.

Mrs. O'Shea was in and out with the teapot. "Poor men," she said, "with all those children up there and not a woman to take care of them, all their mothers under the ground before their time. It's a terrible thing. And digging them up, Lord save us, it's unnatural. No wonder it came to blows. This poor man here," she said to me, "I heard him walking around all night in his room, he didn't get a wink. His head must be hurting him something cruel. There's no good coming out of this for anyone."

The two of them didn't say a word until she left. I said, "I'd like you to wait and not do a thing, until I talk to Dr. Aughney."

"She's not here," said Mister. "She's over in Tralee."

"Well, I'll ring her on the telephone from Dr. Mc-Kenna's," said I. "And where will you get a gravedigger that will open up those graves for you?"

"Don't you worry about that, Father," said Mister. "I'll find plenty who'll be willing when I cross their palms."

"And when they know the police will be there with them," said the other.

I had to cool my heels in Dr. McKenna's waiting room. When I got in he turned around from the sink where he was washing his hands. His stethoscope was around his neck and a bit of egg from his breakfast on his waistcoat.

"Doctor, there's terrible things going to happen!"

"They've happened already from what I hear," says he.

"Blood has been spilt, Doctor," I said, "and there's more waiting to be spilt. Isn't there any way we can call off this business?"

"We've had that discussion, Father," says he, "and as Coroner, I'm answerable. This has to be done, there's no two ways about it."

"Would you listen to this," I said, "and talk to Dr. Aughney?"

"I'm past listening," he said, "and I have patients out there waiting for me."

"Doctor," I said, "you were the very one that didn't want any more about this in the papers. If your men go up and start digging again tomorrow, police and all, there will be warfare. It'll be in the *Press* and the *Independent* the next day for all to see. And the *Independent* won't be nice about it. Would you listen to me, in God's name, for there's no comfort to anyone in all this?"

"Come back in an hour, Father," he said, "and we'll sit down."

Back I came. There were still people waiting. It was another hour before the last one was gone.

"Now, Father," says he, "what's on your mind?"

"Only this," I said. "Five women are buried up there.

Three of their graves have names on them, and two have no names, though there are names for them, but they're not on them."

"I don't have the foggiest what you're talking about, Father," says he.

"It's this way," I said. "After the snow and ice melted and the stream rose up, the coffins were tossed about like matchsticks—and apologies for coffins they were to begin with. Two of the coffins got mixed up and we don't know which of the two women is in them."

"It's romancing me you are," said the doctor. "Any man would recognise a coffin he'd made himself."

"After three or four months out there in the freezing cold and wet?" said I.

"Why didn't they open a lid and take a peek?" said the doctor.

"Doctor," I said, "you know the answer to that. Would you like to open your own wife's coffin—"

"God between us and all harm!" said the doctor. "Leave my poor wife out of it."

I answered him, "To open those coffins would have been a terrible shock. Who knows what state the poor bodies were in?"

"What are you trying to tell me?" said the doctor.

"Look at it this way, Doctor," I said. "There are two

coffins up there with two women in them and we don't know which is which. We don't know which is Oweneen Mahon's wife and which is Séamus Mór O'Sullivan's wife."

"I'll be damned," said the doctor.

"Now listen to this," I said. "If the party that came up yesterday and wants to come up tomorrow settled on one of those graves, you might have less trouble. If you touch any of the other graves, there'll be a power of trouble."

"But we have to have all five of them!" said the doctor.

"Dr. McKenna," I said, "it's your own self I heard say that they all died of the same thing. If it's the same thing, why do you have to dig up all of them? Couldn't you talk with Dr. Aughney and see if she'll settle for the one post-mortem? I swear to you, I was there when every one of them died, and they all died as if they were the one person. All of them blue in the face from coughing and lack of breath. The lungs are what you said yourself when I described it. In the name of God, Doctor, you can help us all put an end to this. You'll have the thanks of everyone far and wide. It's what the Canon himself would advise if he were here."

"Have you talked to him?" said the doctor.

"I have not," said I. "He's not well as you yourself know better than anyone. I've spoken to those two men from Cork over at Mrs. O'Shea's. You need to speak to them yourself, for they're sore as blazes. If you can persuade Dr. Aughney, you'll be doing a service to everyone in this town."

"How would they know which grave to go to?" says he.

"I'll leave a white stone on it," I said, "God forgive me."

"Which one would you choose?" said he, with a bit of mischief.

"One or the other," I said, "for they're both the same. In my mind's eye I can see the one I'd mark. It's on the right."

"I have a few sick calls to make," said the doctor. "Come back in an hour and I'll telephone Dr. Aughney then. She's a hard woman, mind. I can't promise you anything."

I spent the hour in the parish church, storming Heaven, and asking the Blessed Virgin to intercede for us. When I came back, his car was in front of the dispensary.

"I haven't had a chance to talk to her yet, Father," he said.

"Doctor," I said, "they're getting ready to go up to-morrow morning and there's no time left."

"Wait here," he said. "I'll telephone Tralee right now. She's at Cashin's Hotel. It's better that you wait here, Father."

I heard him on the telephone through the door. He came out after fifteen minutes. Never was there a longer fifteen minutes.

"It's done, for the moment anyway," he said. "If I can find a cause of death with that man from Dublin and the pathologist from Cork, I think we might be able to keep her hands off of the other graves. I don't want to have an inquest no more than you do. But she'll not be put off easily."

"God and His Holy Mother will reward you," I said, "for you've done a great thing."

"We'll see how great a thing," he said. "You better get back up the mountain and start telling your people to draw in their horns. I'm going over to Mrs. O'Shea's to talk to those two, though they'll want to get the word from Dr. Aughney herself."

Up the mountain I went again. The sun was blazing down. You'd think I'd rise like a bird with the news I had. But my bones were heavy with fatigue and every step was worse than the last. I thought of Christ Him-

self on the way to Calvary, and I offered up the pain,
imagining I was walking in His steps. There were so
many things on my mind that I suddenly remembered
that I hadn't paid a visit to the barracks to try to have
them hold off on Oweneen. They were probably waiting to take him in tomorrow morning when they came
up in force. I thought of going down again, but it was
beyond me. When I passed the graves, Séamus's young
Brendan was there guarding them. Twelve years old
and nearly six feet already. I didn't like the stick he had
over his shoulder at all.

By the time I had all the men in the church, it was
nearly nine o'clock and still bright as day. It was the
kind of evening you could relish after a day's work. But
there was no pleasure in it for me. "I've been down
there all day," I said, "running back and forth from the
parish house to Dr. McKenna's, and I went to see the
Corkmen, including the one Oweneen left his mark on.
They'll be up tomorrow morning with the police and
there's no stopping them. But if you listen to me, there
may be a way to satisfy them without digging up what
shouldn't be dug up."

The way they were looking at me, I knew they had already decided on how to deal with this. I'm sure there
was no shortage of sticks in their cottages now, and I

wouldn't have put it past Séamus Mór to have gone and
got his cousin's gun. You know the country as well as I.
People have been killed for far less reason than these
men had. I prayed to God to put the right word in my
mouth.

"The first thing I'd like for you to do," I said to Oweneen, "is not be here when they come. We're trying to
get that fellow with the broken head not to lodge a
complaint."

"I'll be here," says Oweneen, "for we'll need everyone
we can muster."

"It's not a war we're considering, Oweneen," I said.

"If I'm not here," said Oweneen, "they'll have my
poor wife out of the grave in no time."

"Out of which grave?" I said. "It could as well be Séamus's here.

"What we don't want to see," I said, "is five empty
graves this time tomorrow night. Nor do we want to
see four. Nor do we want to see two."

"We don't want to see any!" said Séamus Mór. "We're
all together on this."

"Why wouldn't you be?" I said. "Who could bear to
lay their eyes on such a sight? They have the law on
their side though. And we don't. If Oweneen takes off

like I want him to, that leaves just the four of you. But
if you tell them no graves at all, they'll arrest you all."

"What are you saying to us, Father?" said Muiris.

"Only this," I said. "All the poor women, God rest
them, left us in the same way, with the same distress.
Why should they take up all five of them when each one
went the same way as the others?"

Muiris was always the smartest. "Which one of our
wives did you decide to give to them, Father?"

"I didn't decide anything," I said. "All I did was get a
promise from Dr. McKenna after he spoke to Dr. Aughney, who promised as well. It's up to you whether you
want five open graves or one. Whichever poor woman
it is, she'll be back in her grave before the week is out."

"It's easy for you to talk, Father, with no wife out
there in the ground."

"Not a pinch of earth will be turned," said Séamus
Mór. "Not as long as I can draw a breath."

"We can spare four graves from being turned inside
out," I said. "But it's up to yourselves."

"How do we know we can trust that promise?" said
Muiris. "When we turn our backs they may make off
with everything. It wouldn't be the first time the police
broke their word."

"It's not the police," I said. "It's the doctors that promised. And if they break their word to me, you can do whatever you wish."

"You give us a bad choice, Father," said Muiris.

"It's not a choice I would ever have countenanced," I said, "if there wasn't a worse one behind it." I kept looking at Muiris.

"It's a shame on this village," he said, "to have a grave opened by strangers."

"Maybe," I said, "you could open one of the graves yourselves without having Oweneen or Séamus do it."

"What kind of savages do you think we are," said Séamus Mór, "to desecrate the grave of one of our wives?"

I bent my head and asked God for guidance. "Better a friendly hand than a stranger's hand," I said.

"And better no hand at all," said Séamus. To everyone's surprise, Thady Kelleher, who never said much of anything, spoke up.

"And better one than five," he said.

"Well it won't be mine," said Séamus Mór.

"Nor mine," said Oweneen.

Thady Kelleher spoke up again. "If you knew which was which."

"It goes against my nature," said Muiris, "but I suppose the two of you could draw lots."

"I won't draw lots," said Séamus Mór.

"It would leave it to chance," said Muiris.

"And Providence," said I.

"It's not a greyhound race," said Séamus. "I'll have no part or parcel of that."

The others were looking at Oweneen and Séamus Mór. "You can stop looking at us," said Séamus.

"No graves will be touched, whether it's half a grave or not," said Oweneen.

"And that's certain," said Séamus.

The others said nothing. Jamesy, who hadn't opened his mouth while all this was going on, never took his eyes off the floor.

"I'm trying to spare you all," I said. "If it's one grave, it spares four. Like it or not, they'll be up here in the morning. I have their promise that they'll disturb but one. And if Oweneen is gone by that time, we'll try to avoid any trouble from the man with the broken head. If there's no trouble, he half-promised he wouldn't put the police on to you," I said to Oweneen.

"I'm not leaving," said Oweneen.

"Maybe it's better for you if you do," said Muiris.

"Is it to run away from my own home and my wife's grave I'm supposed to do now?" said Oweneen.

"It'll be only for a few hours," said Muiris.

"If that long," I said. "What have you all decided?"

"We haven't decided anything," said Séamus.

"Do you have to go down to tell them tonight, Father?" said Muiris.

"No, I don't," I said.

I walked over to the door of the church. The shadow of the mountain was across the graves. Young Brendan was still there.

"Maybe Oweneen and Séamus might come down to the graves with me," I said back into the dusk of the church. Nobody said a word. Then Séamus suddenly stood up.

"To hell with the lot of you."

When he got to the church door, Oweneen came after him.

"You're not going down alone," he said.

"Who says I'm going anywhere?" says Séamus.

"I'd be obliged if you did, Séamus," I said, "for you're a man who has great respect from everyone in this village. And you can do something that takes more courage than is asked of anyone. If the two of you come down with me now, we can put an end to this pain we're going through."

"Easy for you to say, Father," said Oweneen. "Easy for you to say."

The three of us stood at the two unmarked graves. "God guide you both in your choice," I said. I looked up at the church. The men were standing outside the door, looking down at us. It was ten o'clock and the sky was beginning to turn blue as velvet. I could see the horns of a new moon over the church.

"Which one is it to be?" I said. Oweneen blessed himself, and pointed to one. Then his finger wavered and fell.

Séamus Mór said, "This one." Then he said, "No, no, the other one." I could see a tear in his eye, and that hurt me as much as anything that had gone before, a powerful man like him, who'd always been certain of everything. He had a fit of coughing. Oweneen was kneeling by one of the graves. Then he stood up and walked away and looked back at the other. Séamus looked at him and turned to me. "Father, I'd be obliged if you would make the choice."

"Why don't you both go home now," I said. They went up the hill and stopped a bit away. I lifted a white-washed stone the size of a baby's head and placed it on one of the graves.

"I see you had it all planned, Father," said Oweneen.

·   ·   ·

I looked out the window in the early light. I glimpsed a coat disappearing into the mist high up the mountain. Oweneen was away and clear for the day. A few sheep were grazing among the graves. I went down and shooed them away and waited. It was only about ten minutes until I saw the heads bobbing over the ridge below. One—two—three—nine of them in all, and one in black. I recognised Fr. Staunton. What was he doing here? Three were policemen, including the Sergeant. He wouldn't have been much good in a fight with that belly on him. The two others were strapping young fellows well over regulation height. Country boys. That left five. The two Corkmen, one with the broken head—you could see the bandage a mile away. He stayed behind the others. And three laborers judging by their clothes. One of them was the young fellow with a bit of spunk who'd been up before. I suppose he was eager for a fight now with the company he had. The two others I'd never seen before, but I learned that one of them was the gravedigger from the town.

I waited halfway between the graveyard and the nearest house. I wanted to be in-between if any of the men came out. When they got to the graves, the Sergeant looked up and touched his cap. Fr. Staunton looked up and nodded and looked away again. The

Corkman with the bandaged head looked up at me and said nothing.

There was that hush just before morning breaks. The top of the mountain had cleared. The mist had spilled into the valley below as if from a ladle. Only a twist of smoke out of a chimney here and there. It was six o'clock on the morning of June 30th, a Thursday. A young lad appeared at a door and was pulled back suddenly. I knew there were eyes at every window. I had their promise that they wouldn't stir out of the houses. But I never felt their presence more.

The Corkman went straight to the marked grave and tossed away the stone. Fr. Staunton came up the hill towards me.

"The Canon asked me to come, Father," said he. "He's as troubled by this business as much as you and I. He's far from hale and healthy these days, poor man."

"Dr. McKenna says he'll be fine," says I.

"We'll see," said Fr. Staunton.

We looked down at the fresh brown soil mounting up beside the grave. They were working fast. The sounds of the spade and shovel were as sharp as if I was using them myself. You know these sounds. The wet slice of the spade as it goes in, the suction of it lifting, and the hiss and scrape of the shovel against an odd stone.

"It's nice of you to come up with them, Father," said I.

"Well," said he, "you've been alone in all this, Father." I couldn't believe my ears. Had the Canon put in a good word for me? Or the doctor?

"When they're finished there, Father," I said, "maybe you'd like to come up with me and see our little church of Our Lady of Perpetual Succor?"

"I would indeed," he said. "I see we can expect no violence this morning."

"These men have been sorely tried," I said.

"That they have," he said. They were bending over the grave and lifting. I tried to stand between Séamus Mór's cottage and the grave.

"Would you stand over a little this way, Father?" I said. "I don't want the man whose grave this might be to see what we're seeing."

The coffin was coming to bits even as they took it up. The three diggers had white masks on their faces. What looked like a black rubber sheet was spread beside them and a big white sheet over that. I was glad there were a few of them between us and the grave. The Sergeant was standing a bit up the hill over the graveyard. One of the policemen had his back to the grave watching the houses. The other policeman, a young fellow he was, was looking into the grave. He half-turned and put his hand over his mouth, bent over and made an offer of his breakfast. The diggers laid the body on the white sheet. I said, "I think we should go down, Father."

The body lay there, wrapped in a shawl. I recognised the shawl before I looked at the face. The face was as wizened as a crab apple that's been in a cupboard over winter. The hair combed back from the forehead was as scanty as if it had been plucked. The face was half covered in dirt where the coffin had let in the soil and there was a line of dark green mould around the mouth and on one cheek. It was Peg, Séamus's wife. Her hands were like a skeleton's. The fingernails looked as they did when we buried her. I got a whiff of a smell that you get from a dead dog on the road. God help our mortal selves. It's in store for all of us. They wrapped the body in the white sheet, and after that in the black rubber. Then they took each end like a hammock and lifted it onto the cart—the same one they'd had up before.

"Are they going to fill in the grave, Father?" said I to Fr. Staunton. "That open grave is an insult to heaven and it'll remind the men of what has transpired."

He went over and talked to the Sergeant. Two of the men began to fill it in. The young policeman that had vomited stood up, grabbed a shovel, and helped them furiously. I wanted the grave to look as it was with flowers on top as before. They finished and Fr. Staunton came back up. After that it was like when the air goes out of your bicycle. A feeling as empty as the grave itself. They started down the hill. The Sergeant looked back and shouted, "I'm much obliged to you, Father. If you see Oweneen Mahon, tell him I'd like a word with him." They dropped over the ridge and it was as if they'd never been there.

We stood looking at the grave—filled up and empty at the same time.

"It's a strange thing," I said, "that something has to be done wrong before it can be done right."

"Which of the wives was it?" said Fr. Staunton. "I'd like to talk to the husband."

"Séamus Mór is the man," I said.

"I'd like to have a word with him, Father," says he.

"Indeed you shall, Father," says I.

We went up and into Séamus's house. A kettle was boiling on the fire. Mugs were on the table and a jug of milk. He said little. That Brendan had a puss on him, and he cast me an angry glance. I didn't need to tell Séamus anything. By our visit he knew. Fr. Staunton didn't say much either. We just drank the tea. I talked to the little girl. It was an honor for Séamus to have two priests in his house. "I'm saying Mass this morning for your Peg," I said as we left.

"Wherever she might be," he said, dark as a cave.

"In Heaven surely," said Fr. Staunton.

I brought Fr. Staunton over to the church. He looked around and suddenly it looked very pokey and bare to me. "I'd like to serve your Mass," he said. I couldn't believe he was being so friendly. I'd made up my mind about him as a young whippersnapper from Maynooth who'd never get mud on his boots, though he had his share on them now. I expected no great kindness or understanding from him. Some of the younger priests felt that the way to heaven was clearly indicated by rules and regulations and that sin was sin and that was that. They lived their lives clearly between heaven and hell and had no doubt of their destination. I started the Mass and God forgive me, I was still thinking about Fr. Staunton even as he was making the responses. I was angry at him for a strange reason. I didn't want him to be better than my idea of him. Even as I said the *kyrie eleison* I was thinking what right had he to disturb my notion of him. By the time I got to the first gospel, my mind was saying to itself—he's up to something, for the first impression we have of someone usually proves itself to be true. I turned to open and close my hands and looked down on his bent head and was ashamed of myself.

A few of the men and children had come in at the back of the church. No Séamus though. I gave the final *Ite, missa est*, and by the time Fr. Staunton helped me take off my vestments, they were gone. Back at home, Old Biddy had a breakfast steaming away—porridge and fresh milk and butter and the best of brown bread and black tea. Even as Biddy was annoying me by the way she was fawning all over him—Would you have this, Father? Would you have that, Father?—I was beginning to favor Fr. Staunton. Until he said, "Father, the Bishop wants to see you next Thursday."

My breakfast came together in the pit of my stomach.

"Is that what brought you up here?" I said.

"I wanted to be here," he said, "for I felt—and the Canon agreed—that you shouldn't be left alone to carry the weight of all this when they came up. The Bishop's message arrived late yesterday and I didn't want to send up a young lad with a note. Now that I've been here, Father," says he, "and seen the way you've kept things going after that terrible winter, have no doubt but that I'll speak up for you whenever I can. It's no pleasure for me to bring you that message. I fear the Bishop may want to close your little church."

"He and the county manager are talking of bringing the islanders in from the Blaskets," I said. "Is it nothing to him that decent men want to live their lives as their fathers did before them?"

"Father," he said, "I shouldn't be saying this, but it's the way he is. He likes everything nice and tidy." No more than you do yourself, said I in my own mind. "I'll have the Canon speak for you," said Fr. Staunton, "for he likes you and always has. But it seems to me you need more people up here than a handful of men and children. I can see his side and I can also see yours."

"There are men here who'll have no trouble getting a wife."

"I hope you're right, Father," he said.

"There'll be wives and children skipping around here yet," I said, "for bad as it looks, there's a fair bit of land out there and the grazing isn't bad when the winter is mild."

"I'm sure you're right about that, Father," he said.

I saw him down to the ridge. A few of the children were playing higher up on the mountain and stopped to look at us. The men were already in the fields. A few sheep were nosing around the opened and closed grave. I watched Fr. Staunton's hat bob under the ridge.

My mind was in a confusion about him. But I had to put my thoughts to the meeting with the Bishop. I went back to the church and prayed.

· · ·

You wouldn't credit the difficulty of getting from the village to the Bishop's Palace outside of Killarney. The only good thing was that the day looked as if it had been provided for my journey. Not a cloud in the sky and a fresh morning breeze. I was to be there at three o'clock, so I left early to give myself plenty of time. I had an old bike under a shed in the heel of the mountain and I pedalled along the rutted road to the big one. I got a lift in a pony and trap and the old man who picked me up— he didn't have a word out of him—let me off right at the station where I got my return. I hadn't been on a train for a while. It was a pleasure to rest my mind on the telegraph wires, watching them relax before being slapped to attention by the next pole, then relax again in a long scoop. The carriage was empty except for myself. There were photographs of Glendalough and The Giant's Causeway let into wooden frames over the plush seats which smelled of must and smoke as if they'd never been aired out. I opened the window, letting the broad strap into the next to last notch, and sat with my back to the engine so that I didn't get too many of the smuts.

The rocks as you know stick up like old teeth and bald heads through the scruff and heather until you get past Tralee, and then there's the cattle and sheep in those green fields that never see a plough, as they should if there was sense in this country. Sometimes you'd be thinking it's a mild dictatorship we need, like Salazar in Portugal. Not that O'Duffy would fill the bill.[17] The Bishop's Palace was three miles out the road. I'd been there once before when I was a young priest. There wasn't a bus leaving for another hour, so I took off on shank's mare, keeping an eye on the traffic coming towards me. Many's the poor lad has been swept away from behind, especially at night if he had a drop in. Joanna Mulligan from the town and her man were walking out a year ago and he was stripped from her side and carried a hundred yards and more. God bless and save us and where 'tis told. She never got over it.

17. General Eoin O'Duffy (1882–1944) was the charismatic founder of the Blueshirts, the inept Irish version of Nazi Brownshirts, for whom the poet W. B. Yeats composed some marching songs. After several clashes, riots, and a profusion of rhetoric, the General took his men to Spain to fight for General Franco. The good Father's comment about the desirability of a benign dictator was often heard in the economically stagnant thirties.

The day was without a breath of wind. The sun was high over my head and I was drenched in no time. There was no sign of the bus and when it came I was nearly there anyway, so I let it go. It left behind a blue haze of smoke that to tell you the truth I don't mind the smell of. The smell of summer from the fields and the hedges thick with Queen Anne's lace and fuchsia were a joy to me, for you rarely get that rich smell up the mountain. The tar was melting with the heat and a little cloud of midges came along with me. On a hot summer's day there's a profusion of creation.

I recognized the gates of the Palace. No one was in the lodge. When I stepped into the long avenue—the Palace was more than a half-mile up it—it was like stepping into another world. The parkland stretched out, undulating in little hills like a golf course. One of those white wooden X's set on the grass at intervals beside the avenue was a bit askew. I went over and put it back into line. The chestnuts were heavy with foliage and the willows stood apart from each other as if they'd come to an agreement on the distance between them. There wasn't a rustle or a quiver among those leaves. Walking up that avenue, the crunch of gravel under me, I felt I had entered paradise. Even the midges had stopped outside the Bishop's gate. It was so still I could hear the whine of a bee in the rhododendron bush at the curve of the avenue. Every sound was magnified. It was cooler than outside on the road. When I passed under the shadow of a tree, I felt the slightest of breezes on my cheek. After the three miles I'd walked in the heat, you'd think I'd be tired, but I'd never felt more at my ease. I was convinced I could see every leaf and blade of grass. The gravel became so fine I felt I was walking on velvet. The air was so fresh, I drank it in with each breath, and with each breath I felt I was expanding to include all that perfection—the trees and the green lawns and the blue sky were all part of me—don't laugh, it was the best feeling in the world. Then I turned the corner and there was the Bishop's Palace with its stone front and porch and white windows and I was back to myself in a whisker. The cause of my journey was before me and I didn't relish it at all.

It was ten to three by my watch so I was in plenty of time. I hesitated on the half-circle in front of the house. The windows were all curtained the same way and the blinds all pulled down to exactly the same length. The big front door didn't offer an invitation, and I was wondering how to get to the back door, maybe, when I remembered I was standing on the very spot of an unpleasantness during the Troubles. For this had been old Colonel Sanderson's mansion, and we all know what happened to many of the Big Houses. They came up to burn it and out he came brave as can be with his wife and daughter looking through the window. They took him and stripped the clothes off of him in front of his wife until he was naked as a bulldog. They made him bark and beg and run around on all fours or they'd burn down the house[18] the next minute with his wife and child in it. All the time jeering at him. He'd fought in the World War against the Kaiser and I saw him once in his scarlet coat at the Hunt when I was around Cork years ago. Well, he did what they wanted, and when the Troubles were over, he took his wife (she was delicate, they say) and his daughter over to England and we never heard of him again. And he wasn't a bad man, mind you. The house lay there until the Bishop bought it.

The front door looked so unfriendly and to go to the back didn't feel right. You'd never have this hesitation except with so grand a house. The back door is always

18. Burning down the Big Houses—the Georgian mansions of the Anglo-Irish gentry—was a favourite revolutionary amusement, as the oppressors and their culture were perceived as identical. Treasures were consumed by republican zeal as the present purged the past. How the masters had treated the "natives" often determined whether or not a house was spared.

more friendly and many's the back door where I've had
a warm welcome, for the kitchen is the center of things.
I stood looking at the house, the bishop somewhere inside, not knowing what to do. No point in coming so far
and standing there all day. I went to the porch and
couldn't make a decision between the big brass ring
of a knocker or the bell. I gave two light knocks and
no one came. So I knocked again louder. I was wondering whether to try the bell when the door was opened.
A maid with a white apron and cap showed me into
a parlour off the hallway, and it was the same parlour
I've been in a thousand times before, only bigger and
grander.

There was Jesus opening His chest with His two
hands to show His Sacred Heart, a crown of thorns on
His heart with His head tilted sideways. His gentle eyes
followed you all over the room. And there was the
Blessed Virgin on a pedestal with a blue and white
shawl trimmed with gold over her head. There was a
small statue of St. Bernadette, her eyes turned upward
to the heaven that had sent her the shower of roses in
her arms. On the sideboard, among the silver, was a little statue of St. Anthony holding the Baby Jesus, with
the same upward look, and on the other side, one of
Blessed Martin de Porres, the black Dominican from

Peru. I was in the company of Jesus, His mother, and the saints, but I was far from at my ease. The smell of the room was very familiar, a hint of Jayes Fluid and of waxed table-top—a big oval table, a square of lace in the center with a bunch of white roses in a vase. In the rippled shine of the table, I could see the moulding of the ceiling, with a small chain hanging down, but no chandelier. It must have been getting fixed. Even though I was expecting it, the door opened so suddenly I was surprised.

It's a small world surely. For there was Fr. Darcy, from the same seminary as myself though a few years after me. He still had that shiny dark hair and the same quick way about him. We talked a bit about the old days but I could tell he didn't want to be reminded of them. He'd been secretary to the Bishop for the past five months. I asked what had happened to old Fr. Grainey.

"He's not well at all," says he, which meant he was dying and I was sorry to hear that. We sat on the dining room chairs at the table and he gave me the impression he was very busy. He came to the point right away.

"His Lordship is worried about you, Father," said he.

"Sure the poor man has a lot more to worry about than to be worrying about me," said I.

"These are difficult times for all of us, Father," says he.

"Indeed none knows that better than myself," says I.

He was always at the top of his class, I remembered, and there was a feeling back then that he was well on the way to a bishop's palace himself. His nickname was "The Nuncio." I'll bet you a bottle of Locke's that secretary to His Grace was not what he had set his sights on.

"His Grace is meeting with the permanent secretary to the Department of Education, and he will be with us shortly. He's meeting with the Minister next week."

"In Dublin?" I said, just to keep things going.

"No, the Minister is coming to Killarney," says he.

"Is there a problem in Killarney, Father?" says I.

"There are problems everywhere. What else can you expect with the films they show, in spite of Dr. Hayes.[19] The English Sunday papers are a disgrace—"

---

19. Dr. Richard Hayes (Risteard Ó hAodha, 1882–1958) was the Republic's first film censor. A noble old man, former revolutionary, historian of the Irish Diaspora in France, director of the Abbey Theater, and medical doctor, he was a typical Dublin polymath. He protected the vir-

"I don't read them myself, Father," I said. There was a silence after that. He started to say something when the door opened and in a flash of purple there was the Bishop in his soutane and biretta.

"Ah, Fr. McGreevy," he said, holding out his hand, "how are we today? It's good of you to come down from your mountain eyrie to meet us." I kissed his ring.

"Your word is my command, your Grace," I said.

"Well, now," he said, "I'm sure Fr. Darcy has settled everything with you."

"I was just leading up to it, your Grace," said Fr. Darcy.

"Ah dear, well, I'm sure you can settle it well enough together. I'm afraid I have to go. Some things can't wait, Father." He looked at Fr. Darcy. "Have you offered Fr. McGreevy a glass of sherry?" he said. "He's come a long way to see us. And never hesitate to come see us, Father," he said to me, "any time there's a problem."

"Well, there's a problem now, your Grace," I said.

"Indeed there are problems everywhere you look,"

---

gin sensibilities of the Irish people with tact, and shared with the clergy a suspicion of genito-urinary matters. The censor's post still exists, but with a diminished capacity.

he said with a smile. If I had a smile like that I'd be
Bishop myself. "Fr. Darcy and yourself must have a
good conversation and worry things through. You'll
find Fr. Darcy very helpful. A bundle of energy." He
nodded his long head gravely, took a step backward to
the door and quick as a flash Fr. Darcy was there to
open it for him. Fr. Darcy came back to the table and
the two of us looked at each other.

"I think it's time to talk about what's on the Bishop's
mind," said he.

"Indeed," I said, "isn't that what I came for? But it
looks as if he's not going to tell me himself."

"He's a very busy man," said Fr. Darcy.

"Indeed he is," I said.

"The declining population in the rural areas is a
cause of great concern to us," he said.

"That I know," I said. "It's a worry to myself also."

"So we must consolidate," he said. I said nothing.

"Your little church on the mountain has served its
purpose very well these many years," he said.

"That it has," I said.

"The Bishop is worried about you and the terrible
winter you went through. There's less than a handful
of people left and not a woman among them."

"There's my housekeeper," I said. "By the time they're old enough to work the fields they're off to England."

"Emigration is draining our lifeblood," he said. He looked out the window, then turned around and looked me straight in the eye. "The Bishop would like you to close your little church and join with Canon Sheehy on a temporary basis. I think the time has come, Father. You have served your flock long and well but they've flown the nest."

"What do you mean by a temporary basis?" I said.

"That remains to be seen," he said. "But we can't stand in the way of progress."

"Coming down from the mountain may be progress to you," I said, "but not to the people that live on it. What will the poor men and children up there do without a priest to tend their souls? They've been up there a hundred years and more, God knows how long."

"There's no living for them up there," said Fr. Darcy.

"It's a hard living indeed," I said. "But it's better than none. Nor would they be welcome if they came down."

"They can come down to your Mass every Sunday, and you can visit them yourself when needs be."

"How could they have come down in the winter that's

past? No more than I could have gone up if I had been down."

He looked at me from a distance though we were no farther apart than you and I this minute. "This is not an easy decision for the Bishop, but the time has come, like it or not. All of us are under the law of obedience, Father. I've no doubt they can let out some of their land for grazing, if they wish."

"Is it thinking of moving them down too, you are?" I said.

"There's plenty of grazing for their own livestock around the town."

"There is if you pay for it," I said. He didn't know the first thing about farming. He'd been with the Bishop too long.

Then he said, "There's many a way for them to ease their own hardship. It's only a matter of setting their minds to it."

"The Blasket people[20] won't take at all happily to the mainland," I said.

---

20. The Blasket Islands are located off the Dingle peninsula. There, a community of some 150 survived for hundreds of years. At its apogee it boasted some thousand sheep and thirty cows. Lacking a bull, cows were forced to swim to the mainland for insemination. In 1953, the Government resettled the inhabitants on the mainland. The islanders spoke Irish, had no church, pub, or store, made their furniture from driftwood,

"We're not talking about them," he said, "though I don't agree with you about that. If the village had been resettled last summer we wouldn't have had all those deaths. It's created quite a lot of concern in high places."

"Well, Father," I said, "there's no higher place than the mountain and there's no greater concern than among those that bore the brunt of it. And the chance of another winter like that is as likely as another Big Wind.[21] If we wait around for a hundred years, maybe we'll see the like, but even then I doubt it."

"The Bishop is very serious, Father. I want you to give this your full consideration. We don't want a repeat of last year."

"There are no more women left to catch the sickness," I said, "even if it should come back. And the men are hard at work this very minute, decent, God-fearing men, every one of them."

"I'm sure they are," he said.

---

their houses from local rock. From this bleak environment came three classic texts of the Gaelic Revival as the islanders set down their stories. Much prized by the language revivalists, the books, elegant in their primitive directness, became vulnerable to the ironies of those who detested the lumpen mentality of the revivalists.

21. The Big Wind of 1839, still alive in the national memory. One of

We each said nothing for a while.

"Is that all there's to it?" I said.

"The Bishop has spoken to the Canon," he said, "and it's arranged for you to help the Canon—he's laid up as you know. The town is growing and he needs you, Father."

"Can I talk to the Bishop about this?"

"It would be very difficult for me to get him out of his meeting. He would tell you the same thing I've told you," said Fr. Darcy.

"Father," I said, "what you've told me is a great torment to me. You're telling me to abandon my flock that I've tended for thirty-three years and make an end to a village that goes back beyond our grandfathers' fathers and has its own ways. The *gaeilgeoirs* come up every summer just to hear the Irish spoken."

"They can come to town just as well when the men move down," he said. "It's not the end of the world we're witnessing here."

"It'll be the end of their world. And the language will be gone in no time once they come down."

"Well, that won't be a great hardship," said Fr. Darcy.

---

its lethal tricks was to reverse the flow of air down chimneys, jumping the fire out of the fireplace and setting the house on fire.

"If you have a choice between the language and a better way of life, which would you choose?"

"You can't teach old dogs new tricks, Father," I said.

"Fr. McGreevy," he said, "I'm sympathetic to your objections. But the Bishop is not in the habit of changing his mind."

"When is this event to take place?" I said. "When am I to be taken down from the mountain?"

"As soon as possible, Father," he said.

"Father," I said, "It's too soon. Let another winter go by at least. Give the men a chance to recover and bring things back to the way they were before. It needs to be more gradual. I promise if His Grace gives me the coming winter, I'll come down next summer for certain if he still thinks we should. Only let me try and support these poor men a little longer until they find some peace in themselves. They are not themselves right now."

"I have my orders from the Bishop," he said.

"Fr. Darcy," I said, "do me this one favour and I'll never forget it for you. Ask the Bishop before I go to grant my request and I'll do whatever he says without fail next summer. I'm begging you on my knees, Father." I started to get off the chair, which I knew would embarrass him.

"Please, Father. Please! Please!" he said, shutting his eyes and holding up his hand. "Please."

"Father," I said, "do this for me in the name of God."

He walked over to the window and turned around, dark against the light. "Father," he said at last, "the Canon says you're a good man and you've been through the mill, there's no doubt about that. Wait for me here. I can't promise anything."

He left me alone with the Sacred Heart and St. Bernadette and the Blessed Virgin and you can believe I prayed to all of them, particularly to the Virgin who has a way of approaching her Son. When he came back he was so solemn my heart sank.

"Well, Father," he said, "the Bishop says to let you have your own way this one time."

"God bless you, Father," I said. "I'm sure it was the way you put it to him that did it."

"But next summer without fail," he said, raising a finger.

"Without fail," I said.

The shadows were lengthening on the lawns as I walked down the avenue and the birds were starting their evening clamor. By the grace of God and His Holy Mother I had a chance to show the Bishop that we could rebuild our village and preserve our ways.

It was nearly nine o'clock when I got back to the town, and it was not the town I had left. It was well after tea-time but there were people at street-corners, talking away in that secret manner of theirs, looking right and left and then leaning forward to deliver their words in a half-whisper, though you know as well as I that there's usually no secret at all but a way of talking. To look at them, you'd think the town was full of secrets, but you'd be mistaken, for every secret in that town was as public as a notice on the church board. The secret is that everyone pretends it—whatever it is—is a secret, otherwise there wouldn't be much sport in gossip at all. As for the secrets of the confessional, you wouldn't give a penny for them. There seems to be a poverty of invention on the devil's part. Sins are all much alike and the same ones keep coming up.

I ran into the doctor's wife, Mrs. McKenna, talking to two other women. One of them was the solicitor's wife. She fancied herself as a singer. When she first came to town, she gave a concert in the Hall, her hands clasped in front of her bosom with one of the nuns on the piano. She was singing "The Kerry Dancing" and when she came to "Oh! To think of it! Oh! To dream of it!" Oweneen, who was standing at the back near the door, shouted out, "Did you ever get a slap of it?" and there was a commotion, I can tell you. I shouldn't be telling stories about her, but pride goes before a fall and she had her share of pride. She was looking at me now, as I was talking to the doctor's wife. It was unusual to find women out at this time of night. There was a restlessness on the street and I had no notion what it was. It was a bit like when Kerry wins the All-Ireland, or after an election speech in the square.

"They're moving the body in a minute, Father," said Mrs. McKenna.

"Who died?" I said. "The Canon?"

"It's the German, Father," she said. "The German," as if I should have known.

"What German would that be?" said I.

"He was washed up today," she said, "with not a mark on him. The children found him at four o'clock after school over in the rocks at the Point. He's in the hospital now and they're moving him any minute. The doctor did a quick job on him."

I'd never heard of anything happening so fast. "What's all this hurry?" I said.

"The Protestants wanted it hurried up," she said. "They found out he was a Protestant."

"Did he tell them," said I, "dead and all?"

"Of course not, Father. They went through his pock-

141

ets or his uniform or whatever it was he was wearing. There was great confusion, because the boys hooked it over to the presbytery and Fr. Staunton was there in a flash. He gave him the last sacraments lying there on the rocks. Then the word got to the minister that he was a Protestant, and he claimed the body in the name of the Protestant community and said it would be buried in the Protestant cemetery."

"They have a real shortage of burials there," I said.

"Well, that's what happened, Father," she said, nodding and turning back to her two companions.

There was a knot of people outside the hospital door, including young lads in their short trousers and gansies. In I went and there was Matron, a big woman with her hands tucked into her sleeves.

"Where's the poor boy, Matron?" I said to her.

"He's not one of yours, Father," she said.

"Nor one of yours either," I said, "but he's here all the same."

"It's causing a great disturbance," she said. "The nuns should all be in bed by now, and everyone's running around like they're demented."

I didn't see a soul around except herself. "Is the doctor here?" I said.

"He's in there with Fr. Staunton and the Protestant minister," she said. "Mr. Devany his name is."

"I hear he's a kindly man," I said.

"Kindly or not, I don't want him gallivanting around my hospital." I didn't say, such a big hospital with all its twenty beds. Anyone really sick was bundled off to the county hospital. With the Irish Sweeps we have hospitals everywhere. She was a Sister of Mercy as you know. There was a big framed picture of Mother Mary Aikenhead on the wall opposite the door.

"I'd like to go see them," I said.

"Please yourself," she said. "Just follow your nose down the corridor to the second door on the right."

When I opened the door my eyes went to the high aluminum table like it was a magnet. But Mr. Devany's grey back was in the way. Then the three faces turned around to look at me, and Fr. Staunton said, "What are you doing here, Father?"

"The same as yourself," I said, "to see if there's anything to be done."

"It's kind of you to come, Father," said Mr. Devany, whom I hardly knew. He had all the looks of a Protestant, with the collar over that glossy bib and that secular grey suit instead of black. "But I think it's nearly all taken care of now." I wasn't delighted to hear a kind word from the Protestant and an unfriendly question from my own kind.

"Reverend," I said, "as long as the lad gets the last rites of his proper church and I hear he's been twice blessed for the next world."

"How did you hear about this up on the mountain, Father?" said Dr. McKenna. "News travels fast around here indeed."

"I heard it from your own wife out on the street," I said. "And as for being up the mountain, there's no law against me being here at this hour, is there, now?"

They were silent as I stepped around to the other side of the metal table and looked down. The body was stark naked with a great cut down the middle from the throat to the privates. It was held together with big black stitches and crude knots. He was blond as a woman with a small nose and a heavy chin. His eyes were closed but not so fully I couldn't see two slivers of ground glass between the lids when I bent over. It's hard to see the nature of a person's face when he's lying down. He was about twenty-two or three I'd say. There were purple stains along the body where it met the table, as if it had been bruised. The body was swollen, as if it were made of heavy dough.

"God rest the poor lad," I said. "What killed him, Doctor?"

"He drowned," he said. "He must have got out of his plane all right, for there isn't a break or a bruise on him."

"What's all that bruising?" I said.

"That's not a bruise, Father," he said. "Post-mortem lividity. We're all going to look that way in good time." He always tried to lighten things. The room was getting warm. There was a smell of antiseptic and of sodden clothes.

"He was alive when he got out of the plane, no doubt of that," said the doctor.

"How do you know that?" I said.

"We've been over this ground, Father," said Fr. Staunton.

"Easy to tell," said the doctor. "Look over there." He pointed to a basin of water with a pale wedge of something lying at the bottom. "That's a bit of his lung," he said. "If he hadn't drowned it would have floated."

"What's his name?" I said. Mr. Devany answered.

"Captain Heinrich Wohl, fighter command, squadron 6, Western Theater, Luftwaffe. His things are over there on the table."

I hadn't noticed the table against the wall with the sodden heap of underclothes. To the right of the clothes were documents and an empty wallet. What took my eye were two photographs, one of the young man on the table, smiling, with some writing in German on it—his identification, I suppose. The other was a snapshot of a young woman that looked so familiar, it shocked me. I'd seen her before and it confused me. All that great turmoil raging away across the sea raised a painful echo in my chest, and I didn't know why.

"Let the sisters dress him now," said Dr. McKenna, "and then he'll be ready to go over to your church, Reverend."

"He should be buried in his uniform," said Mr. Devany.

"It should be dried by now," said the doctor. "You'll hardly be needing the underclothes here."

"We've already taken up a subscription among the Protestant community for a coffin," said Mr. Devany. "I'd like to wait here until the coffin comes, set him in that, and bring him over in the morning."

"Whatever you please," said the doctor.

It made me smile, for Matron wouldn't relish a Protestant boy—and a German at that—lying in state in her little hospital all night.

"Are you burying him tomorrow?" I asked. Fr. Staunton looked at me.

"That's no concern of ours, Father," he said. "That's for the Reverend to decide."

"Indeed it is," I said, "and it's a consolation for all of us to think of the poor lad in friendly hands so far from home."

"Thank you, Father," said Mr. Devany. "I appreciate your sentiments."

While we were talking, there was a fuss at the door and Matron came in with one of her nuns.

"The coffin is here now, Reverend," she said to Mr. Devany. "It's here now, and I expect you'll want to take him over to your church right away. They're waiting outside."

"I was planning to leave him here overnight," said the Reverend.

"Well, they're here now to take him away," said the Matron.

"I'll have to open the church and we're not ready for it. My wife is the only one up there at the moment."

"Well ready or not, the coffin is here," said the Matron, turning around and leaving.

I wondered how much she had to do with the coffin arriving so quickly. Her first cousin was married to O'Connell, the undertaker.

"It's up to you, Reverend," said Fr. Staunton. "If you wish we'll stay until the body is clothed and ready. That's if you're thinking of opening the church tonight."

"It's nearly ten o'clock," said Fr. Devany. "I'll see what can be done." Off he went leaving the rest of us in the hot room.

"Poor lad," said the doctor, throwing a sheet over the body. "It'll be a sad day for his family."

"From what I can get on the radio, they're probably dodging bombs this minute," I said. "I suppose Mr. Devany will write to them since he has all the particulars."

"He'll have to go through the Embassy in Dublin first," said Fr. Staunton. "There are ways of doing these things."

"Maybe the Embassy in Dublin should have been contacted before it was decided to bury him," I said.

"What are they going to do?" said the doctor. "Pack him in ice and send him back safe and sound to Germany? There's a war on."

"His family will get him back when the war's over," said Fr. Staunton.

"If there's any family left," I said.

"I wouldn't recommend that you leave that body lying around," said the doctor, "or it'll make its presence felt in a few days."

The Matron stuck her head in the door. "Are you bringing him back to life?" she said.

"That's beyond my abilities," said the doctor. "But with the two fathers here, you'd never know."

"Thank God Dev [Éamon de Valera] kept us out of the war," she said, "or we'd have dozens of these poor bodies lying around here." She withdrew her head and shut the door. It was easy to see she wanted an end to this.

"Maybe we should wait outside," said the doctor, "and let the sisters do their work."

From the hallway we could see people waiting in the street. It was still light outside.

"I was on my way back from the Bishop," I said. Fr. Staunton looked at me and nodded. "It's not all bad news," I said.

"Well," said Fr. Staunton, "the news can wait. Are you going up the mountain tonight?"

"That's my intention," I said.

"It'll be dark before you get up there," said the doctor. "I've been up there in the middle of the night and I didn't relish the journey."

"You're very welcome to stay at the Canon's for the night," said Fr. Staunton. "There's a bed for you there and you can go up first thing in the morning."

"That's very kind of you, Father," I said. He was always confusing me, that man.

Mr. Devany was back in twenty minutes. The doctor had gone to his office to sign the death certificate. The Sergeant joined us in the hallway. Waiting for the doctor I suppose. The coffin was brought in. The sisters dressed the body. I stayed in the hallway with Fr. Staunton. Four men I didn't know went in to put the body in the coffin. They brought the coffin out and lifted it into the back of the hearse. Mr. Devany was making sure the proceedings had a measure of dignity. I wondered if we'd have done as well. O'Connell would stick him for that hearse. In the last twilight of the evening, close to eleven it was, we followed the hearse to the Protestant church on the hill. Fr. Staunton and myself left off at the bottom of the hill. The hearse went slowly up followed by Mr. Devany and his wife who'd

come down to meet him and by a couple of dogs that
would follow anything.

·   ·   ·

Halfway up the mountain early the next morning and
a bit breathless, I turned to look back at the town. A few
tiny figures were going to Mass. I could see the Protestant spire rising out of the trees. They always had the
best spot. There were tall cypresses in the graveyard,
black as exclamation marks. I thought I saw a few
people in the graveyard, but it may have been my imagination. It's handy to have the graveyard next to the
church. The Catholic cemetery is outside the town, but
then that gives people a chance to walk in the funeral.
Up through the light air came a distant bell, Protestant
or Catholic, I couldn't tell. Beyond the town, I could see
the rocks where the body had washed up. The sea was
shining out to where the horizon dissolved into a haze.
I turned back to my climb and to the greatest shock of
my existence.

I hadn't gone more than a few steps when I heard
a sound that frightened me. It put me in mind of a
woman in labor when the pains come thick and fast.
Many's the time I've heard those moans and grunts as

THE DEPOSITION OF FATHER McGREEVY

I waited outside the door while Biddy and the doctor were delivering a child. I say grunts, because new life arrives by stretching our animal nature to its limit. *In sorrow shalt thou bring forth children.* It's the poor women that have to bear the brunt of original sin. It wasn't the same sound, mind you, but it was an urgent noise repeated like a blow, and it struck me in a way that made the bile rise in my throat. It was coming from behind a rock near a bunch of gorse and the bushes were shaking. I thought for a second that a wild beast was about to spring out at me. But as I looked up—for I was still climbing—what did I see but as strange a beast as ever man did see. It had four spindly legs or maybe more and a man's head, and out of the man's stomach— the shock nearly knocked me back down the mountain—was a sheep's head with the eyes staring at me. I lost all words. For a split second I had a nightmare of centaurs and giants, as if Old Biddy's stories had come true, as if the whole mountain had been pulled back thousands of years.

Then in a haze of rage, I saw the face of Tadhg the idiot. Sheep and man were facing me so that they seemed like one. Our eyes locked into a stare. His were wide as saucers. The sheep's eyes were staring at me too. Between man and beast I had a confusion of glances.

THE PRIEST'S STORY

Those strange sounds suddenly ran into a long cry.
Tadhg's eyes opened wide until I thought they'd fall
out. The sheep came towards me as if driven by a blow.
I thought for a moment he was torturing the sheep. He
was always bothering that old ram of ours. An eerier
cry than before came out of his mouth and hung in the
air like a strip of torn skin. He raised his hands from
the sheep and staggered back, hobbled by his trousers
around his knees. I saw glistening in the sun the sign
of his manhood, purple as heather and disgusting to
the sight.

Then the shock of it hit me. I don't remember what I
said. But when my mind returned to me I was shouting,
"You dirty beast! You filthy animal! You dirty beast!"
The sheep gave a little gallop and strolled away and began to graze. Tadhg pulled up his trousers as I ran up
the hill. I could have run up a cliff I had so much forgotten myself. I fetched him a blow across the face. He
pitched back on the ground and curled up sobbing and
making noises like a changeling. "God forgive you," I
said. "Wait until your father hears about this. You're a
disgrace to the man and woman that bore you. It's a
shame you ever saw the light." I turned around and ran
after the sheep—I don't know why. I wanted to give it a
kick. It ran off up the mountain on those legs like black

sticks and stopped, looking back down at me without a bit of sense in its eyes. There's nothing as stupid as a sheep. My anger spent itself and I turned back. The boy was still curled up, crying away. My stomach was in a cramp but there was nothing in it to come up. But that didn't stop me puking, which brought on a sweat and a weakness until I had to sit down on the ground not far from him. Snots were running down around his mouth and his eyes were swimming in his face. "I'msorryFrI'msorryFr—" was all he could say and he kept saying it again and again. As the anger went out of me, I felt the sadness of it. This had been one of the best lads you'd ever seen, a great worker and a handsome fellow. The girls down in the town would look at him more than twice on fair day, even though he came from the mountain. My heart broke and I started sobbing and crying. After all we'd been through—

I took him by the scruff of the neck and marched him up the mountain over the ridge and past the graves. I saw Muiris high on the mountain turn and look at us. I was marching this boyo to the church to relieve him of his sin before his poor deformed soul fell into total darkness. But then, how could he understand confession? It's clear to me now I didn't know what I was doing. Muiris started down to us. As we passed the graves, my heart was in my boots. The lad kept on snivelling and mouthing with hardly a sound. At that moment I recognised the face of the girl in the German pilot's photograph. I knew where I'd seen it before. It was buried right next to me. For it was the spitting image of Máire Rua's face when she was young, before the mountain life had wearied her. That image of her face rose in my mind like a flower opening, for a beautiful young girl she had been. Now her husband was almost on us. And here was I with their demented son, not a trace of either of them in his face, and a stink off him that would knock you over. I saw the great cut down the pilot's front, the black stitches, the purple sex of the lad as he pulled away from the sheep, all mixed up with the face of young Máire Rua and the German girl. The image of that face, only a memory in my mind and in the mind of the man coming towards us, gave me such a turn that I began to vomit again, but nothing came up.

"What's the matter, Father?" said Muiris. "Where are you taking the lad?"

I was swallowing the bitter stuff so I could answer.

Muiris took me by the arm. He still had a lot of strength in him. "I'll take the boy back to the house," he said.

"You will not," I said. "I'm taking this fellow to the church to hear his confession."

"What has he done now?" said Muiris.

"He has shamed us all," I said.

"How?" said he.

"With a beast! With a beast!" I said.

If I knew then what I know now, before God and His blessed angels, I'd have had more to say. What Muiris said astonished me. You could have knocked me down with a feather.

"Sure the lad doesn't have enough sense to see any harm in it," he said.

"Well if he doesn't I do," I said. "It's a crime against the law of God and nature, not to speak of the law of the land." All the while the lout was mouthing away "Fr.Fr.Fr." until it drove me to distraction.

"And well you might be sorry," I said to him.

"And you too for standing up for him," I said.

"Steady on now, Father," said Muiris. "You know yourself he hasn't a notion of what's right or wrong."

"Does that mean he can go around degrading himself and this village and every man in it, not to speak of this parish and the whole of Kerry and the entire country? If this were known, what would be said of us?

156

They'd say we were savages. What if the bishop heard of it? Did you think of that?"

"The lad doesn't know what he's doing so how can it be a sin?" says he.

"Is it a theologian you are now?" I said.

"All I know, Father," said Muiris, "is that he's beyond blame. When the weather's harsh we take in the sheep. You know that yourself, Father. You've seen the children curl up with them for a bit of warmth. So with his mind gone, he sees no harm in it."

"And what's that supposed to mean?" I said. "That when they grow up they can't tell a sheep from a woman? If I listen to you, men and animals will be getting married in the church. An evil thing has happened here, and the devil himself is laughing this very minute. Have you no shame for your son?"

"Soft in the head or not," he said, "he's still my son."

"His immortal soul is trembling on the edge of damnation as we stand here talking. I'm taking him to the church to cleanse his soul, and if a lightning bolt knocks him dead between here and there, he'll burn forever in hell."

"I'll come up with you, Father," said Muiris.

"You can have him when I've absolved him," I said.

157

"And you better keep an eye on him every time he stirs. He's out at night at all hours. God knows what he's up to. What if the police knew what was going on?"

I grabbed Tadhg's arm. He was standing there like a scarecrow. Muiris took his other arm.

"I'm walking my son up to the church with you, Fr. Hugh," he says, "and I'll wait outside for him." We climbed up to the church with the lad between us dribbling away and muttering what was once "I'msorry I'msorry" but was now a "sa-sa-sa" that never stopped as he nodded his head to it every time. There was no way of hearing his confession so I gave him a general absolution. And as I prayed, I knew his father was right and I was wrong. And with that I felt a great shame slowly come over me. I brought him out to his father who led him off without a word.

· · ·

When a bad thing happens, it happens again, as if the evil couldn't wait to force itself on your attention. I was in such a fever I paid no heed to what was going on around me. The sight of that *amadán* as he tore himself away put itself between me and anything I looked at. And when it did, I started to lose my breath as if I were climbing the mountain. I'd stand there panting until

THE PRIEST'S STORY

Old Biddy, with her nose into everything, would say, "Is it sick you are Father? Why don't you lie down and I'll bring you a cup of tea," and the way I'd jump on her, you'd think I was a dog and she'd come between me and a bone. In my mind's eye, I saw all kinds of assaults by that half-wit. Now don't think me innocent. I've heard of such a thing. But in all the time I've heard confession, not a soul had ever asked penance for that sin. I could hardly go to sleep that night and when I did my mind offered me such pictures that I was in an agony of scruples. For when you're half-asleep your mind goes down paths where there's no light at all, only the shine and glow of images you wouldn't want to admit were your own. You have to ask yourself where they come from. And that I knew. The devil was doing his work.

As sure as I'm sitting here, I knew I was going to see what I feared most to see and that no matter how much I expected it, it would be a surprise to me. And so it was. Early one morning before Mass, on impulse—God knows why—there I was stepping over to Máire Rua's grave, for she was the one closest to my heart, a noble woman surely. It was a grand morning with a hush to it. The sky was as blue as Our Lady's robe. Again, it was the grunting I heard this time. I thought for a moment it was a stray pig, or maybe a badger, but then we don't

159

have a pig and I haven't seen a badger in years. Without thinking, my feet brought me over to the ridge where the ground falls down the mountain. Tucked in there behind a fuchsia bush was the madman himself with a lamb no bigger than a little dog and fluffy as a cloud. My mind refused to see what it was looking at. But the eyes have their own appetite as the church always preaches and they stamped that moment on my brain. I saw mostly his back as he bent over for he was holding the lamb off the ground. He staggered forward out of the bushes into clear ground and my eye took in the long shadow that raced ahead of him—the sun was low—and a strange shadow it was, though it lasted but a half second. Two long legs without a torso, for the ground dropped away. Two long legs with four little legs sticking out of them. The lamb was bleating away. The whole scene wavered as if under water with the tears of shame and rage and sorrow that started from my eyes. I heard a crackle of bushes and a power of bleating. When my eyes cleared the lamb was running off, its tail whisking back and forth in a blur. Somehow the shaking of that tail—if you've ever seen a spring lamb's tail go a mile a minute like a woman shaking out a duster—made me feel sick in my bowels. The *amadán* must have heard me for he turned his face up to me, open as the sky—going "he-he-he, he-he-he" as if he'd done a great deed. When he realised what he saw, he yelped like a dog hit by a stone and ran off with his legs wide apart, hobbled again by his pants halfway down his legs. Thank God I didn't see the wicked source of his shame. I stood there with my eyes closed. And up through the air disturbed by his passage came the sour smell, like old cabbage, of his clothes, mixed with a smell my nose didn't want to mention.

I said Mass but I didn't hear a word I said. I tried to put what I'd seen out of my mind by thinking of all the Masses being said at that moment, rising up to the throne of the Almighty as the consecrating Words[22] reenact the miracle of the Body and Blood of Our Savior, who understands all and forgives all the sins of the world from the beginning to the end of time. And though the Latin consoled and fortified me as it had every day of my life since I was ordained, my mind kept wandering. I'd find myself at another place in the Mass without a memory of how I got there. That's no way to honor the Lord. So I was asking Him to forgive me my inattention at the same time that I was trying to be present at the Mass. I kept asking myself: How long has

22. *Hoc Est Enim Corpus Meum.* With these words, the transubstantiation takes place.

161

this been going on? Does anybody know of it? What's to become of us if Fr. Staunton or the Bishop hears of it? I didn't know where to turn.

So it was that I found myself sitting in Dr. McKenna's surgery with the window behind him so I couldn't see him too well. That's what the Sisters do—sit against the light so you don't have a notion how your words are being taken. I moved my chair over to the side to see his face better and said, "Doctor, I have a terrible occurrence up the mountain and I don't know what to do." He was used to hearing nothing but the sickness of the body just as I hear nothing but the sickness of the soul. So we had all the troubles of the world between us.

"What is it now, Father?" he said. "Don't tell me it's more of the same."

"It's an affliction of body and soul," I said, "that has made me so sick in my heart that I'm shamed to speak of it."

He had an easy way of getting over that. "There's nothing that hasn't been heard in this room, Father," he said. "You'd be hard put to surprise me."

"Surprise you I will," I said. "Do you know young Tadhg that was hit by a stone and hasn't an ounce of sense from that day?"

"Indeed I do," he said. "Wasn't it I that brought him

into the world? A fine young lad he was before that accident."

"Now that Máire Rua is gone," I said, "his father has the minding of him and the other young lad that's left."

"It's to your credit the way you all mind him," said the doctor. "What's the matter with him now?"

"It's a matter of the way he's behaving himself," I said.

"And what way is that?" said the doctor. "There's no doubt he has a strange way about him. Whenever I've been up there, he pops up everywhere like a jack-in-the-box. You'd think there were ten of him."

"Thank God there's only one," I said.

"The poor lad's not responsible for himself, Father," said the doctor. "So whatever he's done, short of killing somebody, there can be no great harm to it."

"Harm there is, Doctor," I said. "And if what he's done ever gets out, we'll all suffer."

"Well, now," said the doctor. "It must be something special indeed."

I felt like a sinner with the weight of a great sin on him, going to confession. I couldn't bring it out. The doctor didn't say a word. We could hear the occasional murmur and stir of the patients in the waiting room.

"It's a matter of him and a sheep," I said, and as I said it, I could feel the flush rise over my neck and cheeks. The doctor kept staring at me. "He's attacking the sheep, Doctor, a sheep yesterday and a lamb today. I can't sleep a wink."

"He's buggering the sheep, is he?" said the doctor, leaning back on the two hind legs of his chair. "Well, from the way you were talking I thought it was something worse."

"Worse?" I said. "What could be worse? I caught him in the act twice in the past two days and I'm destroyed thinking about it. What's he up to this very moment? There isn't a sheep on the mountain that's safe from him."

The doctor's face turned red. His eyes opened wide and his lips pursed as if he were about to blow up a balloon. "Are you all right, Doctor?" I said. I thought he might be having a turn. He burst out in a big explosion and started to jerk in spasms. Then it dawned on me he was laughing.

"If that's the response you have," I said, getting up, "there's no reason for me to burden you further!"

He waved at me to stay and took out his handkerchief. "Father, forgive me," he said, blowing his nose. "It's the way it took me when you said what you did. I

164

apologise. I'm not taking what you say lightly. But re-member it's not the first time I've heard such a story in this very room." He started to laugh again but kept it in, holding up his hand again for me not to budge. "Bear with me, Father," he said. "It's a serious business indeed. Father, far be it from me—" He stopped and went on again, "But surely, Father, it's not the first time you've—"

"Never," I said, "except in the seminary and then only in a book."

"Now, Father, you have the practise to go with the theory."

"It's a vile thing to see," I said. "It's worse than a man going with a man."

"Ah, Father," said the doctor, "sure we're all made different. You know the old medical joke? Between man and woman there's a vast difference."[23]

"I haven't a notion what you're talking about," I said. "I came here because I had no one to turn to and I'm beginning to be sorry I did."

He got a hold of himself after that. He came out from behind the desk and sat in a chair beside me. "Father,"

---

23. What the doctor said was probably "vas deferens," the tiny tube that carries sperm from the testicle to the urethra. A standard medical joke of mild wit.

he said, "what do you think men do with the passions God gave them? They have to come out some way."

"Not that way," I said. He held up his hand again.

"Father, hear me out," he said. "I know this is a great shock to you. But I can't say it is to me. I sit here at this desk five mornings a week from half past eight to twelve, and if you were a fly on the wall, there would be times you'd hear things you wouldn't credit. Human nature is human nature and it has its own way of going about its business."

"There's a natural law," I said.

"And what is it?" said he. "What is natural anyway? If I were to take my penny catechism and live by every word, I couldn't turn around but it would be a sin."

"Without the church," I said, "where would we all be? A step above the beasts, that's where we'd be. It's the church that raises us above our own nature. And where would women be without the worship of the Blessed Virgin? Treated like beasts of burden. Where would we be without God's grace?"

"I know what you're talking about," said the doctor. "I spent a year in the seminary myself."

"Well that I never heard," I said.

"I didn't do it for myself, Father. It was to please my mother. She had four sons and no priests and I was the youngest. Poor woman, she never got her wish. I didn't have the vocation."

"She got half her wish," I said, "because you're a healer of bodies, if not of souls. But while we're talking like this, there's a terrible perversion of nature going on up the mountain. I thought you'd be the one person to have some advice for me."

"I don't want to shock you, Father, but there's many a tale between man and beast in the country. If I had a penny for every time this came up in the past thirty years, I'd have a few pennies to rattle in my pocket. Listen to me, Father. Is there an injury to anyone here? Is the sheep going across the road there to the solicitor, to sue the poor fellow for breach of promise? We use the beasts for our own purposes, Father, often cruelly. Have you ever seen a tinker beat a donkey to death? Of course you have. There isn't a fair day that goes by but you don't see that or something like it. We beat them, we fatten them, we sell them, we slaughter them, we eat them. And if we didn't, where would we be? So if a poor half-wit that doesn't know his top from his bottom relieves himself of the needs that nature put into him, who can blame him? Would you prefer he was getting some young girl in the family way? Putting another little bastard into the orphanage in Cork?"

"I've heard enough, Doctor," I said.

"I'm not sure you have, Father," said he. "I know you've had a shock. Let me tell you a story and you tell me whether I did right or wrong. This strapping young lad comes into me this morning, just married he was. He couldn't look me in the eye and his face was red as fire. Eventually I got it out of him. He couldn't do any good with the wife at all. Sometimes this happens with fifty-year-old farmers who get married after their mother dies. But this was a young lad of thirty-five. A fine-looking young fellow he was. I asked him if he'd been with a girl before and he said he hadn't. I said that's a strange thing for a good-looking young fellow like yourself. I was getting nowhere until I asked him about the farm and the cattle. He said, looking strange as can be, 'I used to go to the barn a lot, Doctor.' 'I'm sure you did,' I said. 'Taking care of livestock never ends.' 'I don't mean that way, Doctor,' he said and then it dawned on me. We never mentioned anything directly, mind you. I said, 'There was no problem in the barn then, was there?' 'None at all,' says he, 'but with the wife at home I don't go there any more.' 'Well, now,' I said, 'we can't have this go on, can we?' 'No, Doctor,' says he.

"Then I had a bit of an inspiration, Father, though I'm not sure you'd call it that. I said, 'Take the wife down to the barn tonight and make a nice bed of hay and see how you do.' He came back in two days with his face shining. 'No trouble at all, Doctor.' 'Isn't that the good news?' says I. 'Now move the hay closer to the house over the next few nights.' What happened? Eventually there may have been a bit of straw in the bedroom, Father, but that marriage was a marriage. I haven't heard from him since, though his wife has been in and she's due in November. Now, Father, did I sin in condoning the lad's business with the cattle? Is there a fine theological point here? Did I encourage bestiality, if we want to give it a harsh name, in the interests of having this young lad service his wife? There's stories I could tell you, Father. But I'm not sure they would sit well with you. If what's done in the darkness up there doesn't hurt a soul, what does it matter?"

"Hurt a soul? Hurt a soul, is it?" I said. "Mad or not, is casting his immortal soul into the shadow of dam-nation not a danger here? With his father's approval, mark you—that I didn't tell you. I'm responsible for the boy's salvation. What else goes on up there that I don't know about? It's shaken me to the core. And then

I come down to you and look at the picture of the parish you've just given me. Men degrading themselves with their livestock whenever darkness falls."

"From what you've told me, they're not shy of the daylight either. Father," says he as calm as you like, "there's a lot goes on that we never hear about. There are worse things, as I'm trying to tell you."

"It makes me want to puke my insides out," I said.

"Well," said the doctor, "it wouldn't be my fancy."

I left with my head *tréna chéile* for the last thing I expected was for the doctor to take it as lightly as if talking about his Sunday golf. It confused me, for he was a good man—at Mass every Sunday with his wife, who used to be a nurse. Then I remembered he golfed every Sunday with the Canon, when the old man was up to it. I ran back and knocked at the surgery door and stuck my head in. I shut my eyes and held my hand in front of them because a young girl was standing there in her shift.

"What is it, Father?" he said, none too kindly, looking over his glasses and pulling his stethoscope out of one ear.

"Doctor," I said, "not a word—" I didn't want to say the Canon's name with the young girl there all ears.

"Not a word," said he, "not a word. You can count on it."

Going back up the mountain, I had the weight of the world on my shoulders. You never know people until there's trouble enough to bring another side of them out. If you're thinking I was shocked by the way the doctor took what I'd told him you wouldn't be far wrong. And him a spoiled priest and all.

·   ·   ·

What thoughts rubbed together inside that poor *amadán*'s skull, I could not fathom. If the half-words or sounds that he spoke, if speaking it was, were any sign of what was within, there was only a dark sea of tumult and disorder, awash in images and desires that spouted out as the water spouts up out of a blow hole. Sometimes your ear would be about to fathom some sense in his mumbling, but then it would be gone. There was nothing in there but a constant roiling and moiling with no window or way into it.

I brought it up to Muiris as best I could. "What transpires here on the mountain," I said to him as he looked at me without a blink—he was a man who never shirked a stare—"belongs on the mountain."

"I always thought it did, Father," says he, misunderstanding me on purpose, which is often the way with country people and I'm one so I should know.

"I don't have to tell you," I said, "for I know we're both thinking the same thing."

"What you're thinking and what I'm thinking are two different things," says he. "But if you're thinking about what I think you're talking about, then we don't have to talk about it."

I thought that over and was satisfied. "The less that's said the better," I said.

"Isn't that always the case, Father?" said he.

"A loose lip brings trouble," I said.

"That's no more than the truth," said he. And that was that.

But not for me. The shock had so disturbed me I gave myself no peace. I kept a vigil on my eyes, never knowing what they might witness. The image of that sin fastened itself on everything I looked at, so that it took a second glance to unfasten it. A cluster of dead branches or a sack against a rock might shape themselves for an instant in an obscenity. It was as if my eyes had been corrupted. Even when I closed my eyes to pray, that image of what I'd seen was there against the lids. I tried with all my might to substitute the image of the Holy

Mother and Christ Child, but would you believe it, even that image would betray me—the Christ Child would play with a lamb and the lamb would lead to you know what. It was as if my mind were intent on profaning the Holy Image of its own accord. I knew the devil was at work. It's in images that the devil makes his mischief, for his very name is deception and his nature is vile.

I began to look at the sheep and think which had suffered. I couldn't help it. I tried not to look at the sheep and it almost made me laugh in my distress. Here I was, a country lad born and bred, up there on the mountain and afraid to look at a few sheep. The cattle never entered my imagination in that way, thank God. But I'd find myself staring at a sheep. They'd lift their heads from grazing and look back at me. I was trying to stare down not the sheep, but the very thoughts that entered my head when I looked at them. If I looked what troubled me straight in the eye, that might banish it. It became a habit with me, God help me. Occasionally one of the men would see me studying the sheep and join me for a minute and say, "That's a fine piece of mutton, Father." Or, "She'll fetch a good price at the fair, Father." "She needs to be shorn soon, Father, or she'll fall down with the weight of wool on her." Or,

"That's as good looking a sheep as you'll find on the mountain, Father." I had to say "Aye, surely" and "You've never said a truer word" or "It's the care they're getting from such as yourself." And that would break my concentration while I was wrestling with the devil.

There came a time when the sheep paid little heed to me. One of the dogs would sometimes come and stand by me. The sheep would never take their eyes off the dog. Someone would call the dog and then they'd drop their heads to the heather and grass, what there was of it. I couldn't break the habit. The sheep would turn their big bubbles of eyes to me, chewing away in that sideways grind and I'd be wondering—you'll think me as mad as the madman himself—which of them he'd interfered with. The sheep became so used to me they'd turn away and their bottoms would come into my sight, tail twitching, bits of dirt hanging from the wool, and I'd avert my eyes. No wonder I began to think I was going out of my head. I prayed that God would remove this burden from my eyes. The more I tried to fight it, the worse it got.

When you're worried to death about something, it's only a worse worry will push it out of your mind. I avoided the *amadán* whenever he showed his face,

though I couldn't miss hearing him snuffling and muttering around the corner of a house or behind a bush.
He had a way of lurking, that fellow. His father didn't
fail to take him to Mass on Sundays. There was nothing I could do then but ask how he was, and Muiris
would say, "He's as well as he always was, Father."
Thank God I didn't see that terrible sight again the
rest of that summer. The summer lets the light into the
dark corners of the mind. But the darkness of that
never left me. No matter how bright the day, there was
always the night to bring me back to it.

Many's the night I got up in the wee hours, looking for the first light around the side of the mountain. Sometimes I'd hear sounds that my imagination
shaped into something darker than the darkness I was
staring into. At the faint first light, I'd go back to bed.
But of course you couldn't do a thing without that
Biddy. If I walked a foot away from the house—suffering the cold for the sake of penance—she'd be waiting
for me in the darkness when I got back through the
door. "Would you like a cup of tea now, Father? It'll
take the chill off your bones." I'd tell her to get back to
her bed and not be annoying me, and off she'd go in the
dark—she must have had eyes like a cat—muttering
away so that you couldn't catch the words but you were

in no doubt as to their meaning. What other worry that put the sheep out of my mind? I'll tell you, if you only have patience.

I couldn't believe it when Jamesy Donoghue said he was leaving the mountain to marry that MacCarthy girl from the town. I knew he was walking her out. After his mother's death, he was restless and took up with her. But I fully expected he'd bring her back up the mountain. And that when the winter came, we'd have at least one young woman to keep things going, and maybe the promise of a child, with God's blessing. I prayed for that. It's worse when your mind shapes an expectation and is disappointed. But we see what we want to see and don't see what isn't to our liking. He brought the girl up a few times. A fine young woman by the looks of her, but then who can tell? How did it appear to her, I wonder? Meeting an old priest and a few men, not to mention Old Biddy who got her into a corner. Old Biddy would talk the hind leg off an ass. Half an eye would tell you the young woman was above Jamesy's station. When he was with her, he had that embarrassed look young lads have when they're courting. Well-turned-out she was too. When she sat she gathered her skirts close to her, smoothed them out and then bent forward a little with her hands folded in her lap. Very polite she was. When she looked at the lad there was an expression I couldn't fathom. But a woman's look can speak volumes. Satisfaction and appraisal, I'd say, with something hard in it. He was—and is to this day—a fine figure of a lad with curly black hair and dark skin with two blue eyes that jumped out at you. When I caught him looking at her, you could tell he had the fever all right—you can't mistake that foolish look. I walked her around the village and the mountain, telling her about the past and the kindness of the people and the fine future ahead of us all. I hinted at how nice it would be to hear a baby bawling around here, giving the village some life. Muiris talked to her about the old days, the singing and dancing and story-telling we used to have. And how the *gaeilgeoirs* came up every summer. Old Biddy cooked a meal—new potatoes and cabbage and ham from the town and scones and cake after—and the three of us—herself and Jamesy and myself—sat around my table while I tried to fill in the silences, though with Old Biddy coming and going there was no shortage of talk. Of course I had a word with them about the beauty and sanctity of marriage and the Lord's plan. She said her confessor was Fr. Staunton and he was instructing her.

What was going to happen to his little acre, I asked

Jamesy after he'd left her down the mountain and come back up next day. He said he was going to keep it and let it out for grazing; some people from the town wanted it. Then he talked about coming up every week to plant potatoes and cabbage and turnips that he'd sell in town. I reminded him of how his father had carried many a basket of earth on his back to make that piece of land and how sad he'd be to see it deserted. He said it wasn't being deserted at all. I said that's not the way it looked to me. Then he said words that cut me to the quick and that I've heard too many times from many a young lad.

"There's nothing up here for me, Father," he said.

"There's God's clear air and His blessing on all who work the land," I said.

"I'll be working the land for Mr. MacCarthy"—his father-in-law—he said.

"So you'll be answering to him?" I said. "Up here the only one you have to answer to is yourself."

"There's no future up here for me, Father," he said.

"There's the future your father had, and his father before him," I said. He turned silent at that, looking everywhere but at me. "It's the young lady doesn't want to live up here, isn't that the truth of it?" I said.

He had no answer to that either. We both stood there, neither wanting to be so impolite as to walk away. "She has a few brothers, doesn't she?" I said.

"She has indeed," he said, grateful for the relief, "and they don't take too kindly to me."

"Are they younger or older?" I said.

"They're both younger," he said.

"Well that's a mercy," I said and we parted easily enough. I knew he wouldn't have an easy time with the family.

I tried to see the village as it looked at her. It must have looked bare and harsh to her, but not to me. It was grand to be out in God's good air those summer days that went on forever. Every morning the sky would be as clear as your own eye. Down below, the shore would be blurred with fog which would roll over the town before the heat of the sun turned it to vapour by midmorning. Some days with battalions of clouds sailing along, the sun would shoot its rays down through them in a great fan of light. To this day it's a sight that makes me think of the wonder of creation. Every evening there would be terraces of red clouds in the west. My favourite time of day was those long twilights after the sun has gone down and the wind that could be so cruel

held its breath. The birds would have calmed down—
only an odd swift so sudden and low that it drew a line
across your eyeball.

Every week-end that summer we looked forward to
the children coming up from the convent. They'd play
into the twilight to ten or eleven. From my window, I
could hear their shouts and cries and they were music
to my ears. In the dark, you could still make out the
white dabs of the sheep scattered over the mountain. I
tried not to think of them, but sometimes it forced itself
upon me. The *amadán* would join the children playing
football in the dark and the strange, shapeless roar of
his would rise over their cries as they egged him on.

I went down to the town and got batteries for the
wireless so that we could stay up with the world. I followed the war as best I could but no one was much interested apart from Muiris and myself. Whenever I'd
leave the house I'd turn it off and tell Biddy to leave it
be, but on my way back from a visit I'd hear the music
and the minute she heard or saw me, she'd turn it off
and say, "It was me singing, Father."

"With fiddles and a melodeon? Do you think I'm a
real gom?"

Off she'd go to bake bread or clean the pots, mumbling all the time in that way of hers that would try the

patience of a saint. One time I found the *amadán* in there with her, jigging around to the music—that fiddle music that goes round and round with no beginning and no end until it stops as sudden as it began. She was beating time on a saucepan with a big spoon and laughing her head off. When he saw me he was off like a jackrabbit.

"What's he doing in here?" I said.

"Ah sure there's no harm in him, Father."

"Harm is as harm does," I said. "And don't be wasting those batteries, they cost enough."

"Ah, Father, it's lonely here up the mountain."

"Don't you be starting too," I said. "This is as fine a place as you'll find."

"It is, Father, it is. But I was thinking of going up to Dublin to visit my brother. He says there's a power of work to be had up there. I spent time there when I was a young one starting off. Sure my old bones are not eager for another winter like the one just gone by."

You could have knocked me over with a feather. I never thought of her as having any family at all. I always felt I was giving her charity by keeping her. If Old Biddy left, where would I get another housekeeper to come up the mountain and live the life we lived? The young ones have different ideas nowadays. No wonder the world was falling apart. Hitler was going through Europe like a knife through butter. The English were getting the worst of it and no harm in that. I remembered when I was a lad in Eyrecourt the German bands that would come round, always good humored and polite. Now I hear that they were surveying the country for when they invaded us. Or so people said. There were always rumors of German submarines refueling off the coast. It was a submarine that brought poor Roger Casement back to his fate.[24] They were waiting for him on Banna strand. A good man he was, but strange. Even this far away the war had its echo.

As you know as well as I, some of the young lads from the town went off to fight for the British, which made that thin, dark teacher at the National School more bitter than he already was. He was always talking about Ireland's glory dimmed by the occupation up north. I swear he filled some of those young lads' heads with ideas. There's a certain age when you can tell a young lad anything and he'll go die for it.

24. On Good Friday, 1916, the revolutionary Sir Roger Casement was landed from a German submarine on Banna strand on Tralee Bay. He was hanged three months later after a controversial trial marked by forged evidence and homophobic prejudice. The episode has the signature of many Irish revolutionary episodes: high tragedy, devolving into farce, then overtaken by tragedy again.

Never a word was said, but after that, Biddy knew she had permission to play the wireless, even though it irritated me to hear some of those songs from the BBC. Some of them would make a decent person blush. Some were banned, like that one about the Isle of Capri. When she heard me coming in she'd switch back to Radio Éireann. She never went out much. When I'd come back, there she'd be in the dark. First thing in the morning she'd blow on the ashes to start the fire and then sit half over it with her legs apart. Her shins were riddled with ABC, the blotches that map the shins of older women too fond of the fire. And this was the only example of the whole female race in my village.

Muiris had a widowed sister-in-law in Cahirciveen and I asked him if he thought it might be a good time for her to visit. I said she could take care of the young lad during the week when the others were down at school, and he must miss his mother. He was old enough to go down, but he was a bit sickly, always getting colds and coughing. To tell you the truth, I think Muiris didn't want to give up his company. When I mentioned Máire Rua, he looked away and I realised how much he must have missed her. He sent a letter down to the post in the town and she wrote back that from what she heard, it wasn't a place any woman

183

should venture, since none could survive it. She had moved to Cahirciveen when her husband died, God rest him. From what I heard he'd left her well provided for. Muiris wrote again and said the child needed her, and that the summer was mild and she'd come to no harm. She came eventually, grumbling, with a young lad bringing her belongings up the mountain on a donkey. With what she brought with her, you'd think she was staying for life. She wasn't dressed for the country either. As my mother would say, the grandeur of her. I'd met her for five minutes years ago, and she had seemed to me a plain, decent kind of woman then. But many a widow finds her glory after her man dies. At least, I said to myself, she's a woman, and that's a commodity in short supply up here. The first thing she did was turn Muiris's cottage inside out.

She took to me as if I were the only one worth talking to, but that didn't last long. "Why do you keep that old witch around?" she said of Biddy. "She's a disgrace, with that smell off of her." To tell you the truth, if you live with a smell long enough, you don't notice it. "The last time that woman must have washed herself was when she was caught in the Flood," she said. So there I was finding excuses for Old Biddy to this woman who seemed to be making an effort to remain a stranger to us all. The only one she liked was Jamesy's young woman when he brought her up. The two of them would sit and talk all day long. I'd join them for a few minutes, and then take my leave. Sometimes they'd walk out together picking their way over the dried mud and grass as if it offered an insult to their shoes.

She came to the church often enough. Many a time when I came in, there she was, fingering her beads with her eyes closed. She sat apart from the men at Sunday Mass. Muiris sat two rows behind her, and the three other men were here and there. The nun—Sister Mary Attracta—who brought up the children on week-ends had them all gathered in the front bench, though why she came up was a mystery to me since those children had found their way up and down the mountain for years. Muiris's young lad sat beside Mrs. Reidy—that was her name—in the same place every Sunday, the second bench on the left. Old Biddy sat way in the back where you could hardly see her. It was a good feeling to see three women in the church that summer, if you count Biddy and the Sister, and more if you count the three girls up for the weekend. If everything would only stay that way.

That Mrs. Reidy was a bossy one all right, and I wondered how Muiris was getting on with her. At Mass, she'd nudge the young lad to stand up and sit down and she gave him no peace if he fidgeted. She was always bending over from her prayerbook whispering at him. I suppose I should have been paying more attention to the Mass itself, but even with your eyes closed, you can always sense what's going on in the congregation from their rustles and murmurs, the scrape and shuffle of them standing up for the gospels and the spray of coughs that follow the Elevation. Even the way they take the Sacrament tells you something. All the tongues are out, but some are more generous with it than others. Some will hardly open their mouths at all. The children open their mouths like birds in a nest. Sometimes their eyes flutter. After all the instruction the children receive for their first Communion, when they come to the rails they sometimes forget everything they've learned. You catch the eye of one or two of them staring at you as they peel the Host from the roof of their mouths where It got stuck, which they were told not to do. There was one lad—Séamus's twelve-year-old—who always had his eyes wide open and he must have closed them on the way back to his seat, because he'd bump into everything he could bump into. I remember one old man years ago who always chewed It very slowly. Old men's tongues often have a shake in them. The women would get back to their seats with their heads down, and then bury their faces in their hands. After a few minutes of that, some tilt their faces up, eyes closed, hands joined together under the chin, the image of the saints. But the words that joined the moment to eternity always thrilled my soul: *Custodiat animum tuum in vitam aeternam, Amen.* Some blessed themselves quickly after receiving the Sacrament. Others blessed themselves when they got back to their seats. I wouldn't give the Sacrament to the *amadán* after he spat It out on the way back to his seat. I won't go into it. But after that I gave It to him separately when the others were gone and made sure he swallowed it.

Wouldn't you know it was the *amadán* himself that caused more trouble. I looked out the window one morning and there were Mrs. Reidy and Jamesy's young woman walking out. Nothing strange about that. Whenever that girl came up, the first thing she'd do after seeing Jamesy was make a bee-line for Muiris's cottage. The two of them were thick as thieves. They never came near me beyond a polite "Good morning, Father." Mrs. Reidy never got over the way I'd defended Old Biddy, which surprised myself, since I'm always half-mad at her. But it didn't behoove outsiders to make free of their comments about my housekeeper, for that's what she was, despite the fact that she was Old Biddy.

I was watching them out there, picking their way over the clumps of grass and stones, thinking how different they were from the rest of us even by the way they walked, when I saw the *amadán* stealing up behind them. He was taking tippy-toe steps like a chicken, with his elbows out making a kind of undulation across his shoulders from one elbow to the other. They had no idea he was there and the sight—God forgive me—gave me some satisfaction. Even through the windowpane, I could hear his shriek as he suddenly dashed between them, stretching up his arms and waggling his hands and dancing with one knee high and then the other. I could see the two O's of their mouths as they turned around and their shrieks came through the window like the squeaks of a rabbit when a ferret gets hold of it. Mrs. Reidy fell backwards on the ground. Young Miss MacCarthy fetched him a belt across the mouth. I imagined the crack of it though I couldn't hear it. He ran away and she ran after him a few steps, then went back to Mrs. Reidy who was lying on the ground, raised on one elbow, her hand against her chest as if her heart was about to give out. She lifted

Mrs. Reidy up and the two of them made off, all disheveled they were, to Muiris's house. I knew he'd be getting an earful. I started laughing, God forgive me, and Biddy came out of the kitchen and said, "What are you laughing at, Father? It isn't often I hear you laughing these days." "Get back out of that, and mind your own business," I said to her. She went off with her usual muttering. "God forgive your temper, abusing an old woman who never did you any harm." "That's enough out of you," I said. But I felt warm to her all the same, as I did to the *amadán* at that moment.

A small business you might say, but a lot happened out of it. Mrs. Reidy as much as summoned angels with trumpets to accompany her complaints to Muiris. That night I went over to make the peace as best I could, but she couldn't be stopped saying what she wanted to say, which she did standing with her nose in the air, and gathering her clothes around her as if to prevent them from touching anything. Muiris told the young lad to go out and play, but I could see his head peeping around the door with his two eyes big as saucers. She tore into Muiris, saying, "That poor boy— and I know he's your son, God help the poor creature— shouldn't be allowed to run free to disturb decent folk. It's in a home he should be. Up here he has nothing to do but to run wild over the bogs, dirty as if he'd rolled in cow-dung. If Máire Rua were alive she wouldn't have that boyo here for more than a minute. It's down to the asylum he would be, where he could be cleaned up and cared for and get regular food like a Christian."

Muiris said nothing through all this. He just sat there by the hob, with his back to her. I sat at the table away from the two of them, since it was family business. I wasn't at all distressed to hear Mrs. Reidy talk about the asylum. I'd have been in seventh heaven if that lad were taken away. I said nothing, even when Muiris looked at me. He must have read my thoughts. I turned my attention to the lady, though ladylike she wasn't at that moment.

"Mrs. Reidy," says I—but I got no farther than that.

"And you," she said, "and you" then she added "Father" as if it were hard to wring it out of herself. "And you, letting this village go to rack and ruin, with a half-wit running around and an old witch in your kitchen with a stink off of her a pig would be ashamed of."

"Mrs. Reidy," I said, "I'll thank you to keep your thoughts about my housekeeper to yourself and to show some respect to the cloth, if not to me."

She went off again, this time to Muiris. I could see the

young nipper edging in, so I went to him, and put my arm around him, the two of us standing half-in and half-out of the door. The poor little lad was shivering. He must have been flummoxed with the sight of his father and the woman who had cared for him for weeks past hard at it, or rather she was, for Muiris didn't say a word. She'd stirred the lad's affections, I was sure of that. She wasn't a bad woman, but strange to our ways.

When she'd spent herself, I took young Éamonn over to the table and as I sat down, I thought I saw the face of the *amadán* at the window but it was gone in a blink. The only thing to be heard was the clamor of crows in the distance before they settled down. Mrs. Reidy relaxed herself enough to come over to the child. Muiris lit a pipe and stared at the fire. She told the boy it was time he was in bed. Then Muiris spoke for the first time. "I'll have the men take your things down to the town in the morning." With that he knocked the fresh pipe against the hob and went off to bed, leaving a closed door behind him.

Mrs. Reidy strode over to the bedroom door and started shouting at it. "If that's all the thanks I get for coming up here to the back of beyond, then it'll be a pleasure to shake the dirt of this place off my shoes. After all I did for you! God help that boy now without a

191

woman to take care of him beyond the priest's skivvy. What's a Christian woman doing up here? I ask myself. I'm as daft as the rest of you to be here at all. Don't strain yourself with worry for I'll be gone at the crack of dawn. It's a good thing my sister isn't alive to see what's happened after she departed." The young lad began to cry. I left him clinging to her skirts, she wiping his face roughly and talking softly to him.

Muiris was up before dawn. Through the window I saw him go around and wake up Séamus Mór and Oweneen. Then he went up the mountain into the darkness. An hour later, the two men, large and small, carried her chest and suitcases down the mountain, she walking behind them. I was worried sick she'd stop off at the parish priest's with her story. Our situation was bad enough without her making it worse. She had a touch of meanness in her, that woman. But a woman she was and for that reason and more I was sorry to see her go. As I turned away from the window I got a glimpse of the *amadán* high on the mountain where Muiris had disappeared, watching her departure. He watched for a while and then went off slowly, bent over and dejected like a broken puppet.

. . .

THE PRIEST'S STORY

If you think that was the end of it, you'd be wrong. I was dying to have some young woman come up and settle in. But I never saw sight nor light of Jamesy's girl after. I asked him why she never came up now. "Ah, sure she's busy on the farm, Father," was all he'd say. Mrs. Reidy must have given her an earful before she went back to Cahirciveen. How many other people knew about our troubles, I don't know. Rumors get around like smoke and once enough people hear of a thing, they'll swear to the death it's true. I was waiting for a call down to the parish priest's, or even a visit up the mountain from Fr. Staunton, but it never happened. Thank God for small mercies.

I was happiest on the week-ends. Every Saturday, Sister Attracta brought the children up from their summer school, and glad I was to see her and them. A kindly person indeed. She slept at the back of the church behind a curtain. I'd see her out at the well around five o'clock in the morning washing her face. When I went to the church to say Mass she'd already be saying her prayers. A good woman and polite to everyone, including Old Biddy whom she called Mrs. McGurk. To tell you the truth, I didn't know who she was talking about when she asked me, "How's Mrs. McGurk this morning?"

THE DEPOSITION OF FATHER McGREEVY

That summer was so mild you'd think there would never be another winter. And things repeated themselves as if nature was a train going from station to station in perfect time. What you expected came and went. For Lent I'd given up the little drop of wine I'd have at night before going to bed. At Easter, from the valley below, you could hear the church bell all day long. Shearing time came around. Usually I watched that. I liked seeing the great scallops of wool peel back and out would come a small sheep naked and sort of ashamed. I hadn't the heart to watch it this year though. The lambs were growing up and didn't run to the udder as much. When they did they were so strong they pushed the mother to take a sideways step. The sheep never stop eating, even when there's nothing to eat, shooting their jaws sideways in that circular chew of theirs, stopping only to look at you with eyes big and vacant as a bubble, tilting one ear and then the other like the hands of a clock. When they were shorn, their hind legs walked so dainty, like those hussies in their high heels going to a hooly on a Saturday night. The shearing got rid of those curtains of dirty wool from their hindquarters. The ram looked on at all this, with his crooked horns and wicked eye. The lambs had no time for him at all, or he for them. In the few fields the

potato stalks were high and the edges of the leaves beginning to brown. The gardens were full of fat cabbages and brussels sprouts and peas that seemed to
have come up by themselves. Even flowers, though
there was no woman to tend them. But up they came
just the same, with a sprinkle of daffodils here and
there on the hillside at the end of March, the black-
thorn a month later. Then the yellow gorse in May,
with its angry thorns, and in late August, the fuchsia,
regular as clockwork.

Thady Kelleher took his cow down to Shaughnessy's
bull so he'd have another calf to sell next year. That
poor cow never got a rest. When they came back up the
mountain, the men would joke about her. "Did that bull
give her another big welcome this year?" "He must be
a daft bull indeed to be mad for that!" When I was out
of earshot there would be louder laughs. The fair day
was coming, though there wasn't much they had to sell.
But sell they must to get food and fodder for the winter. I still had a picture in my mind of a village full of
women and children walking around well clad and
shod, with good harvests and livestock galore. Then
I'd open my eyes and see our starved acres plucked from
the side of a hill, all of us living on a slope that might
slide us all down into the valley with the winter rains.

But the winds were fresh that summer and the rains light, and they came just when the crops needed them, and the animals flourished. I didn't see the *amadán* for days on end, and that was no hardship for me, for every time I saw him it tightened the knot in my stomach.

The news on the wireless was terrible, but it was far away. It's hard to think of death and disaster with the sun shining and the harvest ripening, such as it was. The worst news wasn't on the wireless. One of the lads from the town was lost in the Battle of Britain. Falling down from the sky, like that poor German boy. Only nineteen he was. When the youngsters came up that week-end I talked to them about it so they wouldn't take it hard. There was no response from them at all, and one of the young lads smiled. I said, "What are you smiling at, God forgive you?" It came out that the dead lad had bullied the young ones and they weren't a bit sorry he'd gone down in flames over the English Channel. Gilvary his name was. No body was ever brought back. The German lad had the better funeral in the end. There's something terrible about a missing body. There's never a chance to fasten your grief onto the remains of what you loved. There's no grave to return to. The imagination never rests, destroying itself with notions of where that poor lost body might be. It's as if the person vanished through an open door, and the door never closes.

The children were coming up as usual every Friday with Sister Attracta. At first they were glad to come up and ran to their fathers. But as we went into August I noticed a change. Not in all of them, mind you, but in some. Séamus's big lad—Brendan—was really sulking and I couldn't get a word out of him. He wouldn't even take his little sister's hand on the way up, Sister Attracta told me. She said some of them had invitations to stay at their friends' houses and they liked the town better than the village. You can imagine how pleased I was by that. I went down to the town and bought a football and hurleys for the lads and dolls for the girls and put them in each of the houses so that they'd find them when they came up. That satisfied them for a while. Biddy cooked a feast for them. "The poor little mites," she said. "There's nothing up here for them but the promise of a hard life." "There's a hard life everywhere," I said, "and if you go on like that there won't be a soul left up here at all!" "Except for you and me, Father," she said.

So first one and then another of the children didn't come up. This wasn't discussed, it being a cause for shame. Sooner or later, you'd know that one of them would do something about it and I thought it would be Oweneen. But wasn't it Séamus who went down on a Saturday in August to the house where they were putting Brendan up for the week-end. Brendan fought and cried, and Séamus had to pull him most of the way. When he got him back up, Séamus gave him a touch of the stick. Not a word out of the lad for the rest of the week-end. The week after, Oweneen went down for his daughter. But the nuns only made him madder by trying to soothe him, with their hands up their sleeves and their heads nodding, smiling all the time. They wouldn't tell him which house his daughter was at, you see. I suppose they didn't want a scene. "I know you're upset, Mr. Mahon," he said, imitating them in a nancy-voice, "but we're thinking of the poor little girl's future." That set him off entirely. "Poor she may be, and future she may have—" he told us he said, "—but I'll thank you to keep your future to yourself. I'm taking her back up to where she belongs." He was still steaming when he got back without her. They said they'd bring her up themselves the next day, but when they didn't, Sister Attracta had to go down and bring her up. A grand woman she was—and is. Not a word of complaint out of her, having to make two trips. Oweneen wouldn't let his daughter go down on the Monday. All she did was cry after that.

I was so upset by all this that I went down to talk to the nuns. They said the best thing to do was to talk to the parish priest. He was sick in bed and I met with Fr. Staunton instead.

"We must think of the children, Father," he said.

"And what do you think I'm thinking of?" I asked him. "And are we to forget their fathers while we're at it?"

"They have to have their schooling, Father," he said, "after missing it all winter, or the Sergeant will be up there at your doorstep and we don't want that, do we?" Finally he said, "I'll talk to the parish priest and he'll talk to Reverend Mother." There wasn't much to say after that. We walked out into the garden. A blessed summer it was. But the trouble with the children was eating away at me.

There was one time after that that I'll never forget. I'm sure everyone has had the same experience. Sometimes in late summer it seems as if the roll of the earth slows and stops, the flowers in full bloom, their perfume hanging in the air, not a rustle in the crops as they stand still, maybe a hint of a breeze on your cheek. Your ears imagine the echo of a long note fading in the stillness. A warm envelope of air around you gives you a feeling of comfort and peace as if everything was right with the world. You don't even feel your own heart beating.

I suppose such moments are given to us so that memory can ease us in the times that go against us. By a Divine Providence, the memory of pain is short and the memory of delight lingers. With the winter we'd had, you'd be justified in thinking we were owed a good summer. But the ways of Providence are beyond paying little debts to our poor accounts. Yet there's something in us that seeks a balance. We were sure that last winter would never repeat itself, no more than lightning could strike the same place twice. I should have remembered the potato famine that didn't pay heed to the normal round of things at all and never stopped year after year until the whole country was a graveyard.

My grandmother was a little girl then and what her father told her about the famine lives in me to this day—passing people by the side of the road with their mouths green from eating grass. There was only one coffin to go around, and that had no top, only a bottom that swung open. Everyone that died went into that coffin and the men, weak though they were, brought it to the grave on the donkey cart, with the donkey half dead. A lot of work that donkey got, going to the big grave that was widened just a bit for the next corpse, for no one, she said, had the strength to go deep. And not a priest to be had. The men would put the coffin on two blocks of wood, open the bottom and the poor corpse would fall out. Then back they'd go for the next. It's a terrible thing, the hunger, she said. In the beginning it tears at you inside like a wild beast, until it quietens down inside you and the long dying starts.

There's enough hardship in the past, if you think about it, to make us never want to face the future. But there's a Providence that watches over us. Whatever happens fits God's plan. In our exile, we can't see its dimensions. We move in the cycles of our free-will on the continents of His mercy, and the tragedies visited upon us we will comprehend in Paradise. What we went through in the past winter had stretched us beyond our limits, as Job was stretched. But whatever cross He gives us, He gives us the strength to bear. When we reconcile ourselves to God's mysterious will, we cease to chafe against our own fallen nature.

It was an evening in late August, one of those days that starts with rain and clears up around six. There

was a drowsy quiet after the wind died down. The
crows were making a thunder in the distance and the
swifts were swooping and dipping in a fever to catch
the last flies. I was listening to the wireless, and the English were getting it hot and heavy. I wanted them to
win, but not before they suffered. Their punishment
was raining out of the sky over London. Hitler's le-
gions were ready to cross the channel after the disaster
of Dunkirk. The world was in a convulsion. But here
everything was as calm as a pond. It's hard to think of
the conflagrations of the world when you look over the
valley and see a few sheep and cattle grazing, then raising their heads to look around.

I had just lit the paraffin lamp and was reading *The
Kerryman* when I heard the shouts, and shouts when
the light is fading make you start up. They weren't the
shouts of fear and disaster, but the aimless bawling
that whiskey forces out of a man's mouth. Fr. Matthew[25] gave the country a great blessing, but I'll say

---

25. Fr. Theobald Matthew (1790–1856) was an immensely influen-
tial Capuchin priest whose temperance campaign in Cork became a national mission. So successful was he that many publicans went out of
business. According to the *Dictionary of National Biography*, the good father "earned the praise of Daniel O'Connell, who said that he could not
have held his mass meetings for Repeal (of the Act of Union) if the population had not first been converted to sobriety. Fr. Matthew urged his

this for our village. It's a long time since the drink was a serious matter for us. For years there was a still up there under the big rocks, until the police got wind of it and up they came. They didn't catch anyone nor did they try. I won't tell you whose still it was but everyone knows, including probably yourself. Anyway, everyone on the mountain would know the police were on their way up. I never mentioned it in my sermons. As long as it didn't get out of hand and start trouble. And from the sounds of it, there was trouble now.

Out there in the twilight shadowy figures were lurching around and bawling like cattle at a fair. Drink brings a man down to the level of the beasts. There they were, staggering around the graveyard, showing no respect for the dead. A few of the men came out, standing in their doorways, looking. Would you believe it if I told you that one by one they turned around and went in again? All but Muiris. I could see him against the light of his doorway. They started coming up in my direction and out I went, Old Biddy shouting after me, "Watch out for yourself, Father. These fellows have the sign of drink on them." As if that had es-

---

converts to replace drinking as a pastime by taking up dancing and music," activities frowned on by subsequent clergy as potential occasions of sin.

caped me. Who they were, I didn't know. But the way one of them walked, if walking you'd call it, was familiar to me. It was young Jamesy Donoghue back for a visit. The others I didn't know at all, but I knew well enough who they were. His butties from the town, with nothing but mischief on their minds. Though they seemed to be moving in all directions, they were coming up from the graveyard bit by bit, bringing both sides of the path with them.[26]

"What in the name of God are you doing up here?" I said to Jamesy. "Get back the lot of you to where you came from."

It was hard to see their faces in the dim light. They were five or six of them around me, smelling of drink to high heaven. What with their heat and their staggers, you're in another world and a dangerous one, for what sets off a man in that condition you can never fathom.

"It's a disgrace you are to your father and mother lying over there in the graveyard. If they could see you now, they wouldn't want to know you," I said to Jamesy. "So take yourself down the mountain with your fine friends."

These very friends were sticking their faces into me.

26. The expression is translated from the Irish, *ag tabhairt dhá thaobh an bhóthair leis.* It is colorful to English ears and easily located in the in-

THE PRIEST'S STORY

You'd think I was in the middle of a hundred people.
"Ah, take it easy, Father," said one with wild hair like a
clump of straw. "We're only having a bit of fun."

"Is that what you call fun," I said. "Disturbing hard-
working people in the middle of the night? You'd best
all turn around and go down the mountain and the way
you are you're likely to break your neck, and then
where will we be?"

"Will you listen to him talking?" said a big fellow
who kept taking short steps sideways to keep himself
upright. "A little priesteen like himself."

"You'll show respect to the cloth," I said.

"Bless me, Father," said another, "for I have sinned."

"It's sinning you are right now," I said, "if you have a
mind to think about it."

"Come on, Father," says another fellow with a quiff[27]
on him. "Leave us be and there will be no trouble."

Out of the corner of my eye, I saw the *amadán* creep-

dulgent category of quaint, thereby removing another particle of seri-
ousness from a language and its speakers.

27. A quiff is a brilliantined crest of hair rising from the forehead in
one smooth wave, a style affected by young idlers and troublemakers
whose vernacular sophistication elevates them above conventional dull-
ards. Hair, as manipulable as language itself, was here speaking danger-
ously. Not to be confused with "bliff," a term applied to the pout of the
covered mons.

ing close with a strange expression of wonder. "You get out of here!" I shouted at him. But it was too late. Two of them caught him and brought him into the crowd—how five or six can make a crowd is no mystery if you're in the middle of them, all standing too close and never still for a moment.

"Leave him alone!" I said.

"We hear he has a great way with the sheep," said a red-headed fellow.

I had my hand raised to strike him before I knew it. But in the space of a long heartbeat I turned my fury on Jamesy.

"It's a disgrace you are to your own kind," I said. "Get yourself and these tinkers out of here before worse happens."

"Aw sure feck it," said a dark one with a mean face who hadn't said anything till then. He raised and emptied a whiskey bottle, drew back his arm, and arched the bottle over my head. There was a crash as it splintered against the rock.

"Aw Jasus, have you gone mad?" Jamesy shouted at him.

"It's you that's gone mad," I said, "so sober up and get yourself down the mountain this very minute."

"It's too dark to go down the mountain now," said Jamesy. "We'd break our necks!"

"And that would be a great loss," I said, God forgive me. "But it won't be too dark for me tomorrow morning to go down to have a word with the Sergeant."

"The Sergeant's my uncle," said the fellow who'd thrown the bottle, "and he wouldn't lift a finger against his sister's son."

"It's a stick she should have lifted to you long ago," I said.

I felt an arm pushing me aside. Old Muiris was there as sudden as an apparition. "Leave go of that boy," he said to the straw-headed fellow who had his arm around the *amadán*'s neck. The *amadán* no more knew his father than a stray dog would. I took him by the arm. Much as I hated to touch him he was still one of God's creatures. Muiris faced young Jamesy.

"There's no place for you here. It's your own wish and desire to have no part of us, and we want no part of you."

"Who is this?" said Quiff.

"A better man than you'll ever be," I said.

"I still have my place," said Jamesy, "and I'm going to it with my friends."

"Well go then," said Muiris, "and make no more trouble here."

Now the men were coming out of their houses again, and starting down. You could see them clear in the light of the doorways because the night was now black. "And when the morning comes," said Muiris, "you can take these fine lads with you and go for there's no welcome for you here, except you come by yourself as your mother's son—who's lying in her grave behind you. There will be no more trouble from any of you—"

There was a horrible sound as Straw-head turned himself inside out behind a rock. Muiris stood looking at them one by one. There was just the sound of breathing and the smell of drink. One of them broke wind loudly and another of them laughed. "Stand aside there, Father," said Muiris, holding the *amadán* by the arm, and so I did. They trailed up the mountain to Jamesy's cottage, giving an odd shout, but most of the evil had gone out of them. Muiris looked at me. It was hard to see his expression in the dark. "Don't let them lads bother you, Father, they haven't an iota of sense, and what little sense they have they'll find in the morning." The *amadán* was already half-way up the mountain—I could tell from the sound of his boots on the rocks. Muiris stood for a moment looking in that direction. Without another word, he turned and went home. I watched until he darkened his door and until his lamp went out.

The men were out early as always. I went over to Jamesy's cottage around nine o'clock. His friends were stretched out every which way as if you'd tossed a bunch of sticks on the floor. And who do you think was at them but the *amadán* himself? He was squatting down and playing with them like you'd play with a doll, lifting a hand and letting it drop, touching a face and avoiding the lazy swipe the drunk lad would make out of his sleep. He was opening one lad's mouth with two fingers when he looked up and saw me. You wouldn't think he could move so fast—he dissolved like a ghost. But not before he dribbled a bit and said "FrFrFr" with a kind of smile out of his loose lips, so red they were.

I shook Jamesy awake. His eyes were screwed up, refusing to meet the light. He looked as if he'd been strained through a sheet.

"Get them fellows out of here," I said. "They don't belong here, and it's a question whether you do yourself."

"There's no cause for me to come up to this Godforsaken place again," says he.

"You never spoke a truer word," I said. "As for God,

there's no place He forsakes, but there's many that forsake Him."

An hour later I saw them preparing to go down the mountain, sitting on the headstones in the graveyard, yawning and stretching, and a sorry lot they looked. The drink is a terrible curse, and there's no shortage of spirits everywhere you go. Indeed I've no doubt there's a stock of whiskey in every cottage here. But there's been no trouble thank God. If truth be told, there's no amusement up here to keep young lads out of harm's way. That's why they're off to Cork and Dublin and England and America.

It was already September and the year was poised for its long slide into winter. And that was the end of the summer for me. There was only one other thing. Séamus's wife was brought back up in a shining new coffin. They didn't even tell us they were coming. They left it at the graveyard with fresh flowers on top. There was a brass plate with her name under the flowers. I'll say that much for the town. We dug the grave. And for the third time, I said the prayers for the dead over that poor woman.

·   ·   ·

I know now I was like a blind man standing at the edge of a cliff—an abyss of sin and desolation that would make the past winter seem as nothing. When the first flakes of snow came, with them came the memory of past hardship and a feeling that this winter couldn't be as bad as the one gone by. Biddy kept saying, "It's the same winter we'll have again, Father." I'd tell her to take her prognostications someplace else and stop her nonsense. The days shortened and the gloom gathered around four o'clock. The first snow came, and walking back to my house one November evening at five o'clock, with the white glimmer on the ground and the dark sky above, the darker flank of the mountain rising above like a whale, and not a star to be seen, her words kept coming into my head.

There was nothing but bad news on the wireless. It was enough to make you think the world was ending. Cities were blacked out across Europe. Over London the planes were fighting, the Germans were pushing towards Baku and Grozny, names I'd never heard of in my life. It was the oil they were after. Belfast was bombed. Then the rain washed away the first snow and the brown earth and the few bare trees and bushes were a pleasure to see. That's the way it went—a light snow-fall, then heavy rains that would wash it away. Your heart would sink with the snow and rise with the rain. When I ran into the men, they'd ask, "What did the wireless say this morning, Father?" My ear was stuck to that wireless and the weather forecast. Intermittent showers, patches of sunlight, barometer falling. The talk of high and low pressure systems was beyond me. Great banks of clouds raced in after passing over three thousand restless miles of water. At times standing on the mountain and looking up at those clouds scudding along, you'd think the earth was rolling under your feet. I'd get dizzy looking up, wondering what the sky held in store. Christmas came with no more hardship than usual. I said my mother's novena about the Babe who was born in a stable in Bethlehem in piercing cold. In my sermon I talked about the promise of the new-born Child and how He was born in a byre no different from our own, with the same animals around and the star of hope in the East. The children were up from the convent and I'll say this for Biddy, she worked hard to make them scones and sweets. They brought up presents the nuns had given them. The men cast a sour look on them, for they had no money to spare for such things.

Christmas puts a glow in the heart but the cold that week would penetrate your bones. The turf was wet and it took a lot to get it going. Biddy kept blowing away with the bellows until she got the red core with steam and smoke coming out of it. She was always afraid it would go out. Every night she'd bank the embers with the fine white ash that keeps the spark of life in the hearth through the night. Some mornings I'd be up before her and push the ash aside—you could rub it between your fingers like soap—and blow on that red spark. You know all that? Well, I'm surprised you do, for it's coal you have down here mostly now, and a black, dirty fuel it is.

We'd laid up our stores for the winter, just in case. If you're prepared, what you fear doesn't come. A decent shopkeeper or two gave credit, I'll say that for this town. There are some that don't, and you know who I'm talking about. But Matt Keenan is a decent man. I'm not sure the son will follow the father as kindly. But the long and the short of it was we had plenty to meet whatever weather overtook us. All we had to worry about was the cold. And there was nothing new about that.

We put a bank of stones above and below the graveyard so that the earth wouldn't slide away no matter how heavy the rains. The barns were strengthened and roofed and sodded. Some of the sheep took to finding shelter in young Jamesy's abandoned cottage. Its thatch began to go. He hadn't been near us since that bad night. When I went down one Sunday to visit the nuns, Fr. Staunton was there and he told me he'd married Jamesy and the MacCarthy girl. A woman can change a man entirely. I've seen it often. It goes that way more than the other way around. We had another dog we'd picked up somewhere. I swear he was a tinker's dog, because he'd leap and take the food out of your hand if you let him. He stole a cake of Biddy's brown bread she'd set on the windowsill to cool. She'd have hung him if she could've caught him. But you couldn't get near him if he didn't want you to. If you bent down, he'd scud off with his tail between his legs. He thought you'd be lifting a stone to peg at him, you see. A big black mongrel with a torn ear and a stump of a tail. The other dogs avoided him after he whipped the best of them.

It was hard for the young ones to go up and down every week-end as the weather got worse. And it was lonely for young Éamonn during the week, and he only six. I took him under my wing a bit. He was growing fast and so were the lambs. You could almost see them grow. A few were sold. There's always one or two of them that are born weak and need a bottle or a bit of extra care. Old Muiris had one of them. It was a sight to see his rough hands gentle as could be with that lamb. Its mother used to stand in the door looking in, until she gave that up. Young Éamonn made a pet of that lamb. She began following him around like a dog, not from affection I'm sure, but for a taste of something she might be offered. I've seen that before. The dogs didn't like that at all. When the lamb was inside, they'd be kept out. You'd see them squatting down with their heads between their paws looking at the door. Then you'd be sure the lamb was in there. They'd give it a nip when it came out, and the boy would chase them away. The tinker's dog was the worst. He had a bad streak in him that fellow. It was good for the youngster to have something to play with, for there wasn't much to do with the other children gone all week. Old Biddy made such a fuss of him, she irritated me. She was always going on about "the poor young lad without kith nor kin." "What do you think his father is?" I'd say. "A stranger?" "Ah, sure you don't understand the young fellow at all," she'd say.

A manly little fellow he was surely. He looked at you so direct and clear, very solemn. He could make you uneasy if he stared at you long enough. Children can hold your eye even when their mother is bouncing them. It was slow leaving him, that child's stare. I've seen many a child grow up but it struck me that this one might be a bit different. And why not with the way he was on his own, the only child in the village, and left without a mother a year ago? He must have felt that loss to his core. He never gave any indication of it beyond a month of crying last winter. You can never tell how deep a thing has gone into a child. Some go through terrible things without a scar, while something that wouldn't bother you or me leaves a mark that will never go. There's a stage when the parents think a young lad will grow up to be this or that. Or that they have a gift that will make the world sit up and take notice. Then they grow up and they're just themselves, like anyone else. But with a boy the hope is there. I suppose we like to believe his future is better than our own. So strong is this hope we see a sign of it in everything a child says or does. In spite of all that, there were signs of something extra in that young lad.

I took to visiting Muiris every night to keep him and the young lad company. Muiris would fix his pipe and smoke and not much would be said. The young lad played with his toys, and was in bed by nine. Sometimes when I was up early, I'd see the boy, dark though it was, playing with that lamb of his outside the house. During the day he began to come over while I was reading my breviary, and Biddy would have a bun or a cake she'd baked for him. I trained him to serve Mass, or at least how to help me, for I mostly served myself. He wanted to play with the wireless, but I wouldn't let him, since it was the only word I had from the outside. I didn't see a newspaper from one end of the week to the other. I asked Sister Attracta to bring one up but she forgot and I didn't want to ask her again.

I got the boy over every day around three o'clock to teach him writing and sums. He didn't like it at first but his Da spoke to him and after a bit he was going great guns. I taught him a bit of catechism and he learned the responses quicker than anyone apart from old Paddy's daughter that grew up and went to America ten years ago. *Where is God? He is everywhere but we cannot see Him. If God is everywhere, why do we not see Him? We do not see God, because He is a pure Spirit, having no body and therefore cannot be seen by us in this life. Does God see us? God sees us and continually watches over us.* He liked to recite the Ten Commandments. It was strange to hear the sins coming out of that little mouth, for he had no notion of what they were. He'd know soon enough. I was trying to give him a good foundation. As the Jesuits say, "Give him to us young and we'll have him for life."

When the others came up on the week-end, those

that did come up, he was always glad to see them. He watched for them from the ridge below the graveyard, but when they arrived he didn't have much to say to them nor they to him. So he stayed with the girls because the lads wouldn't give him any attention except to fetch a ball. That's the way older ones are and shame on them. Often I'd see him staring at them while they played, but they'd ignore him. When they went down on the Sunday evening, he'd wander around where they played and was restless the next day, not wanting to have anything to do with his lessons. But by Tuesday he was himself again. I think he was a smarter lad than any of them.

It was the war that gave me the idea of teaching him some geography. He was at that stage when a young fellow is full of questions. He'd moider you with questions. He took a shine to the wireless, and he came over for that as much as for Biddy's cakes. We listened mostly to Radio Éireann because the BBC Home Service was full of whistles and blurts. It was hard to understand those English accents anyway. They always said who was reading the news. If it wasn't Stuart Hibbert it was Alvar Liddell, or Richard Somebody. Once there was a strange voice that didn't sound like the BBC at all. It must have been that fellow Fr. Staunton told me about last summer, I can't remember his name, some comedian or other. Fr. Staunton said they wanted the listeners to recognise the voices of the announcers in case the Germans were trying to butt in and give them the wrong news with an English accent. You'd recognise the fellow's voice all right but you couldn't make head nor tail of it. Now I remember, his name was Pickles[28] or something. Fr. Staunton said there was an Irishman from Galway in Berlin, Lord Haw-Haw[29] he called him, who was giving broadcasts against the British. I said, "How on earth did he ever get over there?" Fr. Staunton didn't answer that. So there were some things he didn't know.

So it was Radio Éireann we listened to. Sometimes one or two of the men would come over and listen, smoking their pipes. They were more interested in the

---

28. Wilfred Pickles (1904–1978) was an English comedian.

29. Lord Haw-Haw, so named by the British, was born William Joyce in Brooklyn, New York, of an Irish father and an English mother. Educated in Galway, he had an adventurous right-wing career after emigrating to England in 1922. Expelled from Sir Oswald Mosley's British Union of Fascists, he founded his own National Socialist Party in Britain. He spent the war years in Germany broadcasting Nazi propaganda. His commentaries, delivered in a scornful BBC accent, mocked every icon of English culture, including "the stuttering king and the bandy-legged queen." The comedy of accents proved lethal. He was convicted of treason at the Old Bailey and hanged on January 3, 1946.

weather and the livestock and market reports than in the war. I took the first few months of the year off the calendar from Mitchell's Grocery down below and stuck them together so that I had a space on the back large enough to draw the map of Europe, including what I remembered of Russia. I looked around to find a geography book but there wasn't one to be had. I put in the cities I remembered. I wasn't too sure of Moscow and Warsaw. The young lad and I tried to follow the news on the map. Then the young lad started to draw in everything he heard on the wireless. We put in Ireland too, of course, and Cork was bigger than London, and the town below was bigger then Cork. He was learning his letters and his reading was far ahead of his age.

It must have been a terrible winter in Europe and Russia. The Germans were still going through everything like a bull through a fair. I hadn't paid much attention to North Africa. I had no idea of the shape of Africa except that it was like a giant comma. We got interested in North Africa because an Irishman was leading the British Armed Forces. Montgomery, from the North of course. There was talk of another Irishman named Alexander, a Field Marshall, whatever that means. The British always need an Irishman to win their wars for them. I told the lad how Wellington had beaten Napoleon at Waterloo. It struck me that if by a terrible accident we were cut off up here forever, the only history of the world that young lad would have was the bits and pieces rattling around my head. A strange view of the world he'd get from that.

The wireless wasn't working too well, and often the news wasn't news at all except when something big happened, like when the Germans walked into Paris last June, I think it was. Nothing like the Blitz this past November and December. The Tobruk business was beyond me, for I hadn't a notion where it was located in North Africa. There was talk of General Rommel who was a grand man, and El something, and Addis Ababa, which I knew of because Mussolini had attacked it before the war. The newspapers were full of it, and the kids in the streets below were singing, *Will you come to Abyssinia will you come? Don't forget your ammunition or your gun. De Valera will be there, Shooting bullets in the air, Will you come to Abyssinia will you come?*

But mostly the news was about air raids. Sometimes you'd think it was the same news they were reading over and over. *Allied aircraft raided targets in occupied France yesterday, causing severe damage to Axis installations around the cities of someplace and someplace. Six Axis aircraft were destroyed. One of our aircraft failed to return.* I had that off by heart. It was pleasant gathering almost every night around the fire. In spite of the fact that it took thousands of people dying every day to bring us together. And teaching the young lad gave me something to do besides worrying about the *amadán*. There wasn't a window he didn't look into, or a door he didn't poke his head through. Sometimes when his father spoke to him he'd put a foot across the threshold and stand still before he was off again. Biddy was always offering him food. He'd take it and stuff it into his mouth leaving a good bit of it on his face. She seemed to have a soft spot for him. Maybe she had a better understanding of him than the rest of us since she had a screw loose herself in my opinion.

Every promise of snow would put the heart across me. But when it came for certain and without relief, I didn't want to admit it to myself. It wasn't in the forecast. *Heavy rains with occasional thunderstorms developing to light and moderate during the course of the day* was what it said. It began as the usual snow. Then it turned to rain, washing the snow away as usual. The day after there were patches of blue sky and a high wind. That night the temperature went down like a stone. The next day the clouds came rolling in from the

Atlantic. The clouds looked heavy as lead, with a layer like dirty grey wool running fast under them. Then there was just the heavy cloud moving slowly, laden with snow.

The first few snows were light. But the next day the heavens opened. It was a Wednesday. I remember it well because the day before Oweneen said he should go down to the convent for his young daughter since it looked as if we were going to get it. He was right as it turned out. He nor the others didn't see sight nor light of their children until April and by that time the children were like strangers to them.

You can tell what kind of rain it is with your eyes closed. But the snow steals down and you haven't a notion it's doing its business until you try to open the door in the morning. In the middle of the night I woke up full of worries and went over to the window. Gradually I saw the ghost of a glow on the ground as if the sky had fallen. And when I went out the next morning, indeed it had. It wasn't too deep, just a foot or so. There was a hush except for the odd plop of snow dropping from eaves and branches. Every sound was smothered, every edge rounded. And not a bird in sight. It wasn't too cold because there was no wind. The forecast on the wireless caught up with the weather and described a big snowfall over the west of Ireland. We walked a path out to the graveyard and looked down at the town below. A few distant twists of smoke hung in the air without moving, as if frozen stiff.

The men went around their business, feeding the animals and clearing the apron of space before their doors. We trampled a few more paths so that the snow wouldn't keep us in, if it came down harder. And down it came and down again. The gatherings in the evening around the wireless took away some of the feeling that we were marooned. There was a comfort in those evenings, with the smell of tobacco, the men talking in low voices, the boy on the floor with his map, the dogs scratching at the door, and Biddy baking or doing the things that women do in a house. Some evenings all of us would be there, six sparks of life in a wilderness of snow and ice—all of us that is except the *amadán*, wherever he was. You couldn't keep track of him. He was here there and everywhere, so you'd think there were three or four of him. He took to lurking around Jamesy's empty cottage. He knew how to make a fire, but he hadn't learned to stay close to it, for he was blue with the cold half the time.

. . .

THE PRIEST'S STORY

We were as we were a year ago, wrapped in snow. Again
we were shivering as much indoors as out; again the
short days were over before they started; again there
were days of silence when your ear picked up every little sound, and days and nights when all you'd hear was
the wind. I kept the wireless on until the national an-
them at mid-night, and after, until the hiss gave way to
wailing and moaning like lost souls. Again the wind
drifted the snow over everything, so that you lost what
was familiar; again you had to dig the turf out of the
snow and bring it in to dry near the fire before putting
it on; again we walked around hunched and bundled up
like tinkers; again the dogs wouldn't go out and as soon
as they were out they were scratching at the door to get
back in. Again the church was colder than the arctic.
Again the *amadán* knocked at every door and was let in
to shiver until he took it into his head to go out; again
the cattle were gathered into the byre with the new
roof—all six of them with the new calf; again the sheep
gathered near the graveyard in a big ball of wool, hud-
dling together to keep themselves warm; again the ram
stood away from them staring at any dog that looked at
them; again the sheep began to trickle into the cottages
for a bit of warmth. Again your boots got sodden and
dried out and wrinkled so that they started to crack,

225

even the Wellingtons started to leak, and when you took off your socks, your toes would be as white and wrinkled as a drowned man's. Sometimes I went over to Muiris's around five o'clock and you couldn't see your hand in front of your face, but my feet walked me over on their own on top of the dim lake of white light. There would be the boy cuddled up to his pet sheep, finding warmth; again Biddy had nothing but disasters on her tongue; again the wireless began to whistle and blurt and stammer until you'd get only half the news and you had to fill in the rest, which led to some strange speculations, I can tell you. The little group that would gather in the evenings began to fall away, until usually it was only Muiris and the boy that came over, sometimes with that lamb of his in a cardboard box he pulled along on a string.

You couldn't see the town below for days. The clouds were ready to let down snow if you looked up at them crooked. Nearly always an odd flake was wandering hither and tither like a moth. The chilblains—again— made your hands so clumsy that there was a time when I had trouble cleaning the chalice and raising the Host. And raising the Host was one of the few great joys left in the world.

But the hardship went on beyond endurance. Again

THE PRIEST'S STORY

I had to break the ice in the bowl to wash my hands. Again some of the men left off shaving and began to get beards like brigands in a story. And they were even quieter than last year after the women died. I understood that quiet. And it joined itself to a strange memory. There was a Munster football final at Páirc Uí Chaoimh in Cork—between Cork and Kerry it was. It had rained for days and after the first half the mud was as thick as soup at one end of the field. A high kick came down and the ball just stuck in the mud with never a bounce, like it was glued there. I remember the sound of it to this day, a kind of dead thud like a blow, far from the echo of the bounce you were expecting. You'd think the ball was made of lead. I remember the half-second it took for the lads to get over their surprise and start fighting for the ball. Now that no-bounce was like the feeling I had, if you can understand that.

Every night I prayed for the weather to ease itself, but the clouds were so thick, even a prayer couldn't get through them. Sometimes when I got back from the church, there would be Tadhg the *amadán* sitting like a king at the table wolfing down what Biddy gave him. He'd be out the back door the minute he saw me. "I suppose there's a little left for myself?" I'd say, and then stop her before she drove me mad by turning my own

227

words about Christian charity against me. If we hadn't had the Mass to mark the week, the days would have run one into the other. One Saturday I went up to say Sunday Mass, and wondered why there wasn't a soul to be seen. Back I went and tore into Biddy. "Why didn't you tell me?" I said. "Sure I thought you knew the days of the week as well as myself," she said. I swear she didn't tell me on purpose.

I looked into Jamesy's empty cottage one day coming back after a Mass. It had been open to the weather since he went down to marry that hoity-toity girl of his, and if a house isn't looked after, it shows signs of it soon enough. I noticed two sets of footprints leading to the empty house, where none should be except Tadhg's, for that's where he lurked a lot of the time. I could tell his tracks anywhere, for he never put a regular progress of steps together, they always hopped and leapt sideways. Beside them I saw small, deep tracks—there was a new fall of snow from last night—that could be none other than the boy's. I didn't have to think before I added my tracks to those two. Up I went to the half-door. I heard a kind of a scampering like a badger in a bush and then a shout from the *amadán* and a cry of laughter from the child. Then a scream and I was through that door faster than a blast of air. He was chasing his young

brother around a broken table. They both stopped to
look at me, him with his mad eyes and the child's blank
with pleasure, both of them panting. They were playing. That's what they were doing. Playing! It was a
thought that had never entered my head.

The child said, "Hallo, Father" and tugged the arm
of the *amadán* to start their game again, whatever it
was—a kind of hide and seek, I suppose. The child ran
away from behind the table shouting at me, "Watch
this, Father! Watch this!" The *amadán* ran past me
leaving that smell of his behind. The child set up a cry.
"Look what you've done now, Father."

"Quiet! Quiet!" I said. "There's no harm done. Now
you get yourself back to your father's house. The last
thing you should be is out here in this bitter cold." He
started to cry. "Off with you now," I said. "And bring
your father over tonight to follow the war on the wireless."

"No, I won't," he said. I didn't know what had got into
him. I never had the knack with children. With the
women gone, I realised how much they put into keeping the children out of mischief. Men don't have the
same gift, which is why He made men and women
different, I suppose.

"You've plenty of toys to play with back home," I said.

"I'm tired of them," says he.

"Be off with you now, or I'll talk to your father," I said to him. That got him to go, leaving me looking around wondering why anyone would want to spend a minute in such a place as that was.

The sky was already showing through the thatch in just a few short months. A big stone was lying on the ground near a long bench. You could see where it had fallen from the gable. The glass was gone from the two windows. In the hearth was a mound of silver ash. One of the few chairs was knocked over. The dresser still had a few plates on it, its doors hanging open. In the corner beside the hearth there was a bed of straw with some old coats thrown on it. Near the bed, if that's what you'd call it, was a broken plate with a few scraps of food frozen to it. I thought of Tadhg's mother. Poor Máire Rua. If she could stand where I was standing and see what I was seeing, her heart would break. She had a way with him. She could calm him down and turn him into a good imitation of a Christian on Sundays. Her past kindness to him seemed like a rebuke to me from the grave. There and then, I promised her and the Lord that I'd try to show more Christian charity to the poor distracted boy who through no fault of his own had been deprived of his sense.

THE PRIEST'S STORY

As I came out, I noticed the half-door was off its hinges. Who breaks these things, I wonder? Anything that's neglected seems to bring out destruction in people, and who could it be with only a few of us left? It's as if an empty house attacks itself. I went down to my house past a bunch of sheep clustered on the path. Out for a bit of exercise, I suppose, if you ever saw a sheep exercise—they are as lazy as a family on the dole. But what took my attention was the ram, with his two great horns wound like trumpets. Curtains of wool were hanging down from him, and as he stepped along they shivered and shook. He was on a height above them, looking down at them as if he were a king. And to them I suppose he was. When I passed him he turned to look at me, and I saw those fine white lashes long enough to catch flies. Strange that a beast should have such beautiful lashes around eyes with as much expression as two marbles. He was chewing away and so were the sheep, though whatever grass or heather there was was four feet under the snow. They did it from habit, I suppose. Or maybe they were belching up the food they just had. Do sheep chew the cud? I haven't a notion. Cattle are supposed to have as many stomachs as a woman shopping has bags. I'm told the traffic between these different stomachs is fierce. To look at a cow, you'd never think all that was going on inside. Maybe that's why they move as if there was glue on their hooves.

That night Muiris was sitting there smoking his pipe as if he were a thousand miles away. He took the pipe slowly out of his mouth and said, pausing after nearly every word, "Father, I think this winter will see the end of us." As he spoke, he drew with the pipe in the air as if he were writing. With the pauses, you'd think that pipe was making commas and semi-colons. Though it hadn't for over twenty years, his way with that pipe began to annoy me. If Muiris's pipe was bothering me, then I knew I had better pray for more patience.

"The Lord will take care of us," I said.

"He's not doing a very good job of it," said Muiris. "I'll stay up here myself as long as I can draw a breath. But not many of the others will. There's nothing to keep them here now."

"What about your two sons?" I said. We'd not talked about Tadhg since that night when we had walked him up to the church between us. I thought maybe enough time had gone by to bring it up.

"They'll stay up here with me," he said.

"Now is that fair to young Éamonn?" I said. "He needs to be with children of his own age. As for poor

Tadhg, God bless him, every time I see him he's blue with the cold. What's to become of him?"

"He doesn't feel the cold like the rest of us," said Muiris.

"I'm afraid he'll injure himself," I said, "with the way he is in two places at once, jumping from rock to rock like a goat."

"He has a strange fear of the indoors," said Muiris. "I suppose that is why he goes up to Jamesy's cottage to sleep."

"The only one he's content with is his young brother," said Biddy, sticking her head between us.

"And who asked you?" I said.

"I saw the two of them last evening," I said to Muiris. "He was jumping around on the sheep dirt with the boy, the two of them whooping like red Indians."

"He hasn't a soul to play with up here," said Biddy out of the darkness at the far end of the room.

"That'll do," I said.

"He's terrified out of his wits of you, Father," she said. I told her I'd thank her to keep her gob shut. She'd try the patience of a saint.

For a while Muiris and I didn't exchange a word.

"Is there any way of keeping him still for his own protection?" I said.

"Do you want to hobble him like a billy-goat?" said Muiris.

"That wasn't in my mind at all," I said, "but it makes me nervous to see him abroad the way he is. He might fall into a snowdrift and think it was the best bed he ever had."

"If it hasn't happened to him yet, it won't happen to him now," said Muiris.

Biddy had gone to the dark end of the house, and I could tell that darkness was all ears. So I talked low, both of us bending towards the heat.

"Perhaps when the spring comes we can take him down to the doctor," I said. "I'm sure he can find a place for him where he'll be well treated."

Muiris leaned back. "Why would you do that to a lad that can't bear to have four walls around him?" he said.

"I'm afraid he'll catch his death of pneumonia," I said.

"He hasn't yet, neither this year nor last year nor the year before," said Muiris. This was the most I'd spoken to Muiris in many a year. The village was on his mind. "There's not many who'll stay another winter on this mountain," he said. "Not the way we're afflicted. We've lost our women, and there's enough snow on top of us to bury us."

"If that's the case, and I hope it's not, we'll be like the

234

Blaskets are going to be, if what I hear is true," I said.
"They're all coming to the mainland sooner or later.
Did you ever see those beasts swimming over in the
water? It's no way to move livestock."

"What other way did they have?" said Muiris.
"What's pressed on us often leaves us no choice."

"There's been a village here for more than a hundred
years," I said, "and the Mass said here without a break,
because it was a favourite place for priests on the run in
the penal days."

"My grandfather used to tell me that," said Muiris.

"The English never bothered to come up," I said.

I told Muiris of a trip I took one Sunday out to a famine village in Connemara. I walked around all the deserted cottages, with the thatch falling in. Not a sign of
life to be seen. Just the whisper of who had been there
in your ear, like a chorus of ghosts. That was all that
remained. That's the way it will be with us. Someone
will come up and say, "There must have been a village
here once." It was the loss of the women that killed us.
And maybe even with them, the hardship of these winters would have broken our backs.

The next morning the plane came. There it was cir-
cling around, buzzing like a bee, and shining in the
sun, for sun there was, another clear day before more

snow. The child was beside himself, waving and running around. The *amadán* looked up with his mouth
open, laughing and pointing. He'd run a few steps and
fall over and get up and fall over and get up again. The
rest of us were rooted to the ground. You could see the
head of the pilot in the open cockpit, smooth as a nut.
He thumped his hand against the side of the plane several times, whatever he meant by that. Then he started
dropping bags with little parachutes swinging them
down slowly. I was glad someone was thinking about
us at last after they forgot about us last winter. They
had it on their conscience, I'm sure. Where the sacks
fell, they left a hole in the snow like a well, except
where they bounced off the hard ice on the pathways
and split open. One never opened and came down like a
thunderbolt and nearly hit Oweneen. The men waded
through the snow to get the sacks and the child was up
to his ears trying to get a parachute to play with. It was
a sight to see Old Biddy crabbing around sideways after one of the bags. It was raining plenty out of the
sky—hams and meat and canned salmon, even things
we didn't want like potatoes and sugar. One sack was
full of iodine and veganin and aspirin and thermogen
and syrup of figs and cod liver oil and malt and ban-

dages and plasters as if we were all on our last legs. There was even a dose of cascara. What came out of one bag but a few dozen Guinness and six bottles of whiskey. The only squabble was about the whiskey. Muiris, who didn't run after anything, was given the first bottle. They would be added to the store of poteen I knew they must have somewhere. It's a rare house that's without it in the mountains. The men each took home a bag or two.

It was only when the excitement was over that I realised there was no need for any of it. We'd laid in a store over the summer to carry us through whatever winter would bring. So they took care of us when we didn't need it and didn't take care of us last year when we were in want. The world has a perverse wrinkle in it, however it got that way. It was only after everything was gathered that I realised there wasn't a note or a newspaper to tell us what was happening down below in the town, or in Dublin or the rest of the country. The next day Séamus Mór came over and said his bag was from the nuns and the post office. There were toys for the young lad, including some colored chalks, a beadboard, and another *St. Ita's Reader*. But more important there were letters from the children to their fathers. Letters from all but his own son. There was a letter to Séamus from Sister Attracta saying his boy was getting along grand and not to worry about him.

"When the plane comes round again," I said, "I'm sure there'll be a letter from the lad."

"When will that be," said Séamus, "next blue moon? I'll give you the letters for the others. But I don't want them to know my own son doesn't want to send a message to his own father."

"That will be your secret and mine," I said.

The notes were simple things, written on lined copybooks, two lines inside for the low letters and two lines outside for the capitals. Big round hands most of them were. *Dear Da, I hope you're well. I'm very well. The nuns are very nice. Sincerely, Breda or Mary or Kathleen.* Did I open the letters myself? Yes I did. Some of these men were so far from their schooldays it was hard for them to read. So there was no harm in opening them. They were children's letters anyway. Does that satisfy you?

The older girls' letters were longer and more formal. *I trust*—trust, mark you—*that the weather is not too severe and that it will soon thaw. In the town the streets are cleared of snow every morning. A horse slipped on Jail Hill last week and broke his leg. They had to take him out of the cart and destroy him. The sisters have helped me make a new dress. It's made of cotton and has buttons down the front. We are all happy here. So there's no need to worry about me. With best regards, your affectionate daughter, Bridget Mahon.* There was also a letter for me in an elegant hand in a blue envelope with an embossed impression on the flap. Who was it from but the brave Fr. Staunton.

Dear Fr. McGreevy,

We are concerned that Providence has visited such hardship upon you and your flock again this year. Another winter like the one before was entirely unexpected. The town, as you can discern from the supplies gathered for the relief of your community, is concerned as well. The Red Cross has kindly coordinated relief efforts up and down the coast. Some communities are isolated, including one village, I believe from the papers, in the Wicklow Mountains.

I did want to mention to you in confidence some matters that have arisen here in terms of rumor and gossip, though never reported directly to me. While such sources are not to be given credence in the normal course of events, I felt that you should be aware of their nature so that you will not to be surprised to encounter them should they persist until the Spring, which I sincerely hope they do not.

Some young men who are no strangers to drink have been making cruel jokes about your village, impoverished and decimated though it is through no fault of your own. This came to my attention through the son of Manus Folan, the greengrocer, who spent an evening with some of those young men, including one lately from your village, James Donoghue. What they spoke should not pass anyone's lips, so vicious and vile is the subject. Some of your parishioners, the rumor goes, have in the winter just past, consorted with animals, no less. I am confident there is no truth in these rumors, but forewarned is forearmed, and I would be derelict in my duties were I not to inform you on a matter so grievous.

I have not shared this matter with anyone, nor have I spoken to the Canon. I'm sure times are harsh enough up there without adding to your difficulties. I know there is nothing more to these rumors than willful gossip and mischief. I thought it best that you should be informed.

We are getting through the winter down here as best we can. The Canon is finding this a difficult winter. He has been bedridden since Shrove Tuesday. I look forward to seeing you when you descend from your mountain, none the worse, I hope, from hardships suffered.

Your bro. In J.C.
Francis Staunton, C.P.

After the shock was over, I read it several more times. Old Biddy started peering over my shoulder at the letter in my hand and saying, "Is there a bit of news in it, Father?" I shouted at her, "Not a scrap for your eyes!" and went up to the church and knelt before the altar. The light of the sanctuary lamp gave me some peace of mind. That red eye had witnessed worse torment than mine. It had shone through centuries before me and would for centuries after me. But as I thought of that young pup down there spreading his stories and laughing with his friends, I folded my hands and bowed my head over a breast full of turmoil. I read the letter again in the dim light. Anger casts a shadow on any letter. I've read that letter in calmer times and there's nothing wrong with it. But at the time, I could have sworn I could see a smirk on Fr. Staunton's face as he wrote it— glad to have another reason to put an end to the village. And no matter what he said about not speaking to anyone, I knew that it was all over the town.

Nothing about that renegade Jamesy surprised me, with the company he'd fallen into. Between them and his new wife, he was changed for the worse. But the thought of Fr. Staunton ate into me. Was that all he had to do with his day—write letters about rumors and whispers? It was a dark day that brought that letter. And whenever I turned on the wireless, all I heard was of the darkness that was eclipsing the light of faith and reason all over Europe and beyond.

But even as I'm telling you this, things got better. Why? I think part of it was because we knew we hadn't been forgotten like last year. The extra food made living a bit easier, no doubt about that. For those few days the wind died down and you could see patches of blue sky like a promise. For a few days our spirits lifted. Even Old Biddy stopped her prognostications. We all stepped out a bit and looked up at the sky, making predictions about the weather. All the beasts were safe and sound. I even enjoyed seeing young Éamonn, all bundled up, leading his lamb around on a piece of string. The dogs were friendlier, perhaps because they were better fed. Even the tinker's dog, but that may have been because he ate something that made him turn himself inside out, and after that he didn't have the strength to be so vicious.

For some reason he and the *amadán* made a pair. Like to like, I suppose. That dog would lay around the empty house with the *amadán*. For the first time since that terrible sight, I felt more kindly to him. Even though he was the cause of our ruination, as it turned out. I reconciled myself to God's will, though I could no more see the logic of Providence than I could see through a mirror. But at that time, remembering my vows and more than a bit guilty for my harshness to a creature with no mind of his own, I went up to the empty house. There they were, the two of them, the tinker's dog and the *amadán* taking their ease. The second Tadhg saw me he was off his haunches and ready for flight. The dog raised its head and bared its teeth for no reason beyond its own bad nature. I held out my hand and moved a step. He was up in an instant with his back humped and breathing a snarl both in and out. The *amadán* sidestepped over to him and put out his hand. The way that the mongrel was snarling, I thought he'd take the hand off. But the dog started to lick the hand with a big red tongue and swallow with just an odd growl. He lay down again, his head between his front paws, never taking his eyes off me.

So there we were, the *amadán* trying to look at me, as far as he could look at anyone with those slipping eyes. What to do next? Whatever I'd say he wouldn't understand. He started growling as if he were imitating the dog, but there was no evil in it, just madness. I felt I was in the Dublin Zoo. He was in a terrible state—made up of bundles of rags—and I got a whiff of him like rancid lard. His face was chapped and skinned, and he had a stubble of beard. I came across Muiris shaving him once, with a saucepan of hot water steaming on the table, the *amadán*'s head stretched back and a big smile on his face, a sight that would make an angel weep. He had old socks over his boots and a blue toe sticking through one of them like a tramp in a cartoon. His snots were dribbling into his mouth and his mouth was dribbling as usual, and he dribbled more when he made those noises more animal than human. The fingers of one hand were swollen like bananas, and he kept rubbing his hands together as if they were hurting. One of his arms kept shaking as if it weren't a part of him, regular as a clock ticking. His short hair stuck up in all directions. Muiris must have clipped it too. I made myself smile, the way you do to a child, and took a step towards him. He took a step away from the dog to the back door and the dog snarled again. So I went down on my hunkers, even with my stiff bones, so he wouldn't think I was trying to catch him. It struck me that I should have brought some food.

I went back to Biddy and got some hot brown bread, buttered thick, and a scrap of gristle and fat for the dog. Up I went again. They were still there as if they knew I was coming back. I held out the bread, but he didn't stir. At least he wasn't running away. I sidled over to his bed, if that's what it was, and left the bread there on a broken plate. It gave off steam in the cold air. I threw the meat over at the dog. He sniffed it and left it where it lay, never taking his eyes off me. The *amadán* sidled over to the plate, not taking his eyes off of me either. He stuffed the bread into his mouth and looked over it at me directly for the first time. I looked into an ocean of bewilderment, thoughts tossing around like pebbles in a wave.

I was ashamed of myself. I'd left the care of this lost soul to Muiris and Biddy. The old witch had shown more charity than myself. Somewhere his uncorrupted soul reflected God's perfect light, obscured now by his misfortune. Some day that immortal soul would draw to it the poor half-starved body and transform it with its radiance into one of God's chosen. I asked God's forgiveness for my sin. I saw how I had put blame for our sickness and disasters on the poor madman. He was easy to blame for everything. Fr. Staunton's letter was proof of that.

I made peace with myself by bringing the *amadán* something every day. You could never tell what way my visit would take him. Sometimes he'd run outside through the back door when I came in the front and look in at me through the window. I'd hold out a piece of meat or a slice of bread through the broken window and he'd take that. When I left, he'd come in. It was like a game. Once he was trying to build a fire in the middle of the dirt floor. I took the sticks by the cool end and put them in the hearth and made a fire. He joined me, blowing and blowing like a bellows on the embers. I thought he'd burst his lungs. We were all right as long as we didn't stare at each other. It was the same way with the tinker's dog. I got in the way of avoiding them. Once I came out to see Muiris at his door looking up at me. He went back in when he saw me. Old Biddy must have told him what I was up to. It showed in the way he was to me. He started to come over again in the evenings, bringing the young lad with him. We'd listen to the wireless as before, him smoking his pipe and the young lad working on the map. In the meantime, Hitler had taken a big bite out of Russia.

I showed Muiris Fr. Staunton's letter. That shook him all right. After a long time, he took the pipe out of his mouth and said, "That young lad we sent down—" He put the pipe in his mouth, then took it out again, "—we'd a been better off killing him."

"God bless and save us," I said, "don't even talk like that in jest." That was all I got out of him. None of the men were free with words, except for Oweneen, who'd talk the hind leg off an ass.

The *amadán* began to follow me at a distance, like a stray dog I'd been kind to. And the tinker's dog would follow him. A sight the three of us must have been. Some evenings when Muiris and I were talking, I'd see his face at the window looking in. I'd tell Biddy to bring him in out of the cold, in spite of that terrible smell. Of course, no sooner was he in than he'd be off again. I saw his face often enough at the window to wonder what he saw when he looked in. Muiris and myself bent over the fire. The boy on the floor working on his map in the light of the oil lamp. His pet sheep beside him. Biddy hovering around in the shadows being busy at who knows what. And the wireless crackling and blurting and whistling away between bursts of music and news of the great war. The wireless was beginning to die. At least it was in tune with everything here and abroad.

Coming back from Mass one morning, looking forward to Biddy's breakfast, a fancy took me. Who knows where it came from. I went over to my own window and looked in. I suppose a kind of curiosity put me in the *amadán*'s shoes. What I saw rooted my feet to the ground. Biddy was sitting with her back to the table. The *amadán* was standing in front of her, his shirt pulled up and his trousers half down. She had a spoon in her hand. She gave a tap of her spoon on his sex, which was standing out like a signpost. The bob it gave each time she tapped it I see to this day. He was looking down with a daft smile. Through the glass I heard her cackle. I let out a shout that shivered the picture of the two of them like a stone in a pond. In I went like a whirlwind and fetched Biddy a clout. Down she fell on the floor screaming as if she were about to be murdered. The *amadán* stumbled around with his thing waving from side to side like a tail. I leaned on the table panting like a man who'd run a mile. My legs were weak. I sat down like a sack of potatoes. Biddy was crying holy murder in the corner. My breakfast was on the floor. The *amadán* staggered around, hobbled by his trousers. The last I saw of him was his bare backside.

When I got my breath back I spoke these words: "Don't ever address a word to me again as long as you live. I leave you to Almighty God for your sins, for I can't deal with you. To take advantage of a poor gom not right in the head and to lead him on to make an exhibition of himself that way is enough to make the saints weep—And to think that you yourself have been here these past five years, eating from this table and sleeping in this house—God knows who and what your parents were, but if they're in heaven, they're weeping now. If there were a place to send you, you'd be gone out of this house this very minute."

I couldn't bear the thought of her living in the same place with me. "This is what you will do," I said. "You will have the food on the table at twenty of eight and my dinner at one o'clock. I'll take care of the evening myself. And wherever you are when I come in I don't want to see sight nor light of you, nor a sound out of you, not anything that reminds me of you. And the minute the path opens up, you'll be on your way." From that day to this, I never spoke another word to her. I never wavered in that. Except under the seal, and one other time when I had to.

.   .   .

There was one more thing about that witch. A week later she wrote a note and left it on the table. "Father, you cant refus me abslusun. I want to make my confessun." And that no priest can refuse. I beckoned her and we walked up to the church in silence. I can't speak of her confession for that would be breaking the seal. I'd never thought much about her before. Once I did, I discovered there was a well of darkness in her, with her sly ways, as if she was laughing at you inside. I said to her through the grill, "Are you sure you've told me all you need to tell?" "Sure, what else would I have, Father, but what I've told you?"

After I gave her absolution, she said, "Would you like a nice fresh egg for breakfast, Father?" "Don't talk to me," I said, "and get yourself out of here." "Is it driving me out of the church you are, Father," she said, "without me having time to do my penance before the altar?" I shut my lips tight. Off she went, and back the next Sunday morning with her tongue out for the Sacrament. With the Host in my hand, I looked down at those squinting eyes, tight shut in a bed of wrinkles, and that little tongue sticking out like a parrot's. I paused long enough for her to open her eyes and we both knew what was going through my mind. Yes, I put It on her tongue, with an apology to the Lord who finds Himself some strange habitations. But who knows the miracles that His grace can bring.

I had no one to confide in, not a soul I could talk to. No matter how friendly, there's always a distance between a priest and his flock. I had to possess my soul in patience and wait for the Spring, a Spring I wanted and didn't want to come. For now I knew what it would bring. All I could do up there was say Mass and pray for the souls of all on that hillside, including that woman cooking my food, which I had difficulty eating, knowing it was from her hands. It's no wonder I began to melt away and you see me now on my way back from being nine stone. Why had God put this heavy burden on my shoulders? This thought nibbled at the borders of my mind when I was half-asleep or lying awake in the darkness of the morning. I had dreams all right. I dreamt of sunlight on green fields and tall trees laden with leaves. But it was the dark dreams that took me unawares and shook me like a terrier shaking a rat.

I'd see Biddy grown into a giantess, stepping over the mountains and looking down at me with that red grin of hers, all gums and no teeth. I saw again that frozen picture of her and the *amadán* bending towards each other, but so indistinct I couldn't tell what they were doing, which made it worse. I saw the young boy stretched out and the two of them bending over him. He'd give out a scream to wake the dead and myself to boot. I had dreams you couldn't make head nor tail of. I'd be in the middle of a terrible tangle of guts and blood, twisting and turning with a life of their own. I'd see flayed bodies and torn limbs like in a knacker's yard. In one dream some of those limbs got up and started walking towards me and I was paralyzed with fright. If they reached me, I knew I'd die. I heard a shout and woke up, and knew it was my own. I'd lie there in the pitch dark listening to myself breathing as heavy as if I'd run a race. I was so worn out from the dreams and nightmares that I'd even listen for a stir out of Biddy. For a sign of life you see. No matter how cold it was, I'd wake up in a sweat and throw the clothes off. In five minutes I'd be shivering and trying to get warm again.

Then came a stretch when I couldn't sleep at all, and didn't want to. I had no desire to meet what was waiting for me in the darkness of sleep. It was a terrible persecution I was visiting on myself. One night after waking up in the darkness, it struck me to wonder what dreams the others were having, for dreaming never stops. Lying there in the darkness, I began to imagine Muiris's dreams and Séamus Mór's and Oweneen's and the boy's. I fancied I could see all those dreams hovering over the mountainside. And then I imagined the *amadán*'s. That opened a dark well, with horrible things glistening below, and out of it rose that shining obscenity that tormented me, so that I didn't know whether I was asleep or awake. I thought I was asleep and trying to wake up when I was already awake. That happened more than once. There were times when I thought my mind was giving way, and there would be a mad priest locked in his room and a madwoman outside his door. The thought made me laugh and that was a help.

When I looked in the little mirror in the morning, I saw a face that wasn't my own. I thought if I missed a day or two shaving, it would be no harm. Then it became a week and I'd see black eyebrows and a white stubble, and two sunken eyes. It became such an effort to shave, I don't rightly know why, but it did. It was an effort to say Mass on Sunday.

I still had a trace of feeling for the *amadán*, if you can believe that. He wasn't to blame for the accident that had made him what he was. I always understood that. But the difference was I felt it now. I brought food up to him every day. Biddy got into the habit of leaving a piece of fresh bread or a bit of stew on the table, without a word being said. I'd go up to Jamesy's cottage—what was left of it—about three before the night came down. But now he'd run away on all fours the minute he saw me and he'd wait until I left before he came back in. He always seemed to have a fire. Maybe Biddy was helping him with that. There hadn't been a snowfall for over a week. When I came in the dog would stir itself and walk towards me, his legs stiff as splints, baring his teeth. It never got used to me, nor I to it. I met the young lad with his lamb once or twice and chased him away. He didn't understand that at all.

Sometimes I'd run into one or other of the men. We had less and less to say to each other. What was there to say? They'd touch their caps and we'd pass. Except Oweneen. He had an easy way with people, including the *amadán*. He'd talk to him as if he were sane as a bank manager. I've seen the two of them, him chattering away and the *amadán* nodding and dribbling and looking at him as if he understood every word. Now there was a pantomime for you. Oweneen would find something to talk about when there wasn't a word to say. This day was no exception.

"I wonder if they've closed the convent," says he. "Isn't it glad I am that my little girl isn't up here with the rest of us misfortunates. I saw a thrush the other day frozen to a branch. His claws were closed around the branch as if they were growing out of it. It was still there an hour later. There was a cover of snow on him like a winter jacket. Not much life around here now. And what there is mostly hiding under the ground. The birds should be coming back soon. I wonder if they'll send up that plane again. It'd be nice to get another bottle or two to keep us warm." I always let him rattle on and didn't pay much attention. Five minutes with Oweneen would cheer you up and ten minutes would leave you wanting to get away. But he had a way of not letting you go. It's as if you were an excuse for him to talk to himself.

The only thing that kept me sane was the wireless. Whatever terrible news it brought at least it was out in the world and not here. I had only the voice on the wireless to vouch that it was true. There were days when I had a notion that it was all a lie they were making up. Just for our benefit. The next day I'd wonder what was wrong with me to think that way. But living in our white prison, tramping down every new snowfall, scanning the sky for a hint of change, can thwart your spirit. That was the way it went on into April. The thaw couldn't be far away. The wireless kept fainting and after I'd switch it off, it seemed to gather strength and recover. The announcers' voices went farther and farther away. So I'd have to put my ear against the golden cloth between the diamonds of bakelite as if I were hearing a confession. I felt the world was dropping away from us into the distance. Then there were times when I thought everything would be all right. A strange optimism we have sometimes in the midst of disaster. I'd see us all from a distance and say to myself all we have here is an old rascal of a woman and a madman and the men you'd be proud to meet that never did anyone harm. But these moments were few and far between. I always had that cloud of worry hanging over me. I got into the habit of thinking something terrible was going to happen. I kept waiting for it. When it did I wasn't ready for it, nor had I a notion of the shape it took.

You think things can't get worse and then they do.

From that moment on there was no rest between one disaster and the next. What happened next made my heart shrivel so that I felt there wasn't a drop of blood left in me. Did you ever notice how sound travels in icy air? It contracts and sharpens and comes to your ear as if it were a shaft of ice itself. When I heard that sound, clear and distant as if it were coming from under one of the glass domes in the graveyard, I didn't notice it at first. I thought it might be a cat. Then a bird caught in that sticky stuff young lads smear on branches. Or a rabbit in a snare. None of which was possible. I was walking up and down outside my door on a path I'd made in the snow, reading my breviary. I lost my place a few times on the page. When I realised what it was, it swelled up all of a sudden in my mind. I was rushing up to Tadhg's house—for that's what we called it now—before I knew I was on my way at all.

Every terrible thing he did was a puzzle to me when it burst upon me. I suppose the eyes and the mind separate when you get a shock. You see what you see but you don't know it. There's the space of a second before it explodes in your head and you're blind with rage. So in a heartbeat you go from blind to blind, from not understanding what you're seeing, to understanding it all too well. It's a strange way we're made surely. He had his back to me. I felt a spark of pity for that scrawny neck of his between his shorn hair and his collarless gansy. There's nothing sadder than the back of someone you pity. He was having a fit. His lower quarters had a St. Vitus attack, shaking in and out as fast as a fiddler's elbow. I couldn't see anything else. Who was crying then? The young lad twisted into my line of sight, just beyond the *amadán*. He was screaming and pulling at something. For a minute I thought they were playing a game. I heard another sound like an animal in pain. Then the *amadán* staggered sideways. There was a blur of curly white, and there was the pet lamb, all four legs off the ground and he holding him like he was putting on a boot. The child lost his grip and I glimpsed the soles of his boots as he fell over. The *amadán* staggered around and let out a great cry. It sounded as if all the banshees in the world were falling off the edge of the earth. It went up and down the scales for a long time, that cry—he must have had a power of wind in his lungs—half-way between torture and triumph. I heard a great bellow. I didn't know I could shout so loud. All those noises were mingling in a confusion—the young lad sobbing, the *amadán* panting and screaming, the lamb bleating, and my own voice strange to my ears. There was another snarling sound

I didn't recognise for a moment. I got an arm around the *amadán*'s neck and pulled. He came back, staggering me. His hands flew up and he fell on the ground, the lamb on top like a lump of cream on a cake. The child rushed up and plucked the lamb off of him and cuddled her, whimpering and crying. That terrible shiny shaft of his, which I'd seen too many times, was waving around like a mast in a storm. He tried to get up. He was stronger than you'd think. "No, my fine bucko!" I said in his ear. "You'll stay where you are till your father deals with you." Then I heard that snarling again. I'd forgotten all about the tinker's dog.

He was showing so many teeth you'd think he had two sets of them. "Go get your father," I said to the child. He stood looking at us with round eyes, holding his lamb half off the ground. "Go get your father this very minute," I said, and off he went half carrying, half dragging his lamb. I hadn't remembered it getting so big. The next thing I knew that dog was leaping at me like a wolf. I fetched him a kick that lifted him out of it, and bent down for a stone beside a big rock that had fallen from the gable. The minute I went for it, he slunk over to a corner where he kept pointing at me, still snarling.

Then the exhaustion overtook me. I felt I weighed a

ton. I dragged that madman over to his bed in the corner and sat in front of him on a broken chair. The dog started to come at me again, but I threatened him with a stone. The *amadán* was dribbling away and casting his eyes on either side of me. "You may not understand a word I'm saying, but in the name of God as I live and breathe, you'll not budge from that spot until I'm done with you." He crouched over, holding on to his shame and rocking back and forth like an old woman at a wake. I sat there looking at him. Innocent himself, but wherever he went, evil followed. Truly, he was the devil's instrument.

Muiris came in with a face like thunder. I stood up and the two of us looked down at the son of his flesh.

"What's been happening here, Father?" he said, as if he didn't know. He wasn't in a friendly mood.

"It's the child's pet he was after this time," I said. "He was hard at it when I came in and in front of the child." The *amadán* was looking up at us as if Judgement Day had come. "This has got to stop, Muiris," I said. "There's no two ways about it."

He said nothing. He closed his eyes and ran his hand from his forehead to his poll. He did that twice. His face was a picture of pain. He reached out with his foot and touched the *amadán* gently in the side. That surprised me. The *amadán* clutched the leg as if it were his last hope of salvation. There was a scuffle behind me.

"Watch out for the dog!" I said. He had Muiris by the leg and was looking up with one evil eye as he dug deeper.

Muiris fell down by the big stone, one leg stiff as a poker. The *amadán* still held the other. Muiris leaned sideways as if he were pulling a bucket out of a well and lifted that stone with both hands. He crashed it down onto the dog's back. The dog let go, his hind legs stiff and shaking. He scrambled with his front legs like a child trying to swim. His back was broken. Muiris took his time getting up. He lifted that stone again, walked slowly around, and crashed it down on the dog's head. The dog's tongue came out and his eyes started out as white as two pigeon's eggs. His body vibrated and the toes of his four paws twitched. Blood was pumping out of his nose and mouth. It was steaming in the cold air like the food I used to bring up. My stomach gave notice to me. Muiris peeled up his trouser leg, sodden with blood. A lump of flesh was hanging from a deep hole. "You'd better watch that," I said, "or you'll get lockjaw. I have the iodine and bandages they dropped from the air back at the house." He moved the flesh on its hinge like he was closing a little door in his leg.

There was a shadow at the door. Oweneen and Séamus Mór were peeping in. Séamus had a shovel over his shoulder. With the dead dog on the floor still steaming, Muiris holding his leg, and the *amadán* shaking in the corner, we must have been a sight.

"Did you kill that mongrel?" said Oweneen. "A vicious one he was surely—it's no loss."

"Has he taken a turn?" said Séamus, nodding towards the corner.

"He's as he always is," I said. "There's nothing to worry about now."

"Do you want us to take that dog out of there?" said Séamus.

"It would do no harm," said Muiris.

They each grabbed a pair of legs and swung the dog out. Séamus came back for his shovel. The two of them always cleared the graveyard after a snowfall. Séamus looked at Muiris's bloody leg and said, "Well if there's nothing wrong—" and off they went, leaving a silence broken only by the *amadán* whining and sucking up his snots.

What happened next is hard to credit. He got up and burst between us like a rugby player, stopped at the door, and turned round wearing that loopy grin of his. He raised each elbow in tune to the same leg. I thought he was having a fit. It dawned on me just as Muiris said it: "He's dancing!" And indeed he was. Maybe he was trying to please us. Then he started to yowl, still dancing away. His voice went up and down without rhyme or reason to it. "He's singing!" I said. He stopped and looked back, his eyes going from side to side at a mile a minute. Then he was out the door.

Muiris went off in a hurry to his cottage. He had a limp he wouldn't give in to. I could tell there was a volcano inside of him. And why wouldn't there be with his mad son making his young brother witness a sight that should never be seen by mortal eyes? You never know what a quiet man like that would do. Not that there was anything to do as long as Tadhg was let run wild. I hoped this event would make Muiris lean towards putting the daft boy where he couldn't harm himself or anyone else. I made my way around the bloody stone and looked out the door. The sky was darker than the earth. Oweneen and Séamus were over at the grave-yard, one bent over the shovel, the other—Oweneen of course—looking as if he were giving instructions. Muiris was entering his own door. I noticed the ram. But then how could I miss him? He was standing still as if a hand had lifted him from where I last saw him and put him down again on the slope just above Muiris's cottage. I went and got the iodine and bandages, then went over to Muiris's. When I dropped the iodine into the open wound he turned white and threw his head back, but he didn't utter a word.

.   .   .

There's only so much can be squeezed out of you. There comes a time when you wonder if you've any feelings left. I was in a state of simultaneous calm and confusion, if you can imagine that. I was thinking of the young Éamonn. What he had seen would never leave him. I wore out my knees praying for all the souls on the mountainside, including those flawed and twisted. But God had turned a deaf ear as it turned out.

The week after, I had the child serve Mass a few times. He was proud of the way he'd learned the responses. He'd be seven in July—the age of reason. After Mass, I taught him his catechism. He'd sit at the edge of the chair casting his eyes in all directions but on the book. But that's the way the young are. On a Saturday, I think it was, he brought his lamb with him, but I wouldn't let him bring the profaned creature into the church. He tied it outside the door where he could see it. When I looked out what did I see but the ewe out there with her lamb and the lamb nuzzling her udder.

She hadn't given her lamb a bit of notice since it became a pet. I couldn't understand it, but there it was. Éamonn went out and tried to chase the ewe away. He didn't want to share his lamb, I suppose, though that had already occurred, in a terrible way. The ewe wouldn't go. The lad said, "I have to go home now, Father"—he was glad for an excuse not to be put to the catechism again. Off he trotted leading the lamb on a string. The shadow of his mad brother was on my mind and it cast itself over the two of them going down the icy path. The ewe followed them slowly.

That's when the wireless gave out. The British had just captured Addis Ababa, where Mussolini had done such evil things, bad cess to him. The last I heard was that the Germans were in Greece. After that it gave out a confusion of whistles and blurts, then it whispered like a wind rising and falling, then a long *brrrrrrr* loud enough to drill into your teeth. It had gone mad too. I went over a few times and dressed Muiris's leg. It was healing well enough, with a good fringe of laudable pus. He'd have a dinge there for the rest of his days to remember that dog by.

I saw the *amadán* a few times in the distance, always on the move. I left it to Biddy to take up food to him. I hated being in the house with her. I spent more time in the church because of it. Just a week after the business with the lamb, someone came in for confession. I pulled the curtain over. It was Muiris's voice. You know better than to ask me what he said. After giving him absolution, I asked him if he'd sit on a bench and talk to me. Of course that was what he was expecting.

"Muiris," I said, "the winter is ending and it has been a terrible scourge. Soon we'll be making our way down to the town and I don't know what we're going to meet there. It's best we try and settle on how to deal with poor Tadhg. We can't have him running around like a wild man. You and I can find a place for him where he'll be well taken care of, and never in want of food and shelter."

"He has food and shelter up here," said Muiris.

"If you call that shelter," I said, "shivering in Jamesy's place. He's likely to freeze to death one of these nights."

"The cold doesn't take him badly," said Muiris.

"He's a danger to himself up here," I said, "and who knows when his sickness will take him another way."

"There's no harm in him," said Muiris.

"There was harm enough in him a week ago," I said, "providing his young brother with a sight his eyes will never forget. You have your responsibility as a father and I have mine as a priest. There should be no quarrel between us doing what's right for him. He might even get some of his sense back with proper treatment."

"I know well what's on your mind, Father," said Muiris. "You want to put him in the county asylum in a room like a prisoner. A lad that has the run of the whole mountain. With the four walls coming in on him day after day, it'll kill him in a month. It's bad enough for the rest of us, stuck up here, with the sky pressing down on us."

"Muiris," I said, "you're a man of great sense in everything. But what I've witnessed with my own eyes demands a solution."

"As if there never was a worse sight," said Muiris.

"I don't believe I'm hearing right," I said, "your own child scandalised."

He rubbed his forehead back and forth with his fingers.

"I'm in no two minds about this," I said, "for man is made in God's image and to sink to the level of the beasts—"

"I'll thank you not to speak that way of my son," he said. "He has no sense of what he does."

"But the rest of us do," I said.

266

"Have you heard any of the men complain?" he asked me.

"No I haven't. But that's neither here nor there." I wanted to tell him about Biddy but the words wouldn't come out of my mouth. "It's not a matter of complaints. It's a matter of what's right. Through no fault of his own, the poor afflicted lad has become an instrument of the devil, sowing dissension and scandal."

"And we know who God's instrument is," he said, raising his head and looking at me for the first time directly. "So you want to kill my son to kill the devil in him?"

"Do you hear yourself talking?" I said. "I'm asking you as a Christian man I've known for thirty years to listen to reason."

"There's reason and there's reason, Father," he said. "I must be going now."

He went off, deliberate and stiff with anger. It hadn't gone the way he'd expected. But how else could it go?

The next morning he was pounding at my door at nine o'clock. "You'd better come with me, Father," said he.

A soft, mottled light in the east was soaking up the

darkness. The battlefields of Europe were already in full daylight. As the two of us walked up the hill to Tadhg's house my legs were so heavy they didn't want to go with me. Every step I took, I felt I was walking in my own footsteps. I didn't ask what was wrong. Muiris's face was sealed. I knew old Biddy was at the door behind me, watching every step. I saw in my mind's eye the *amadán* blue from pneumonia, gasping his last. I saw a broken leg and him squirming around like a fox in a trap. Had he taken the child and gone off? The lamb? No! The imagination is eager to oblige with the worst. Except for the crunch of fresh ice over yesterday's snow, there wasn't a sound as we approached.

Muiris let me through the door first. "He's not here!" I said. Without raising his arm, Muiris made a jerk of the wrist and a long forefinger towards a bundle of rags half-under the table. Muiris stayed by the door. It was him all right, what was left of him. Whatever had opened his skull had done a good job of it. A pool of frozen blood had lapped over the blood from the dog the day before. It had a sheen like spilled oil. A splinter of white skull, like a piece of broken crockery, was sticking out from a wound on the left side of his head. His left hand looked as if a giant had stepped on it, squashed like putty and swollen with the colors of the rainbow. I turned him over gently. His mouth was wide open. He had only black stumps for teeth. His dead eyes were looking up at the gable. I looked up. Part of the gable was gone. There had been a heavy wind the night before. A few stones the size of footballs were lying around. I lifted him and put him on the table. He was light as a chicken. Muiris came in and stood beside me. I closed the eyes, and tried to cross his hands, but his arms were sticking straight out, stiff as oars.

"Stay with him," I said. "I have to get the oils."

I ran down the path on my own footsteps again. Biddy had the oils laid out on the table as if she knew what had happened. She spoke her first words to me: "Is he dead, Father?" I nodded. I went back up in my own footsteps again.

I put my hand under the clothes to see if there was a touch of heat left in him. He was a block of ice.

Muiris said, "What are you doing, Father?"

"When did you find him?" I said.

"Just now," he said.

"Would you help me now?" I said. Muiris tried to help me pull off the gansy but we couldn't manage it with the arms stretched and stiff. There was a rope around his trousers and a knot I couldn't loosen. Muiris cut it with a big pocket knife. We pulled down his trousers, stiff in the groin from his frozen urine. I pulled up the gansy. The belly was pale and yellow and streaked with dirt that had got into every crease and pore so that it looked like a map. As I pulled down the trousers, the tip of his shame, blue as a robin's egg, appeared, laid back on his stomach. There it was, that tiny thing, the source of so much trouble for all of us. I pulled the trousers up and covered him as best I could with the remains of a sheet I found twisted in his bed like a *súgán* [a rope made by twisting straw during harvest-time, used to hold down haystacks].

Muiris knelt on the floor beside the table. I gave the dead man the last sacraments, anointing his eyes, his lips, his ears, his nose, his hands. *Visum, tactum.* His soul was now bright as an angel's, his troubles over. I remembered him as a strapping young lad. What was before me bore no relation to that memory. The smell of him was pungent enough to cut through the cold air. Now it was mixed with the sweat of death.

Muiris stood up, looking down at his son. If there wasn't a tear in his eye, there was something like it.

"He was the pride of this village once," he said.

"That he was," I said, "and he's running around now as perfect as he was before the blow that took his mind from him. He's with God, Muiris. You did all you could

270

for him. You were as kind a father as ever was. Máire Rua would be proud of you. Now she has her son back, the way he was."

"I'd be obliged if you'd leave me with him for a minute, Father," Muiris said.

As I went through the broken half-door, a little voice inside me expressed its satisfaction. I raised my fist against it. As I did I looked up and there were Oweneen and Séamus like apparitions in the grey light.

"What's happened now, Father?"

"He's dead!" I told them. I saw Biddy coming up the slope, bits of mist around her feet.

"When did it happen?" said Oweneen.

"How did it happen is more like it," said Séamus.

"It looks as if maybe a stone off the gable hit him on the head," I said. An image came into my mind of Muiris lifting that stone and killing the dog. I saw the stone come down, but it came down on his demented son. Cold though it was, I felt myself break into a sweat.

The two of them started to go in. "Leave him with Muiris for a minute," I said.

Biddy went past us without a word. We could hear her voice inside lamenting. She was out in no time. "I know you won't address a word to me, Father," she said, "but that poor boy has to be taken care of unless you want to take care of him yourself." She had that authority that births and deaths gave her. Well she knew she was the only one to undress that body and wash it and pack it where it was needed. I nodded my head. She went in again. Muiris came out.

"I'll go down and prepare the table to lay him out," he said, "and we'll have to find wood for another coffin."

Thady joined us. Since he'd lost his wife, he was always up later than the others. Never a great man for hard work, was Thady. The plumes of our breaths congealed in the cold air.

I saw the boy coming up the path. "Muiris! Go down and stop him!" I said. "This is no sight for him to see. She'll wash and dress him up here, Muiris. I'll go down with you and get a shirt and a clean gansy." I didn't like the thought of that body laid out on Muiris's table with his young son there beside it. Even dead, I didn't want Tadhg in Éamonn's vicinity. "He's better laid out up here, Muiris," I said.

"That's true," said Biddy from the door. "This was his place as far as any place was his. He was king in his own castle here."

"I'm taking him down when you're done," said Muiris.

"It'd be better for the boy if you left him here," I said.

"What's wrong?" said young Éamonn, arriving.

"Nothing," said two or three of us.

"Your brother has gone to heaven," I told him. He looked at us with round eyes.

"Come on with me," said Muiris, putting his arm around him.

"We'll make a fire up here that will warm the place," said Biddy, "and these lads will give me a hand. There's a good table here to lay him out on, and if you don't like what we've done, Muiris, we'll bring him down." Muiris started to say something. Then he turned and went off with the child. The lad kept looking back, stepping sideways so that he almost tripped over his feet.

"He won't leave him up here," I said. Biddy followed Muiris down to get the clothes.

"Have a fire roaring when I get back," she said.

"Look at that ram," said Oweneen. "You'd think there was more than one of him." The ram was on a slope near the church, looking down at us. I was sick of seeing him. Why should I be? There was no reason at all. He seemed to be always in the wrong place, if that makes any sense. He had as much right to be here and there as any other beast, but the sight of him was an irritation to me. The ram went up the hill. A patch of fog drifted across. Through it we could see his white blur.

"Let's make that bloody fire," said Séamus. "Excuse me, Father," he added.

Oweneen and Thady went out to get the turf. Séamus took one of the broken chairs and tore it apart like it was made of cardboard. There was no paper to start a fire. I went down and brought back some brown paper bags. Then no one had matches. I had to go down again. The three of them started a fire, arguing about the best way to do it. Biddy came back with a long shirt draped over her arm. I tried to clean up the cottage to make it half-way decent. I threw the broken plate, bits of food stuck to it, in the hearth. When the fire got going, we dragged the table and body closer to it. Biddy was already well along with her work. What clothes she couldn't get off easily, she cut off with a big scissors. I hadn't realised how thin he was. His chest was like an old boat with the ribs sticking out on either side. I threw his coat and gansy in the fire, holding them as far away from me as I could. She had a hard time getting the trousers off. None of the men helped her. She pulled so hard on one leg that the corpse almost fell off the table. She threw the trousers at my feet.

By the time Muiris came back, a great fire was burning. Someone had brought two candles that were lit on the windowsill. The body was naked on the table.

There were bruises on the body where it met the table. I remembered the German airman. Biddy saw me looking.

"It always does that, Father," she said, "it's the way the blood settles." "I know that!" came to my lips but didn't pass them. Muiris went to the head of the table and cradled the head in his hands and called me over. The wound on the left side of the head had a blue rim. In the clots were toothpicks of bright bone. A couple of grey streaks, like snots, trailed onto the damp hair. I didn't need anyone to tell me what they were.

Muiris said, "That's what did it, Father." I thought he was talking about the wound. But his fingers were searching on the right side of the head. "Put your finger in that," he said. I felt nothing but the hard nut. He took my fingers and guided them. "There," he said. I felt a dinge in the bone over the temple, enough to hold a spoonful of water. I realised he was talking about the blow that long ago had robbed his son of his senses.

"I want to lay him out proper," said Biddy to Muiris, standing at the side of the table like a shopkeeper at a counter. Muiris didn't seem anxious to go. Then he nodded his head briskly and stepped back. Biddy took one of the arms sticking out askew and tried to fold it across the chest. She strained, but it wouldn't break. "I need to get the stiffness out of him," she said to Séamus. Séamus put his knee in the elbow and broke the rigor mortis. He put the arm on the corpse's breast. It flopped back on the table. He broke the other arm the same way. Biddy crossed the two hands, one twice the size of the other, across the breast. "I've things to do here there's no cause for you to watch," she said to Muiris. "Nor you neither, Father. If Séamus will stay." She leaned over and closed the eyes which had half-opened, and stroked the face, smoothing it out. She was in her element. Séamus took off his coat and hung it over the back of the bockety chair. The air was getting warmer. The flames of the candles in the window were pale against the morning light. Icicles hung down outside the window, like lace curtains. They began to pick up a gleam of sun.

"We'll take him down when you're done," said Muiris.

"We'll come tell you," said Séamus. Muiris left again. Like myself that morning, he was up and down, up and down. I couldn't keep track of who was there and who wasn't.

"He'd be better off here," I said when Muiris left. "It's close to the church and we can bring him up in mid-morning and bury him the next day."

"If you can strike a spade into that ground," said Séamus. "We've had an experience of that before, Father."

"Let me dress him up and lay him out and maybe Muiris will agree to leave him where he lived, if living it was," said Biddy to me. I didn't answer.

"That's a good idea," said Oweneen. "Every bird likes his nest and every beast his lair. If ever there was anywhere he could call home, this was the place. And a palace it is surely. Look at it. Look up there. There's a danger of more stones from that gable. The last wind must have shaken that whole wall. That's what happens to a place when there's no one to take care of it. And that's the stone that did it." He kicked a heavy stone and picked it up. He offered it to me. "See, Father, there's a touch of hair on it." I stared at the stone. He held it up. "Now there's a stone that killed a man. A wicked stone it is surely. It had a mind to do its mischief from the moment it became a stone." He laughed at his own fancy. "I'll leave it far up the mountain. Someone will give it a kick in the summer that never will know what it did. I'll be back in a minute. I'll bring back something to keep us warm."

Biddy looked up from the table and grinned at him. She was washing down the body from a bucket of hot water. A round-bellied pot was hanging on the hook over the fire.

"We need some chairs and a lamp," said Oweneen.

"I'll get some of mine," said Séamus.

I didn't want to be alone with Biddy and her master-piece, God forgive me for saying that. I followed Owen-een and waited for him to come back down the moun-tain, minus the stone.

"I hope Muiris will leave him there for the wake to-night," I said.

"I'm sure he will," said Oweneen. "When you're dead, one place is as good as another. It's the living that think otherwise. It's where you gave up the ghost that you should be waked. We'll bury him in the graveyard when the weather eases up, which won't be too long now by the looks of it. So his soul won't lose any time searching for his body when the time comes." He was taken by his own thought. "Think of the lost bodies in the war over there, Father. Lost in the air, or deep in the sea, or blown to bits. Their ghosts will have a hard time finding them. Imagine," he said, "coming to the last judgement in pieces!"

"You're talking about the temple of the Holy Ghost," I said, "and you might show some respect for it."

"Indeed I should, Father. Indeed I should. You never

spoke a truer word. Where would we all be if we didn't have the faith to guide us? That's all we have in the end. Everything else is cold comfort when you're drawing your last breath."

I had a notion he was having me on a little. Oweneen's thoughts slipped around like a ferret in a warren. You'd never know where they'd come out. I remembered what I'd come after him for.

"Oweneen, we need a coffin."

"That we do," he said, "that we do. And where are we to find the wood for it?" We looked down at the smoke rising from the chimney of Muiris's cottage. "Speaking of coffins reminds me of things I don't want to remember," he said. "Indeed the whole of last year I don't want to remember. It rarely leaves my mind. We'll have to sacrifice the kitchen table. We'll use the table he's lying on. We'll put him on a board near the fire. Or maybe not, it mightn't be good to warm him up. We'll make the coffin early in the morning, put him in it, and bring him to church by the time you're striking the bell for the Angelus."

"The least moving of the body is to be desired," I said.

"Sure we wouldn't wake him up anyway," said Oweneen.

"We'll find a place for him next to Máire Rua," I said.

"Where else?" said Oweneen. "But you know as well as I that you'll never get the edge of a spade into the ground if we could find it under all that ice."

"It isn't past the ingenuity of man to find a way," I said. "I don't want him lying out there like last year."

"I'll get Séamus and Thady to start digging down there," said Oweneen, "if I can get Thady to work up a sweat. You wouldn't have any wood in your own kitchen, would you, Father?" said he.

"You can talk to Biddy," I said.

"Where is she now?" he said.

"She's still where we left her a minute ago—with the dead, where else?" I said.

"Of course," he said, "of course," and off he went. We were all a bit distracted. Muiris came out of his cottage and made his way up the hill slowly. He was holding a pair of boots in one hand. I turned and went up to the church to pray for the dead man's soul.

.   .   .

There's an orderly way of doing things that takes you back from the borders of chaos. You wouldn't have conceived how that pig-sty could look after a day of gathering and cleaning. A breath of heat met you when you entered. A mound of turf was stacked up by the hearth, and more turf against the outside wall. Most of the heat escaped through the broken roof. But like every cottage it had thick walls, built for all kinds of weather, and the thatch, falling down as it was, helped keep the heat in. The men kept coming and going, bringing what they could spare. Biddy had done miracles, I'll say that for her. There was a fresh tablecloth on the table. I recognised it as my own. The body lay on it, the two uneven hands folded over the breast on my mother's crucifix, the one she held when she died. Of course it would never strike Biddy to ask my permission. The soles of his boots faced you when you came in the door. There was a bandage around his head, like a wounded hero, and another bandage held up his jaw. Two more candles had appeared at the head of the table.

"Isn't he looking lovely?" said Biddy. I turned away. There was straw on the ground over the blood and someone had brought a few more chairs. On a small table by the window was a bottle of Powers. On the windowsill between the candles was a fat bottle of what looked like water, but I knew better. Beside it were two other whiskey bottles. With the light coming through them, they looked as if they were made of gold. Black bottles of stout were in a cardboard box under the little table. On a bench next to it were a few tumblers, cups, and plates, waiting for the fresh bread and scones I knew Biddy would bake. A lot of respect had been shown for Muiris.

"Where is he?" I said to Oweneen.

"Back in his cottage," said Biddy as if I were talking to her.

"I'm going down to the house now, Father," she said.

I was glad Muiris was staying with young Éamonn. I could imagine what he was thinking down there. Two desperate winters and a dead wife and now another loss to add to that.

"Has he seen what's been done?" I asked Oweneen.

"Not yet, he hasn't," said Oweneen. "But when he does I'm sure he'll be pleased. It wouldn't take too much to do this place up. A new door and a new thatch and you wouldn't know it. Indeed there's some of us that need a thatcher this summer, if it ever comes. But for thousands of years it's come, so I suppose nature won't change its mind this time, although we've had cause to wonder for two winters now."

As I was wondering whether I should go down and get Muiris, in he came. He looked around and said, "It's a shame you've gone to all this trouble, for I want him down in the house where he belongs."

"Muiris," I said, "he'll be in the church tomorrow as sure as I'm standing here. He's not a stone's throw from it now. He's laid out proper as he is. Everyone has brought something as a mark of respect. Just look around you at what's been done. This isn't the worst place in the world for a wake. It's where he was most himself. He's resting here so easy it'd be a shame to disturb him who had no peace in his life—"

"Where's the coffin?" said Muiris.

"That has to be done yet," I said. Muiris went to the door and looked out. "Muiris," I said, "I know you'd like to have your son down there where you want him to be. That's the most natural thing in the world. But we must remember there's a young lad down there who's had a shock. He lost his mother last year, and now his brother. He needs all the care and consolation we can give him. Is it the best thing for him to look death in the face again? He's seen more than a lad of his age should." Not a word out of Muiris. "He made this place his own," I said. "Well you know he never stayed more than a heartbeat anywhere else. If he ever had a happy minute it was here. Who knows but God himself what went on in his head. But he always knew his own father." God forgive me for saying that, because it wasn't true.

"And his priest," said Muiris. There was a bitter edge to that.

"Doesn't he look lovely, Muiris?" said Biddy. "You'd think he was sleeping." Indeed the dead face didn't have a line on it. With the poor distracted mind taken away, you could almost see how handsome he had once been. Biddy undid the bandage that had held the chin up. "It'll hold now," she said. "Everyone has brought something, Muiris. You'd never think that this place could get so cozy. We'll give him a good send-off. And as his father's son, who deserves it better?" Muiris tilted his hat, briefly scratched the side of his head and was off without saying a word.

"He'll let him stay," said Biddy. "I know the way his mind goes." I almost answered her before I bit my tongue. I went to the door and watched Muiris going down the path. He went through a few sheep that scattered in that slow-motion way of theirs. He slipped on the ice and staggered. He still had a trace of a limp. Passing the ram he gave it a kick that lifted it. It looked after Muiris and limped off up the hill, dragging one of its hind legs. I remembered the way Tadhg used to tease that ram. He'd stand in front of him and wag his finger and tilt his head and make noises. When the ram lowered his head, he'd take the crooked horns and wag

284

the head from side to side. Then he'd try to mount him backwards and ride him. You can break an animal's back that way. I suppose he thought he was still six years old, like his brother. Why he had this set on the ram, the Lord only knows.

It was a long day that day. I had an ache in my calves and tiredness in my bones. At three o'clock the sky clouded over and everything lost its edge. A few branches above the snow looked like black spiders. The animals were driven back to their barns and one or two gave trouble. The dogs chased a sheep up the mountain until it was up to its neck in snow. The dogs jumped through the snow and almost disappeared with each leap. They got to the sheep, nibbling at it until it panicked and sprang out of the snow. With its white fleece it looked as if a black head was jumping down the mountain. If the snow had been deeper up there, there might have been one less sheep. The windows and doors were black holes in the white mountain. Some of them turned orange as lamps were put in the windows.

There's no rest for the wicked. I had to prepare the church to receive the body in the morning. There was the ram on the other side of the church. I began to think he was persecuting me. I know it makes no sense. He was always let wander, that animal. No one came after him. It always surprised me, that. It's as if the men didn't care about him, and yet they couldn't do without him. Like a goat that's crowned over in Killorglin each year.[30] A hardy beast he was. You might find him pressed against your door in the morning for the heat.

When I got back to my house there was the smell of baking bread. We gathered around six o'clock. Muiris brought the child with him, his hair slicked flat on his head as if he were going to his first communion, which indeed he was to make that summer.

We sat around on the chairs and on an upturned bucket. Biddy was at the hob as usual. There was a plank of wood on the ground by the hob with fresh baked bread and scones, and what looked like a barmbrack. I led them in the rosary. The joyful mysteries it was. Thady sat by the window leaning forward with

---

30. At Killorglin's Puck Fair every August, a goat from the hills (King Puck) is captured, clothed, garlanded, and raised on a high wooden platform over the town to preside over the fair. The origin of this pagan ritual is lost, and few of those below know that they are celebrating the lust of the goat. When I spoke to Biddy McGurk she gave a vivid description of one such goat: "A mighty fellow he was with a great bollocks on him, swinging two cannon balls the size of Jack Doyle's fists." Jack Doyle (1913–1978) was an excessively handsome Irish heavyweight of little distinction, who married Movita, a Hollywood "actress" of some notoriety. Movita divorced him in 1945 and married Marlon Brando.

his elbows on his knees. Séamus and Oweneen knelt on one knee. Biddy knelt with her bottom to the fire. The beads swung as they went through finger and thumb. The part of the litany I most enjoyed came and went. *Tower of Ivory, House of Gold ... Morning Star.* The men made the responses in their deep voices. Biddy of course was always a whisker late so that her voice lingered. It irritated me. But the men's voices consoled me. And the litany too. It gave me a glimpse of the Virgin's wonders. Once at a Trappist monastery on a retreat I heard monks sworn to silence sing the Salve Regina. It sent shivers down my spine to hear those deep celibate voices raised in praise of the Virgin.

Muiris sat near the corpse's head, Éamonn between his father's legs, his hand on his father's knee. The lad took one look at the body when he came in and after that he looked everywhere but at it. He had a startled look to him. During the rosary he was restless. After the prayers, Muiris kept one arm around him and in the other hand he had a glass of whiskey. He drank steadily with long, slow draughts. For as you well know, no sooner was the rosary over than the drinking began. The men sat or moved around in that clumsy way of theirs that is half respect and half embarrassment. Biddy had her knees open to the fire, her skirt drawn up so that you could see the ABC on her shins. There was talk about the dead man before he was injured, what a fine lad he was, always a smile, always ready for work.

"What a way he had with the hurley," said Oweneen. "Another Mick Mackey he was going to be." I didn't want that talk to begin just yet. I wanted to pay respect to Muiris.

"Tadhg had the best of mothers and fathers," I said. The dead boy's name sounded strange on my tongue.

"None better," said one or two.

"The woman over there in the graveyard was the finest of women."

"That she was," came from Thady.

"Many's the time I saw her lead Tadhg back from his travels over the mountain, wash his clothes and bathe him and send him off bright as a new penny." I didn't say that in five minutes he'd be back to his previous state. It struck me as I spoke how the boy had been neglected after his mother died. There was no one who had a way with him after that, not even his father.

"We're mourning not just Tadhg," I said, "but making an act of faith through the hardship that has been visited on us. All our sufferings join with the suffering of Christ on the Cross for the redemption of sins. We know what Providence in its mystery has taken from us. We do not know what Providence in its wisdom has given us. Not a sparrow falls but that He knows. He has not forgotten us as we gather here. He knows the troubles of each and every one of us. We will keep our faith as our fathers did, through the darkest of times. Now we see through a glass darkly. In time we will understand, if not in this world, then in the next."

After a silence Oweneen said, "Do you remember the time he came running down the mountain and flew over the graveyard out over the ridge, his arms spread out like an aeroplane? I saw him disappear. He must have fallen twenty feet. We all ran down thinking he would be dead as a doornail. And when we topped the ridge, there he was picking his way back up as if nothing had happened. That fall would have killed any of us."

"He was protected from harm surely," said Séamus.

I was glad to see Muiris smile as he raised his glass. "I remember the time," he said, "he took the bone out of the mouth of that gypsy dog that no one could go near. I ran over to stop him, but begob there he was with the bone in his hand, holding it up in the air and the dog jumping for it. Then he threw it and raced the dog for it. Didn't he beat the dog to it. He gave the dog a push as they were racing and the dog went head over heels. It's a sight I'll never forget. He could run like the wind." The dead face lay there with its blind eyes to the ceiling. The very same dog that Muiris had killed, I said to myself.

"Wouldn't you care for a wee dram, Father?" said Oweneen. Sometimes his way of speaking reminded me he must have travelled to the north. Maybe that's where he'd been when he disappeared for two years during the Troubles.

"Well, maybe a little drop." He poured me nearly a full tumbler.

"You've left no room for the water," I said.

"Sure the whole mountain is covered with water that we're half buried in," said Oweneen. "It'd be a shame to let a drop of it into that good stuff." Everyone laughed at that.

Biddy spoke up from the hob. "I remember the time he came in and I was after cooking a whole leg of lamb to last the week and beyond. It was gone when I turned around. I thought one of the dogs had taken it. But no, it was my brave fellow. I saw him here later in this very house working on the bone and giving lumps of meat to that tinker dog of his. There were times he had the appetite of three men. You'd think he had an *ar-*

pluca in him. Then there were times he wouldn't eat at all."

There were some stories I'd never heard. You learn more about people when they're dead than when they're alive. I had my own stories, but they weren't ones I'd want to share.

There's a time at a wake when silence falls as thick as a blanket. And there's a time when a priest should leave. I stayed for Muiris's sake. There was only the sound of someone breaking wind or exhaling after a draught. And the click of a bottle being set into one basket or being lifted out of another. Biddy would throw a few pieces of turf on the fire and it would sigh and settle after a little explosion of the ash that bearded the turf. When the fire was stoked, the white face of the corpse seemed alive as the flames leaped. The bottles of whiskey on the windowsill were empty, but a few more had appeared on the floor next to the stout. Séamus Mór was drinking the poteen. He was the one who'd brought it. I was feeling lightheaded after finishing the full glass. When I looked back, it was full again. The child went over to Biddy. She bent down to his ear whispering who can tell what. She fed him some of the cake. He yawned and came back to Muiris and climbed onto his lap. I wanted to tell Muiris to take the child down to bed, for beyond a certain time, a wake isn't the best place for a child to be. And that moment was not far away.

The heavy smell of porter and whiskey was making me sleepy. The fire and lamp and candles cast shadows every time anyone moved. Our shelter was ablaze with light compared to the endless darkness outside. I had no desire to face the cold. But it was late—eleven o'clock—and there was to be an early start next morning. The coffin hadn't yet been made. The child was asleep in Muiris's lap, head stretched back, his mouth open. He looked like an angel. Muiris's chin was on his chest. He'd start up now and then, and when he did, he'd reach down and lift his glass. Biddy was looking into the fire, sometimes throwing on a bit of wood for a quick blaze. Now and then she'd look in my direction, her eyes glittering in the firelight. I sat at the wrong end of the corpse. The men went out now and then to relieve themselves. I went over to Muiris. "It's time for that young gosoon to be in bed," I said. Muiris looked up with blind eyes. "It's time to go, Muiris," I said.

I lifted the child from his arms. There wasn't a stir out of him. Muiris stood up and tried to steady himself against the table. He knocked over a candle but it had gone out by the time it hit the straw. Biddy looked over and started to get up. I turned my back on her. "I'll go down with you, Muiris," I said. I held the child in one arm and picked up one of the lamps. The men started talking as we went out the door.

Outside Muiris insisted on taking the child from me. The cold seemed to steady him. I held the lamp high as we walked over the ice down to his cottage. He toppled the child into his bed near the hearth. There was still a spark in the ash. I stirred it and threw on a few bits of turf. "Easy now, Muiris," I said. "It's a good sleep you need." He sat at the kitchen table and put his head on his arms. I'd never seen a man so tired. I left the lamp on the table. I was out the door when I worried that he might knock it over in his sleep. I went back and put it on the dresser under the shining row of plates—Máire Rua's pride.

In the dark, I stumbled on the ridges of ice now and then. I kept my eye on the lighted door of Tadhg's cottage. Even though I knew the way like the back of my hand, the dark confused me. Passing the barn, I saw the animals in my mind's eye, waiting patiently for the light. I could see a glimmer of snow on the roof. As I passed I felt the animals' sum of life as if one great beast were breathing in the darkness. The sound of a cow scratching itself on a corner took away that notion.

Passing the corpse's house I heard an argument and several voices singing. I knew my leaving would be like taking a cork out of a bottle. I bumped into something that ran and put the heart across me. It wouldn't be a badger this time of year—maybe a fox looking for chickens. Or a stray sheep left out with everyone distracted. I saw a shape pass a lighted door. It looked like the ram limping along. I heard laughter and someone singing "For Rambling and Roving." That's a song that can go on forever. It didn't this time. There was a pause and a voice rose up out pure and clear: *If I were a blackbird / I'd whistle and sing / And I'd follow the ship that my true love sailed in / And on the top rigging, I'd there build my nest / And I'd pillow my head on his lily-white breast.* Nonsense, as you might expect from Biddy. There was a burst of laughter and then her voice rose again. I'd heard her sing, but never from a distance. Without the sight of her, you'd think the voice was from a young girl. I stopped and listened, cold though it was. *Cé hé sin amuigh a bhfuil faobhar ar a ghuth / ag réabadh mo dhorais dúnta / mise Éamonn an Chnoic atá*

báite fuar fliuch / ag síorshiúl sléibhte is gleannta.[31] I remembered she often called the boy Éamonn an Chnoic.
I waited until her voice died away. She started up with
another one, *"Seán Ó Duibhir an Ghleanna,"*[32] that has

---

31. Biddy is singing a seventeenth-century song about Éamonn an
Chnoic, or Ned of the Mountains, a mythical rebel on the run from the
English. He, like his fellow wanderers, must join the royal army or be
executed. The song begins as Éamonn knocks at the door of a mountain
cottage for help. The woman who answers him can only offer him a fold
of her gown for protection and shelter. The woman is, of course, yet another personification of Ireland, the lady of the poets' visions (*aislingí*).
The lines above translate: *Who is that outside with a hoarse voice / Knock-
ing loudly at my closed door?* The next two lines answer: *I am Éamonn of
the mountains, drenched, cold and wet / from endlessly walking the mountains
and glens.*

32. Seán Ó Duibhir an Ghleanna is John O'Dwyer of the Glens. He
has been identified with a Colonel O'Dwyer who surrendered to the
British in 1652. Under the terms of his surrender he was allowed to take
three hundred of his men to France, becoming part of the "Wild Geese,"
the Irish Diaspora, fighting the British on several continental fronts.
The opening lines the good Father refers to go as follows: *When I rise in
the morning, the summer sun is shining / I hear the bugle crying and the bird's
sweet song.* The song goes on to lament the loss of O'Dwyer's hunting
grounds and lands, confiscated by the settlers. The settlers had few
graces. According to the poet Dáibhi Ó Bruadair (c. 1625–1698), "All
our castles and big houses are held by the ill-bred upstarts." The class
issue is a recurring one as the two cultures meet over the next two hundred years. The poets continuously lament the lingering death of the old
culture, gradually perfecting their extended note of melancholy and
loss, to be interrupted occasionally by eloquent anger.

the most beautiful beginning of any song I know, especially if it gets the proper trill and break on the right notes. After that there was silence, broken suddenly by a shout. The men's voices started with *I'm a rambler, I'm a gambler*—I bet there's someone singing a Delia Murphy[33] ballad every hour of the day and night. When I got back, my house was as cold as a tomb.

I heard hammering during the night, but I was halfway between sleeping and waking and paid it no great heed. That would be the coffin they were making. It would start regular as a heartbeat, then stop and start again. When I'd drop off, that's when it would start. I couldn't rouse myself, I was tired out. What finally

---

33. Delia Murphy (1903–1971) was a singer of popular ballads, with a vast repertoire in Irish and English and a distinctive brogue. Her delivery was fast-paced and good-humored, and expertly touched the outsider part of the popular psyche with its secular energy and nimble phrasing. Educated in University College, Galway, she spent the war years in Rome as wife to Dr. Thomas Kiernan, Irish Ambassador to the Vatican. The refrain of the "rambler and gambler" goes, "Oh moonshine, dear moonshine, oh how I love thee / You killed my poor father but dare you try me." How did an American colloquialism, "moonshine," migrate from Appalachia to a wake on a remote Kerry mountain? In Ireland, the word for illicitly distilled spirits is "poteen," a transparent potato vodka. The answer lies in cross-cultural migrations and rebounds. The moonshine song, developed as many sentimental Irish songs were by immigrants to the United States, was picked up, brought back to Ireland, and popularized by such as Ms. Murphy.

startled me out of my sleep were shouts and cries. I thought for a moment the *amadán* had come back to life. There was a flickering light in the room. I ran over to the window that faced the corpse's house. The flames were leaping from the thatch in great shimmering triangles. Smoke was rising in clouds that were lit from below. The two windows and door were orange-red. It looked as if the end of the world had come. Black figures were running back and forth against the light. One came out the door and flung something in the snow. Where was Muiris? I was in my clothes and out the door before I knew it. The reflection of the flames on the ice between me and the cottage made it look like a red river. You'd think the ice and snow were moving. I raced up the red ice, rippled like the surface of the sea. The men never stopped shouting. One of them picked up what had been thrown out and flung it in my direction. I thought it might be the corpse, but why would they do that? When I got to it, I saw a singed body, small as a child. It was the ram, all twisted, with one of his hind legs missing. His guts were spilling out through a slash in his belly. Oweneen was running back and forth throwing handfuls of snow at the flames. I ran towards him and fell flat on my face. My shin bone was killing me. I thought I'd broken my leg. I looked at what I'd fallen over. It was a half-made coffin. Séamus Mór was standing, shaking his fist at the flames. I grabbed his arm.

"What happened? In the name of God, what happened? Where's the corpse?"

He shook himself free before turning a wild eye on me. "He's in there!" he said.

"Where's Muiris?" I shouted. Séamus shook his head. A shower of sparks puffed up from the roof as part of the thatch fell in. Some sparks were borne over to the roof of the church and glowed for a moment before the snow extinguished them. I ran after Oweneen, shielding my face against the heat.

"What happened in the name of God?" I shouted at him. I couldn't hear his answer. "Is there anyone in there? Is there anyone who needs me?"

"He was past needing anyone when this all started," said Oweneen in my ear.

"Go get Muiris!" I told him.

The heat was like a furnace. Occasionally the flames would roar like an animal and exhale a burst of heat. A thought struck me. I ran after Oweneen and shook him by the shoulders.

"Where's the auld wan? Where's Biddy?"

He put his face into mine. "That I don't know and care less, bad cess to her!"

"Is she inside?" I shouted at him. He ran down towards Muiris's.

I looked around. Someone was sitting in the snow half-way down the slope with his back to the fire, his shadow stretched out before him, quivering and shaking like the flames themselves. I looked into the dark face. It was Thady. I knelt down beside him and something hurt my knee. I picked it up. It was a carving knife with blood on it. I thumped him on the chest.

"What is this?" I shouted at him. His face was a dark blob. I thumped him as hard as I could. He fell over backwards, his face to the sky. "Where's Biddy?" I said. I reared back as the vomit shot out of his mouth. He turned on his side and drew up his knees.

You've heard of kings and heroes being burned on a pyre. Well, that poor boy had some send-off, but it wasn't the one we'd planned. There was never a thought of going in. The body must have been a cinder by now. The cottage seemed to sink down in a black hollow as the heat melted the snow around it. That was the first sight of the earth we'd had since November. Where was Biddy? I scoured the place, slipping on the melted ice. Séamus Mór kept looking at the fire as if hypnotised. Oweneen was coming back from Muiris's cottage. He must have had a hard time waking him, from the last I saw of Muiris. There was nothing to fight the fire with.

I went to the church, slipping and sliding. With the way the flames were shifting the shadows, you wouldn't know where you were putting your feet. I wanted to bless the burning cottage and the poor body within. On my way back with the holy water, I stumbled and fell for the second time that night. What I fell over gave a shriek like a trapped rabbit. The holy water went all over the snow. I was distracted with relief and terror.

"What have you done up there in that place?" I asked her. She was crawling away from me. You wouldn't think she could go so fast. She turned a mad eye over her shoulder, like a dog looking back.

"Is it talking to me you are, Father?"

I hit her on the head with a heavy hand. I couldn't help it. She screamed and covered her head with both hands.

"I'll tell you who's talking to you!" I said. "Get up on your feet like a Christian, and get back to the house and stay there."

She paid no heed at all. Off she went crawling again. I gathered what was left of the holy water.

There's a lot I don't remember about that night. But I do remember Muiris, when he arrived at last, looking at the fire. He kept shaking his head in disbelief. Oweneen and Séamus Mór and myself stood with him watching the beams shift and fall, listening to the crackles and snaps and creaks of whatever was in there settling down as if it were tired after a great exertion. Muiris didn't say a word. Thady, when I remembered to look back, was gone. He must have sobered up once he got the drink out of him. The boy never appeared. He slept through everything and that was a mercy. We stood there until morning, watching.

The embers were still smoking and crackling at first light. Muiris disappeared and came back with a bucket of water from the well. Would you believe not a bucket was thrown on those flames when they needed it? It was as if everyone was in a state of paralysis. When he threw the water through the door the wet smell of burning was sharp to the nostrils. It was still too hot to enter. As Muiris stood in the door, Oweneen took the bucket from him and came back with more water. That was the way it went, Muiris going in bit by bit behind the buckets that Séamus and Oweneen took turns going for. The sky was grey when we got through the door behind Muiris. There was enough light to see that not a thing was left. A big beam was slanted across from the roof to the floor near where the body had been. It had lumps of charcoal standing out on it like great fissured warts.

"Where did you put it?" I said to Oweneen.

"Over there," he said, nodding to where Tadhg used to make his bed near the hearth. We watched while Muiris stepped over the smoking embers and pockets of blue flame to what was left of his older son.

He stood there looking down. We didn't go near him. When he turned around he was very calm. "I want him brought over to the church now, Father," he said, "and I want a Mass said for him this morning. We'll bury him then." I nodded because any words I might say would be wrong no matter how right they were. As he passed me I put my hand on his shoulder, and went out with him in case he had anything more to say. He just walked on. When I came back, Séamus and Oweneen were over by the hearth. I picked my way over. The three of us looked down on the remains. That pungent wet smell when fire and water meet was irritating my nostrils. My imagination added a charred smell like burned meat.

I could see nothing at first. Then I made out the shape of a man made of charcoal amidst the white ash. I bent down to touch where a hand seemed to be across the chest. My finger came back with sooty flakes on it.

"There's not much left of him," said Oweneen. He bent down and poked his fingers into a biscuit of charcoal. It dropped into a cavity where the chest would be.

Oweneen crumbled a piece of charcoal between finger and thumb. "A puff of wind would blow what's left of him away, Father," he said.

"You heard Muiris," I said. "We'll gather what we can and get it into that coffin out there."

"Thady Kelleher was lying in it stocious the last time I saw him," said Oweneen.

"Well, he was out of it the last time I saw him," I said. "Now get that coffin up here, and be quick about it." I hadn't time to think of how they had saved the coffin and not the corpse.

I stood looking down at the image of a man that was like a negative of a photograph, dark and shadowy. The round head was like a blackened urn. The boots had escaped. At least you could see they were boots. Strange thoughts went through my mind. I thought of the mutilated ram, and it made me shiver. Snow began to fall into the open ruin. I welcomed the blanket it would put over the wreckage. I heard the sound of the coffin scraping on the ice outside.

"Get the coffin in here," I said. "We'll do the best we can."

"We can't tramp over all this carrying a coffin," said Oweneen.

"Well, let us bring out what's left of him and put it in it anyway," said Séamus. "There's no point in you watching this, Father."

"What are you trying to spare me in your foolishness?" I said. "There's the coffin and there's the body. Just bring it in here and put the two of them together in the name of God." I bent down and took the head in my hands. As I lifted it slipped from me as if coated with oil. I stared at my black hands. The chest and head had got the worst of it. Séamus and Oweneen started from the other end. The only bones you could call by the name were the thighbones, the two blades of the hips, and the knuckles of the spine beneath looking like a black centipede. And a few ribs of course. We put the bones in first, then the black ashes.

"How much of this is him, I wonder?" said Oweneen. "It would take the Lord himself to separate it out."

"The silver ash is the turf. Any gom could see that,"
I said.

"We'll be burying as much ashes as the poor boy himself," said Oweneen. I was glad Muiris wasn't there to
see his son scooped into his coffin in handfuls.

The little procession went up to the church an hour
later. By eleven, it was as bright as it would be. I led the
way. The three men carried the coffin, Séamus in front,
Oweneen and Thady—there's nothing good I can say
about him, so I'll say nothing—taking the weight at
the back. Why the small men were at the back going
uphill is beyond me. Then Muiris and young Éamonn.
Wouldn't you know that under the new snow there was
a patch of ice that nearly did us in? I turned around
when I heard a shout. The coffin was lurching like a
boat at sea. But it didn't fall, thank God. Who was waiting for us at the church, blessing herself and kissing
her beads, but the old witch herself, as if she'd never
touched a drop in her life. As it transpired, she'd been
at the church cleaning and setting up. I said the Mass.

When it came time, Muiris and the child went to
communion. None of the other men did. Biddy came up
with her tongue out. The cheek of her knew no bounds.
I passed her by. As for the others, they wouldn't meet

my eye, kneeling with their heads in their hands. Thady stayed in the back as well he might. When the time came for the sermon, I had no notion what I was going to say. Then into my mind, shining and bright, came the image of Tadhg as a strapping young lad, as nimble as a goat and as fleet as a greyhound. I saw Máire Rua's face, with a benign smile, as clear as if she were in the congregation, if six people—seven including myself—make a congregation, waiting for my words.

"There was no one like him," I said. "And all of us can see him now as he was, striding over the mountain as if he had seven-league boots. He was as fine a hurler as this parish ever saw, and it was only a matter of a year or two before he would have been on the Kerry team. He was as decent a lad as ever walked this mountain. He was blessed in his parents and they were blessed in him. If Máire Rua were here now, she'd be sharing with us the pride of what he was. The accident that robbed him of his senses is a mystery. Why did it happen to him? There seems to be no reason for it at all. Like all the mysteries of the world, it never ceases to torment our understanding. But that's why we have faith. Was God in his wisdom telling us something we can only see dimly? Would something terrible have happened to that young man if he had gone his perfect way? Something worse? Something that might even have lost him his immortal soul? Maybe what happened stored up a greater reward for him in heaven, struck down as he was in the full flower of his youth. For it's in Heaven he surely is. And his mother is smiling at him and welcoming him. It's not what lies in that coffin over there that we should think about now. It's the shining spirit that has gone to its reward. And when the Day of Judgement comes, his poor remains will stir under the earth, and join themselves into that perfect young body we all knew, rising, rising from the grave, radiant and immortal to meet his soul, to sit at the right hand of God, the Father Almighty. That's the future, as surely as we sit here. As surely as the time will come when we will join him in the radiance of eternity. Then all his suffering, and ours, will be united with the sufferings of Jesus on the cross, and redeemed by the grace of the Holy Spirit, for ever and ever, Amen."

Muiris sat through this with the back of one hand under his elbow and the other holding his forehead. The child fidgeted. There wasn't a stir out of any of the others. When I stopped there was silence—except for

Biddy's loud Amen. I finished the Mass. It was time to bury the dead.

And of course, we couldn't. And that was no surprise. All we could do was bring the coffin down to the grave-yard—this time it made sense to have Séamus in front—and find a place where the tips of the headstones didn't show through the snow.

"We'll need a few stones to hold it down," said Séamus. We searched but there wasn't a stone to be found. I wondered what had happened to the white stone I'd used to mark the grave for the exhumation. A cold wind was rising. Biddy stood far off.

"We'll put the churn on it!" she said. "That'll hold it down." I didn't know whether she was serious or not. What else could you expect from the likes of her? Nobody answered her.

Séamus Mór went and got a pickax and slung it at the ground. He managed to lever off bits of ice. It was hard as a shield under the snow. We were all shivering at this point, with young Éamonn half-hidden inside Muiris's coat.

"Stones!" said Oweneen. "What are we thinking about at all! There's plenty of stones up in Jamesy's cottage. Maybe I should have kept the one I took up the mountain." Why hadn't we thought of that? Sometimes you can't see what's as plain as the nose on your face.

"We'll take care of it, Muiris," I said. "If you go back with the young lad, we'll get it all done. You can come back later and see if it's to your satisfaction." He didn't answer. Séamus went off for the stones. I told Thady to go up with him. He touched his cap and went off without looking me in the eye. Thady was a man you'd never notice. He was always fawning on Muiris, but Muiris had no time for him. Biddy went up the hill after Thady. I asked Muiris again to take the boy home and for once he did what I asked. "You can come back and look at it later," I said after him. Oweneen, who was the one who thought of the stones, hadn't budged. "Oweneen," I said, "I want to see you after this. Over in my house." For once he had no answer. Séamus brought down two big stones, each in the crook of his arms. Thady followed him carrying a stone clasped between his arms and chest, leaning back as if it weighed a ton. We put the stones on the coffin and wedged it in where Séamus had hacked a ledge in the ice. When I looked back through the swirls of snow, I could see the three stones like three heads. Or so the fancy went.

I made my way back to my house, with Oweneen

trailing behind me. Biddy wasn't around. She'd probably gone to the church. I sat Oweneen down and stood in front of him.

"Owen," I said. "What in the name of God transpired up there last night?"

"My memory of it isn't the best, Father," says he.

"That may be," I said, "but I'll have an answer, if you please." It took a bit of work, but I got it out of him in the end.

"Séamus and myself were working on the coffin outside. We put him down near the hob. We needed the table as you know. Biddy and Thady were inside, that I remember. I looked in once to see what was happening. Biddy was stroking the corpse's face and singing to herself. Thady was drinking from a bottle. He had a terrible thirst last night, if you remember."

"There's no answer yet," I said.

"Well I can only guess at it," said Oweneen.

"Well then, guess away," I said. "For an answer I'll have, if not from you, from someone."

"You might ask Séamus," he said.

"I'm asking you," I answered him.

"We were well on, you know that," said Oweneen.

"I have no doubt of that," I said. "Now what happened?"

"The ram was looking at us," said he.

"The ram? What's the ram got to do with it?" I said.

"I'm beginning to think that ram was bad luck!" said he.

"He was only a ram so what bad luck could he be?" I said.

"He was looking at us making that coffin," said Oweneen, "and Thady came out and he was far gone."

"So what had Thady got to do with it?" I said.

Then Oweneen said, "Did you ever see a dog's eyes light up in the dark?"

"Of course I did!" I answered him.

"Well," he said, "when Thady came out the door, he said the ram was looking at him and his eyes were lit up."

"Thady had the light of the door behind him," I said. "Of course the ram's would light up." I was beginning to think I'd never get to the end of this.

"Well, Thady got it into his head that the devil was in the ram," said he.

"It wasn't the ram the devil was in," I said.

"Thady got the ram by the horns and dragged him inside."

"How could he do that?" I said. "It's hard to move a ram by the horns."

"Well, Séamus got behind the ram, as far as I remember."

"And why did he do that?"

"I don't know, Father. There's a lot that's not clear to me."

"What happened then?" I said.

"We were working away, banging away, turning that table into a coffin."

"What happened then?" I said again.

"We heard some screaming inside the cottage," he said, "and both of us rushed in."

"And what did you see?"

"I'm not sure of what I saw," he said.

"Well tell me what you're not sure of," I said.

"Do you have a drink of water, Father?" he said. "My mouth is as dry as fire."

I gave him a drink of water. "Now," I said, "what did you see or not see?"

"I'm not sure," he said, "for as you know, Father, it was a wake."

"That's no news to me!" I said. I let him drink another cup of water.

"The ram was running around with its insides hanging out," he said.

"Is that where the knife came from?" I said.

"Thady had the knife," he said. "I never saw a sight like it. Biddy had a hold of his entrails and they were unraveling like thread from a spool. I couldn't believe my eyes. And I was so well on I wasn't sure I was seeing it anyway. Thady cut the guts away from the ram. Biddy made a circle of them on the floor. Then the ram broke away trailing the rest of his insides. Thady blocked him at the door where I was standing. Séamus arrived behind me and let a shout out of him. He rushed past me and threw Thady down. We all owned the ram, but Séamus owned most of him. The ram gave a leap and knocked over the oil lamp on the straw. The next thing I know the flames were everywhere."

"And you saved the ram and not the body?" I said. "It's proud you should be."

"That was Séamus," said Oweneen. "It was mostly his ram."

"What was left of him. How did the others get out?"

"That I don't know," he said.

I felt a strange calm. Nothing more could surprise me. What was to be done? Nothing. Nothing at all. It had all gone past me now.

·   ·   ·

The thaw came a week later. I heard it one morning when I slept late, which I never do. I could almost hear the whisper of a drop falling and the sound it makes when it falls—like a pop of the lips. Then another, so that half-awake you listen for the next. That's the way it comes, drop by drop from the icicles hanging around the roof, some sounding a little different as they fall on another place, until your ears plot the space around your house for your eyes to imagine.

We were afraid the thaw would go too fast and we'd be swept with the torrent of last year. But at least God was with us in that the thaw was slow, freezing at night and holding the ice firm until it was released the next day. The thaw undercuts the ice at the edge of the paths, so that it leaves an overlap fragile as a biscuit. You hear the crackle under your boots as if you were walking on glass. Waking up in the morning, you hear the snaps as the ice on the roof stretches itself and falls off. Sounds better than any music.

You'd think we'd be rejoicing. But nothing is simple. We looked at each other and knew what was in each other's mind. We'd lived through this terrible winter, a winter not just of ice and snow, but of the spirit. Not a day had gone by but that we'd longed for the end of it. And now that it was here, was this all there was to it?

THE PRIEST'S STORY

For things to be the same as they always were, only worse? The days seemed dull as lead. There's a boredom that eats into the soul like cancer. The saints speak of it as one of the terrors of the spirit. Now we'd survived, but with terrible memories. And there to remind us, its scorched black walls poking through the snow, were the remains of Tadhg's cottage, open to the sky. Not to speak of the coffin out there in the graveyard, tilting as the ice melted under it. The first chance we had, we buried it beside Máire Rua. A muddy grave to be sure. As the ice melted, corners of the other coffins poked out of the earth here and there. The dead were rising on that mountainside as if they couldn't wait for Judgement Day. We covered them again as best we could. And out again one would poke after a heavy rain, as if someone was pushing from underneath.

The sheep and cattle came out blinking, heads down on the wet earth looking for a blade of grass. The dogs were as full of life as if there hadn't been a winter at all. Hens will survive anything. I saw the old donkey we had, his coat looking like an old rug. I'd forgotten he existed. The men came to confession one by one. The old witch too. What was said is known to God and to me. Not if it would save the soul of this town, wild horses wouldn't drag out of me what they said. Even if the Pope himself gave the order. They came and the Lord, in His infinite mercy, forgave them their sins. They went to communion one bright morning and God's grace flowed into their souls, even into the soul of that old woman, though it went against my grain to entrust Almighty God to that quivering tongue of hers. But the winter was over, and praise the Lord for that. Our thoughts turned to the town below.

Now that we were thinking of the outside, when I looked around I saw the village as a stranger might see it—half-sunk in mud, the burned-out cottage like a black tooth, clumps of thatch lifted here and there on many a roof from the storms. The women's vegetable gardens were a memory now. The church was built on an outcrop of rock, so that it parted the mud that had slid down the mountain. I couldn't open my back door, because a foot of mud had gathered outside it. I took a spade to it, but it was slow work even though the thaw was well along, regulated by the day's sun and the night's cold. Some of the banks of frozen snow would stay there well into June. There's an arctic crystal inside them as cold as the north pole and it takes a power of sun to get to it. That icy snow closes around itself in a grip as cruel as winter.

We wore whatever would keep us warm, scarves

made out of old gansies or whatever came to hand. Biddy was a great one for knitting, and she'd knitted a great scarf for me—it must have been six feet long. She had her moments, I'll say that for her. Our coats were patched, but the patches, without women to take care of them, opened. Every morning we'd put on boots that might have been cast in bronze so stiff with mud were they. We always wore several layers of socks, so that the men took each deliberate step as if their feet were foreign to them. We had an accumulation of old hats and caps, the likes of which you never saw, the shape of old potatoes.

You'd think we'd rush down to the town after waiting all winter. But no one did. Do you think anyone came up from down here to see us? You'd be dreaming if you thought that. I think the men were waiting for me to make the first move, which wasn't the way it had been last year. This winter had taken the heart out of them. I was frightened that the terrible things that had happened would become common knowledge. You could see the memory of what we'd been through behind every face, like a nightmare in which everyone had a part. Séamus Mór went about his business, off early in the morning to the fields. Oweneen, who I thought would be sprightly, had lost his usual chatter. Thady wouldn't cast an eye in my direction at all. Muiris was even more measured and solemn. He'd walk holding Éamonn's hand, but the child wouldn't want that. He'd break away to throw things for the dogs, or rush at a sheep, or go back to the lamb, but he and the lamb weren't as close as before. The lamb would follow Muiris and the boy for a while and then wander off. For some reason it had made its way back to its mother ever since that incident, I don't know why.

When Muiris came over again, we'd stare at the fire without much to say. Since the wireless was out, the war wasn't a source of conversation any more. Biddy kept out of my way, as well she might. She was afraid now that the outside world was about to open up to us. She'd be gone as soon as she could get her old bones down the mountain. The night before she left I heard her crying in the dark, but that was only to get my sympathy. I had other things on my mind. How was the village, or what was left of it, to come through all that had transpired, once they found out below? You couldn't expect it to be kept quiet. After what Jamesy Donoghue had done, who could you trust? We had a secret, and a secret shared is no secret. What would young Éamonn, all of six years old, have to say if he was asked? And what was I to say to the Bishop? In my heart of hearts, I knew things were over for us. At times, since the mind feeds on illusions, I thought maybe everything would pass and we'd take up again as usual.

Oweneen was at my door. "I'm going down, Father," said he. "If you'd like to keep me company." You wouldn't have recognised him. His face was freshly shaved, the pink skin matched his red hair. He had a striped shirt with no collar, neatly studded at the neck, and a pair of baggy pants which I thought for a moment were new. They were simply the old ones washed so they had a different color. He had on his usual coat with long sides and deep pockets and a stick in his hand he was twitching about.

"It looks to me you're off to meet the Lord Mayor of Cork," I said.

"Ah, well, Father," he said, "we've got to put our best foot forward. Don't forget little Bridget is down there with the nuns and I want her to be proud of her Da." He said that by way of a joke, but he meant it.

We started down, sliding and slipping, going sideways half the time. My old bike was still there in the shed near the road, but someone had taken the saddle off it, bad cess to them. The crossbar was cold as ice, the tires were flat, and the pump was gone from where I'd hidden it. I don't know who it was picked us up in a trap, but he did. There's new people in the town I haven't a notion who they are. After the "Good morning, Father," he hadn't a word out of him and I spent the time watching that horse's shoulder blades slide up and down.

The first thing I noticed when we got to town is that no one paid any attention to us at all. The streets looked familiar and strange at the same time, so that I kept looking at everything twice. We parted, me off to the parish priest's and Oweneen to the convent. I had a last word of advice for him—not to pay attention to remarks from anyone, jeering or the like. Of course it was Fr. Staunton at the presbytery. He was in the kitchen—I'd gone around to the back door. Some people fit in a kitchen and some don't. He was one that didn't. He wasn't beside himself with joy to see me, but he made a show of pretending he was. Theresa Mulligan, the housekeeper, was kindness itself. She had scalding tea and scones on the table before I could get my coat off.

"God bless and save you all up there on the mountain this cruel winter," she said. "It's many the howling night I thought of you up there in the pitch-black dark, and not a one to help you if someone got sick. Are you all well? The little children at the convent are getting along grand. Little Bridget Mahon made her first communion, she looked like a little saint. My Dympna made her first communion the same day. It's a shame her Da wasn't there to see her. A terrible time you've had with deaths and troubles. How did you all come through the winter?"

"We lost one soul to God," I said.

"God bless and save us," she said. "And who was that?"

"It was the poor afflicted boy himself, that was never the same after he was hit on the head with that stone."

"Ah his poor father," she said, "he's lost both wife and son and only the little lad left. What happened to him?"

"He was into that empty cottage Jamesy Donoghue left behind him and started a fire we couldn't put out."

"I heard there was a fire up there," said Fr. Staunton. "Someone saw it in the middle of the night lighting up the side of the mountain."

I didn't want to talk about this too much as you can imagine. "There's been no shortage of tragedies up there," I said, "but the winter's over now and we can get back to normal."

"God rest his soul," said Theresa. "God took him

back to Himself when he needed him. His poor distracted mind is at rest at last. I saw him a few times down here with his father and the lads were making fun of him. He'd run up to people and stand too close to them and then run away again. People that didn't know he was a bit soft didn't take to it too kindly. Break your heart, it would. How's the little fellow?" By that she meant young Éamonn.

"He's well enough," I said, "but it wasn't much of a life for him up there this winter without a woman to take care of him."

"The poor little craythur," said Theresa. "How's Mrs. McGurk?" meaning the old rip. I said nothing to that.

Each of us followed our own thoughts and then Fr. Staunton took a last drink from his cup, stirred himself, and said, "Would you like to stretch your legs, Father?" In truth, I'd stretched them so much coming down the mountain they were aching. We walked out into the spring air.

We found a bench in the parish priest's garden. The sun had some heat in it, weak though it was.

"So Jamesy's house burned down?" said Fr. Staunton.

"That it did," I said. "It's a mercy no one was killed trying to save the poor afflicted soul."

"Were you able to bury him?"

"What was left of him, we did, later, when the soil yielded," I said.

"Well, I suppose there will be more about it," said Fr. Staunton. "Does Jamesy know his house is gone?"

"I don't think there will be much distress there," I said. "He left us without a backward glance."

"Still, it's property and has value," said Fr. Staunton.

"He still has his patch of land," I said. "No one's taking that away from him."

"He's settled in with his bride down here," said Fr. Staunton. "I hear she'll have a child by the end of the month."

"How long are they married?" I said.

"Ten months," said Fr. Staunton.

"It's a hard world to bring a child into," I said, "but I suppose it's easier down here. There's no great welcome for him up there."

"Well, as I wrote you, he doesn't speak too kindly of you all."

"He's no cause for that," I said. "He came back on one

occasion cross-eyed, with some of his friends, rowdies they were. Is he still lifting the elbow?"

"He'll be a good enough lad in time," said Fr. Staunton. "It'll take him a while to get used to the life down here."

"That wife of his will make sure of that," I said.

"She's Tom Mac's daughter all right," said Fr. Staunton, "so I've no doubt of it if the lad has more to him than his good looks."

"Good looks can be deceiving," I said.

"He has a strange way of talking when he has a drop in," said Fr. Staunton.

"Sure everyone does," I said. "The drink is a terrible thing when it gets hold of a man."

A fat robin stood in front of us and looked at us, dropped his head to the ground, and pulled out a long worm.

"There's been a bit of talk since I wrote you," said Fr. Staunton. "That young fellow has a mouth on him," he added after a pause.

"That we know to our cost," I said.

Fr. Staunton made a show of looking out over the hedge. There was nothing to see there. "What he started hasn't stopped and people pay attention that shouldn't."

"People have nothing to do but to lend an ear to gossip, true or false," I said.

"True enough," he said. "How did the livestock get through the winter?"

"Well enough," I said. "A lost sheep or two and a calf. It would take the end of the world to kill the hens. We lost the ram too."

"That's too bad," he said. "The two winters you've had would knock anything out. There was hardship in a lot of mountain villages."

"We're still there," I said, "by the grace of God and His Holy Mother."

"That's to the credit of your village," he said, "but as you know the person you'll have to convince is the Bishop. If the talk that's going round comes to his ears, you'll not have an easy time of it."

"There's always talk everywhere you go," I said. "If there's three people in a village, when two meet they're talking about the third."

"True enough," he said. "Who did you meet in the town?"

"I came straight here," I said, "but Owen Mahon went off to the convent to see his daughter."

"When you come down," said Fr. Staunton, "it might be a good thing to advise your men not to linger too long, or wait until some of the young lads have a drop in them. It's best to take things easy until they get used to you again. It's not just the poor fellow that burned up. It's the rest that have been tarred with the same brush."

"May God forgive that Jamesy," was the only answer I could give him. "He hasn't an ounce of sense."

"He had enough sense to resent the welcome you gave him when he went back up last Autumn," said Fr. Staunton. "And I hear the wife doesn't have a high regard for you either."

I felt a chill go through me. I well knew the way the town was always eager to paint the mountain people as savages. "Does the parish priest know?"

"He's the first to hear some things and the last to hear others. He hasn't mentioned it to me," said Fr. Staunton, standing up and stretching his arms.

"There's only a particle of truth in it, Father," I said. "It's mostly exaggeration and evil gossip."

"Sometimes we don't know what's going on in our own house," says he.

"I'll swear to it in the name of the crucified Christ," said I.

"Don't get excited, Father," says he. "All I'm doing is giving you a quiet word for your own sake."

"Why are you cautioning me," I said, "with respect to God-fearing men who have done no wrong, who've lost their wives, who've attended the sacraments, who supported each other through the trials and tribulations of two cruel winters, who have nothing but good words for their neighbours? I'll match Muiris O'Sullivan against any ten men down here."

"No doubt, no doubt," says he. "I'm only trying to help you, Father. People get things into their minds and won't let go of them. True or false doesn't matter. It's the way people take things."

"If you're thinking what I think you are," I said, "it does you no honor. Rumors and gossip are the destruction of the world. And I'm sure there's no shortage of mischief down here in this town if you were to look for it."

"That's as may be, Father," says he. "I'm just trying to help you avoid trouble until other things put this out of people's minds."

"And when will that be?" I said. "Do we have to stay up there quiet as mice until the town agrees to let its memory lapse? You're asking a lot of them and a lot of me."

"Neither of us wants any trouble, Father," he said. "We're on the same side on this."

"Same side or opposite side," I said, "the shame is on the people of this town and not on the innocent people up the mountain. I came here to see the Canon and tell him how we made our way through the winter and have him hear my confession, and all I hear is how evil we are and what trouble we're about to cause."

"I can understand the way you feel, Father," says he. "The parish priest has had one of his dizzy spells today and I doubt if we'll see him up. I'd be glad to hear your confession myself, if you so desire."

It was a struggle for me to summon my humility and bend the knee. But I took it as an occasion to mortify my pride. For Fr. Staunton, like myself, is only God's instrument, and we should never fail to see the eternal light behind the earthly raiment and collar. We went into the parlour with its artificial flowers—why artificial when they were blooming in the garden outside?—and knelt at the *prie dieu* [a low chair, also used as a kneeler]. And through him, I told my Savior my story, holding back nothing. My own sins are buried in the silence of the confessional. I spoke of what you already know. I told him about the sheep and the mad boy and how he met his death, about the evil old woman, and the drunkenness, which drew no question. We're all used to that. When I finished, I realized that he

328

couldn't speak a word of it to anyone else. It was all under the seal. That was not in my mind when I confessed. But I wouldn't be human if I didn't feel a pinch of satisfaction. He couldn't tell another soul. God forgive me if I used the confessional in this way, unknowingly. But if it spared my flock further gossip and shame, no harm had been done.

I've been often enough on the other side of the grill to sense his discomfort when I finished. Embarrassment has a sour smell and there was a whiff of it in the air. He said, "Anything else?" I said, "Nothing else before God." The penance he gave me was a rosary. There was a delay before the *absolvo te*, and then the murmur started. I felt the waters of absolution flow over my soul, washing away the torment and grief and shame. We walked out into the weak sun and shook hands. Very formal we were.

I was planning to go to the doctor, but I ran into Oweneen on the main street looking angry and muttering to himself. He'd lost his hat and his red hair was standing up like fire. He ran up to me and grabbed me by the arm.

"God's curse on all of them for their evil hearts!"

"What are you talking about?" I said.

"Those young tramps threw stones at me," he said. I

saw some boys lurking at the end of the street. Oweneen was in a passion. "Sheepfucker, they called me a
sheepfucker! May their mothers burn in hell, the little
bastards!"

"For God's sake watch your language!" I said, "or
everyone will be looking at us. Have you seen little
Bridget?"

"Indeed I have," he said, "and no good to tell of it. She
hardly knew me. She just buried her head in the nun's
skirts and wouldn't look at me at all. And I her father!"

"It'll take a little time," I said. "She hasn't seen you
through the long winter and has to get used to seeing
you again."

"I was going to take her back up," he said, "and she
wouldn't come with me. She ran away from the sister
and hid. From her own father. Do you know what she
said? 'I don't want to go back up.'" Something fell out
of his pocket and I picked it up. It was a wooden cup
with a handle on it attached to a little red ball with a
string. "I gave her that, and she threw it down," he said.

"Maybe she'd have preferred a doll," I said. Poor
Oweneen was beside himself.

"I'd like to burn down that damned convent. Giving
her airs."

"No, you wouldn't," I said. "They're good and decent people, the holy nuns. They've given up the good things of the world. Did she look well-fed and happy?"

"She did until she saw me!" said Oweneen.

"There you are," I said. "They've taken good care of her. Give her time. It was a shock for her to see you. She's got used to another way of things. Did you see any of the others? When we go back they'll be asking you, and I'm sure they'll be all down tomorrow or the day after."

No response at all from Oweneen. His thoughts had turned inward and from his face they were dark thoughts indeed. "I said I was taking her back up and they wouldn't let me. 'Let her take her exams' they said. Exams at seven years old!"

We started walking along the main street. A few of the women saluted me. As if by accident we ended up at the doctor's house. He was with a patient. The young girl said she'd tell him. I didn't know her—it was a new one. We sat in the waiting room with two women and a young girl reading a magazine. Oweneen leaned forward with his elbows on his knees, turning the red ball and cup around in his hands, winding the string around his finger and unwinding it again. From time to time he shook his head.

The doctor was smiling when he let out his patient,

an old woman with a child. When he saw me, he looked startled and then gave me a warm, "How are you, Father?" and looked at the women. I said, "I'll wait, Doctor," but one of the women said, "You go ahead, Father." I thanked her and said I wouldn't be too long. Nor was I.

I got right to the point. I said, "Have you heard what's been said around the town?"

"About what, Father?" said the doctor.

"It's that young fellow that came down and poisoned the town with his gossip," I said.

"I think I did hear something now that you mention it," said the doctor. "Ah sure it's the only entertainment they have around here."

He was trying to make light of it. "There's no harm to it," says he.

"No harm to it?" I said. "When the first appearance that poor man out there makes after the winter we've had, he has stones pegged at him and called names I can't repeat? We discussed this in this very room last summer. Well, now it's gone from bad to worse. And it's time to put an end to it. What do you think will happen when the others come down?"

"Father," he said, "don't raise your voice or they'll think we're arguing in here. There isn't time to get into this now. You could come back and we'll discuss it. Though it looks to me it's the police you should be talking to. What can I do? Tell the children to stop throwing stones? It's only happened the one time. You don't know if it'll keep up. Anyway, Father, I'm not sure why you came to see me about it. I'm not in charge of these young shavers. I've enough trouble with my own two."

It dawned on me I didn't know why I was there no more than he did. For what could he do? You always think the doctor can help, maybe talk to the solicitor or the parish priest when they're playing cards or out on the links. It's the kind of faith we have in educated people.

The doctor started washing his hands in a little sink. "Maybe you should go and talk to that young Jamesy you were telling me about last summer, if he's the one that started it all. Stop it at the source. His wife is a patient of mine. Now I'd like to talk to you, Father, but I've a few still waiting outside. And I have to drive over to Cahirciveen to see your man's sister, what's his name, up there in your village—"

"Muiris O'Sullivan," I said.

"—she won't have anyone else. No rest for the wicked." He took pity on my downcast face. I didn't know what to do next. I didn't want to go to the station

333

and draw the Sergeant's attention. Now isn't that a joke with you and me sitting down here and me telling you everything?

"If you can wait for me," said the doctor, "I'll drive you over to the farm and you can speak to Jamesy yourself." He saw me to the surgery door saying, "I won't be too long, Father."

I sat down beside Oweneen. Two others had arrived, an old man with a shake in his head, a white stubble on his face, leaning on a stick between his knees, and a mother with a grown-up son who looked a little daft. I was about to send Oweneen back up. But then I thought of going out and meeting Jamesy. He'd deny it all. I wouldn't be welcome. I could see himself and that wife of his sitting there with her hands on her lap, her knees together and her feet drawn in. She wouldn't leave me with him, if I knew her. And I wouldn't be able to talk with her there. If she were there, there might well be talk of libel. And Jamesy probably wasn't the same lad anyway. I said to Oweneen, "We're done here. Let's go back up." They'd be waiting for the news when we got back. I knew Oweneen would have his way, turning bad to worse. But there was nothing I could do about that.

And tell them he did. I tried to make less of it. "What

do a few young ruffians in their ignorance mean to grown men like yourselves? You can't think they're speaking for the whole town. There's people of good-will everywhere and there's no shortage of them in the town below. Mulready the grocer always gives you credit and never presses for what he's owed after a bad season. There's many the time the doctor has been up here in the dark of night delivering a child with never a complaint. Don't judge the town by a few rowdies that didn't get enough of the strap at school."

I might as well have been talking to the wall. There was a restlessness about them that made me uneasy. In the spring the spirit stirs inside even as things are stirring under the earth. It's a dangerous time you might say, often a time of temptation for the young. Oweneen and Séamus went off together. I could see them arguing through the window, and then they left.

. . .

The next day they all went down, including Muiris and the child. You know what happened. They went to see their children at the convent and on the way back the name-calling and stone-throwing started from those with idle hands. We know whose sons they were too, and you could expect no less with the fathers they have.

Although Phelim Galvin is a decent man and he was as surprised as any to find that his son was part of that company. Anyone with half a mind could tell what was going to happen. One of those idlers outside Murphy's pub started egging those youngsters on—worse than tinker children they were. Who do you think went up to him but Thady, the last one you'd expect? He must have had more than a few in. Of course he's the sort that would start something and then let others take care of it. Séamus Mór joined him. There were words and I don't know who struck the first blow. They tried to separate them, then someone else got hit and you witnessed the rest, for I hear you and the Sergeant were soon there, keeping law and order. Séamus Mór ended up in jail as did the fellow that started it. Oweneen got a cut on his forehead that the doctor put fifteen stitches into.

The only one that didn't join in was Muiris. He'd too much sense for that. But when he was standing there, he was hit with a stone. Just like his poor dead son whose wits were scattered by a stone so long ago. It must have gone deep, for Oweneen tells me he went after that boy and shook him like a rat. He screamed for his father, who is a good-for-nothing as you know. And for that you put Muiris in jail. You don't make much distinction between people, do you? And what happened to little Éamonn? Little you cared about that after you took away his father. Those young pups were jeering and taunting him. He started crying, Oweneen tells me, and he wasn't one to cry, for he was manly enough. He must have been as strange to those children as they were to him. Oweneen brought him back up.

Your Sergeant wasn't in a forgiving mood when I went down the next morning. "Every time you people come down here there's trouble," said he.

"And how many times have we been down in the past six months?" I said. Every time, indeed. There's justice for you.

"It's obvious to me you have only one side of the story," I said.

"Were you there, Father?" said he. He's not a man to cross. He's so tall and broad there's too much of him. No wonder he thinks himself above everything. "The next time it happens, it'll be serious," he said.

"And what about the rowdies that started it? There's no mystery as to who they are. What are you doing about them?"

Fr. Staunton arrived as we were arguing, and to give him his due, he was a great help. "It's not a question of who started it," he said to the Sergeant, "it's a question of those children, half of them mitchers as I well know, calling names and making trouble. I have witnesses who saw what happened when Mr. Mahon came down to see his daughter at the convent yesterday."

I saw Muiris and Séamus Mór in their cells before I left. Séamus was too big for his cell and he kept walking back and forth in little steps. Muiris had nothing to say beyond asking me how Éamonn was. It was a crime to see a man like Muiris in a cell. Little did I know what was in store for him.

Fr. Staunton was waiting when I came back upstairs. We left together. And though he'd seemed so calm with the Sergeant, he was boiling.

"What did I tell you?" he said. "We'll have more trouble with this. Once people get a thing into their heads, it takes wild horses to get it out. What goes in first comes out last."

"What are we to do?" I said. "If they come down together there's trouble, and if they come down alone, there's trouble. They have a right to live, like everyone else."

"I feel for you, Father," he said, "but these rumors are

dangerous. They're all tarred with the same brush now, innocent though they may be."

I hadn't the heart for an argument, standing there in the street. But I did say, "Fr. Staunton, let us not see evil where there is none. You'll have us thinking along with everyone else that we're perverts and monsters, and that's a sin against charity and the good name of these poor men. There's no finer man than Muiris O'Sullivan in the entire county. It's the bold Jamesy who did the damage and you know that as well as I, since you're the one that knows the whole story."

"Maybe I'll go talk to him, though the horse is well out of the stable by now."

"Better you than me with that fellow," I said. "God forgive him for the mischief he's caused."

"There was a case of you-know-what long before your time and mine, forty years ago," said Fr. Staunton. "A laborer in a farm not ten minutes from here. The town felt it was shamed, because it was in the papers. There's some that remember it still. Maybe it's that memory that's passing through their minds now in some mysterious way."

"I never heard of that, Father," I said.

"There's a long memory for such things," he said.

"What happened to him?" I asked him.

"They pleaded him insane which is what's done in such cases, I believe, and put him in the asylum. He died there, as far as I know," says he.

That's the way we parted, without a by-your-leave.

The two men made their way back up the next morning. There had been no charges. The charges should have been the other way. Although they said the fellow who struck the first blow was still in his cell when they left. Séamus hadn't a word out of him. He went off with Oweneen Mahon. The two of them sat outside near the graveyard. I could see their cigarettes glowing at midnight. Muiris was as silent as if what had happened to him had happened to someone else. I think he was ashamed he had lost his temper and cuffed that young fellow, which was no more than he deserved. The father wanted to lodge a complaint, but I hear the Sergeant said his boy would see the inside of a reformatory if he persisted. You can tell me if that's true or not.

I sent the old witch down next morning. I didn't want her there a minute longer than she had to be. She said she'd send someone up for her things. That was all she said. She didn't look at me when I gave her the note and told her to go. But out of the corner of her eye she gave me a parting glance so quick I wondered if I'd dreamt it. It was as if evil itself had looked out of her eye. I raised my hand against the force of it. How she got down the mountain, I don't know and I don't care, God forgive me. The last I saw of her, she was inching down the slope, carrying a brown paper parcel under one arm, the other elbow raising her black shawl up and down like a wing as she tried to keep her balance.

You know what happened after that. Everyone does. But no one knows the truth of it. By the time you've heard from everyone, who knows what the truth is. People will swear to things they never saw. There wasn't a scrap of evidence to connect Séamus and Oweneen to that assault. It was a terrible beating, I'm told. I'm not saying he deserved it, mind you. But God will forgive me if I admit that I felt a spark of pleasure before it died away in shame. I know he was badly hurt. No one deserves that, even him.

I was in Muiris's kitchen when I heard it. Thady came in and said, "Have you heard?"

"Heard what?"

"They found Jamesy Donoghue in a ditch early this morning with his face a mass of blood and his arm and thighbone broken. Someone heard him moaning as they passed. They got him to Dr. McKenna in a cart with him screaming at every bump on the road. The Sergeant was there in no time and Fr. Staunton too.

When they asked him what happened, Jamesy said he fell into the ditch. The Sergeant's a cute one. He said, 'Before you fell in, did you get a good look at them at all?' Before he could stop himself, Jamesy said, 'It was too dark to see.' After that, they couldn't get a word out of him as to who did it. He was so bad they had to send him to Cork in an ambulance. It'll be a while before he's any good to that wife of his."

"Who told you all this?" I asked him.

"I was down to get some seeds and it was on everyone's lips. They're still not saying nice things about us either." It would be Thady who'd go down and come back without any trouble.

If Jamesy hadn't had that wife of his and her connections, it might have died away. She was beside herself, I heard later, swearing she'd have the life of whoever did this to her husband. When she screams, people listen, given who her first cousin is and her father's money behind her. The Sergeant and yourself were up the next day, as you know, looking for Oweneen. But he was gone without a word and we haven't seen him since.

You and that new Garda took Séamus Mór back down with you on the strength of some half-wit who said they heard him making threats against Jamesy. After I talked to him, he went without a murmur. If he'd chosen not to, you'd have had your hands full. There's nothing you can do to him when you've no evidence, and when the injured party won't open his mouth. I don't care that his wife said Jamesy named Oweneen and Séamus. She thinks she has a score to settle with us. I don't say what happened was right, but there's been enough trouble already. The latest I heard is you got Séamus to confess in return for a year's hard labor and to be bound over for a year. Now how did you manage that? Yes, I heard about the evidence—the pipe that had Séamus's fingerprints on it. Planted there as bold as you please in the ditch. As if the fingerprints would be on it and it in the ditch after a week of rain. Now there's a mystery for you to solve all right. He says the pipe was taken from him when you brought him down. I wonder how it ended up in the ditch. God forgive you all. I'm sure you made that wife happy, and that's all that matters. Maybe he should have done what Oweneen did and vamoosed. They say Oweneen went to England on the next boat from Rosslare. There was a letter from Muiris's nephew in Australia saying he'd been seen there. It's a great talent he has to be in several places at once. Better that than suffer the same fate as Séamus. You might go back to that ditch and maybe you'll find Oweneen's birth certificate.

It's time for me to go back to the convent, which is where the parish priest placed me on the Bishop's orders. We're all scattered like the wind. Oweneen gone. Séamus in jail. Nobody left up there now. Would you believe they let the auld rip out of the asylum to polish the convent floors now and then? I almost fell over her. There she was looking up at me so polite it would split your gizzard to hear her with her "Isn't it a nice day, Father?" and "How are you today, Father?" She'll never get a word out of me. The nuns like her. "She's a great worker," they say. The nurses send her over when they think she's up to a good day's work. Little do they know. It won't be long before she's back there. For good. What happened to Thady? He went to his brother in Westmeath whose wife just died. They had no children. I heard Thady sold his land for what he could get for it. No flies on that Thady. Do you know who bought it? No?

The worst thing that's ever been done was to go up and take Muiris down and charge him with the vile act that you did. I bet that woman was behind it. She never liked Muiris. His goodness was a reproach to her. Of course the child went to his sister-in-law in Cahirciveen and she must be delighted with that. Why on earth you would charge Muiris I don't know. He came down without a word. I suppose he never thought there was enough madness in the world to believe that terrible lie. Those friends of Jamesy swore to it, did they? It's a sad day when anyone would believe them. He was the only one left and they had to charge someone I suppose. Didn't they know that would only make it worse? It'll be in the papers like it was forty years ago. I swear to you before God that Muiris is without sin. Only a sinner would think otherwise. There was a sheep following him around? You're making me laugh. What happened to all the livestock? Rounded up and kept for the next fair day and sold at bad prices I expect. And how will you get the money to the men that it's owed to? Or does that ever cross your mind? The lawyers are doing it? I bet they are.

What happens to Muiris when the trial is over and he's found innocent as a baby? With that accusation hanging around his neck for the rest of his life? How can he go up there and start all over again, without another soul around, his friends gone and his livestock in strangers' hands? Did anyone go up and try to tend what had been sowed? Of course not. It just became a place for grazing. And what of my church with the Blessed Sacrament in it? Yes, I know, I know, Fr. Staunton went up and brought down the tabernacle and chalice. That church is empty now that was a source of grace and consolation for more generations than we can number. It was built just after Emancipation. Well it's another time that's in it, and we can't blame the English this time, can we?

Did I see the Bishop? So you know about that too? Yes, he sent word for me to come see him, and it was another burning day like the one almost a year ago. This time Fr. Staunton drove me. He's been very decent, I'll say that for him. He drove me up the avenue and asked me if I'd like him to come in with me. I said I'd rather go by myself. I waited in the parlour in which not a thing had budged since I was there before. And same as before, the brave Fr. Darcy came in and did the dirty work. I was not to say Mass and the church, my church would be deconsecrated. "What terrible thing have I done?" I said. "It's only for a short time until everything is cleared up," said he. "And what is to be cleared up?" said I. At that moment the Bishop swept in as if the door had been specially made for his entrance. I kissed his ring and he said, I'll tell you the very words he said: "It's a sad moment for us all, Father, and when things are better, come here and see us again." Then he was out the door. It was all so quick I didn't know what was happening to me. Fr. Staunton drove me back to the convent but I was so distracted I just kept going over what had happened trying to make some sense out of it. He left me at the front door of the convent. "You should come over for dinner some night, Father," he said, and left me looking after his car.

I walked back down the avenue because I didn't want to go in yet. My thoughts were whirling. From the end of the avenue, you can see the mountain and the dark spot where the purple rocks mark the village. A strange thing came over me. It was as if my eye was a telescope, and I could see close as my hand every cottage and house, including my own, and I could see my lost church clear as if it were a toy I held in my hand. All in my mind's eye, you understand. I had a rush of feeling that choked me, and I haven't cried like that since I was a child. It was the shouts of the children coming out of the convent school that brought me back, and there was Oweneen's red-head Bridget, and Séamus's young lad, a big, strapping boy, and Thady's puny little fellow with the big eyes that will follow Thady up to Westmeath when school is over, all of them racing to the playground around the side. I didn't tell you that the Mother Superior said it would be better if I didn't play with the children. What are people coming to at all? As if some terrible shame is attached to me. I don't know the half of what went on behind my back. That's the end of it. And no beginning to come out of it. But like my Lord and Savior, I will bear the cross He fashioned for me and offer up my suffering, and all the suffering of my village, to Him, from whom nothing is hidden.

WILLIAM MAGINN

I read all of this in a room overlooking the Liffey in the Ormond Hotel in Dublin, a fleabag if ever there was one. It's mentioned in *Ulysses*, but that didn't make the sheets any cleaner. There's a good bar downstairs though. I read most of the good Father's account in bed, because that was the only way to stay warm in that room, apart from the bottle of Powers Gold Label I had with me. I started reading on the train and finished in my room at three in the morning.

Afterwards, sitting up high in the bed close to the window, I could see the street lights on the far bank scribbling on the river. I looked at them for a long time because I couldn't sleep, and they kept my eyes busy while my thoughts wandered. Stories of decline and fall leave you with contrary feelings. The events are a closed book with no revisions possible, but your emotions become entangled with the characters as if you could urge a different ending on them. There wasn't one of them that wasn't familiar to me. What's to be avoided—in my view, anyway—are those quasi-philosophical meditations on human nature and its fallibility that give the facts a distant, comforting glow. Things were harsh enough in Fr. McGreevy's story without giving them a lick of that mythological polish. Nothing was surprising to me, and to my mind there wasn't much evil to be found in the whole recitation. No more than Dr. McKenna did I find the seduction of the lamb troubling. I've heard of much worse. People take what they can where they find it. Some older brothers of myself and my friends relieved their budding lusts in the eager suckle of young calves. Nothing wrong with that either, except maybe the calves were short-changed.

There's always conflict between any two villages or towns a few miles apart, especially if one of them is from the mountains. I remember the football matches in the field behind our house when I was a kid. If the teams from two villages didn't end up fighting, it was a bit of a disappointment. The only peaceful event was when Fossett's Circus came around and set up their tent. Gypsy-looking women would come to our back door to have their buckets filled with water. After the circus picked up and left, us kids would play on the circle the tent left behind on the grass, rehearsing all we'd seen in our own minds. There were times when we were as idle as the young lads Fr. McGreevy had a set on. It could just as well have been us throwing those stones. Of course such a magnanimous understanding of everyone in the story offered me a touch of smugness that I had to smile at. It's easy to exercise your better instincts from a distance when you're not involved. Which was part of the reason I went off searching for Fr. McGreevy, to see how things had settled in his mind. There were a few questions I wanted to ask him. As I already mentioned, he had departed for what I'm sure he was convinced was a better place.

I came back and stayed in the Ormond again, not because of its luxurious appointments, but because I'd taken a shine to the girl behind the registration desk. She wasn't there that evening, of course. Serves me right. I telephoned long distance to Dr. McKenna at his home; he wanted to know when I was coming back. You'd think he was my bosom buddy. I wanted to confirm the whereabouts of the two people who most fascinated me, and one of them was no more than a mile from the hotel as the crow flies.

"Still there?" I said.

"Still there," he said, "unless I'm very much mistaken. Once in there, they don't come out as a rule."

I telephoned for an appointment. I was at Grangegorman Mental Hospital as requested at half-past ten the next morning.

OLD BIDDY

I met with Old Biddy in a large, underfurnished recreation room where patients drifted aimlessly, or sat curled up, sometimes facing the wall. There were rockings back and forth, mutterings, and occasional cries and fits of words. Two attendants in white trousers and white short-sleeved jackets talked to each other and stirred occasionally when drawn by a particularly furious shout or gesture. The older one had suede shoes. The room—a corner room—had five windows barred from the outside. Through the windows were views of stone walls and other windows, sometimes obscured by black branches and olive-colored leaves.

Old Biddy was brought in by a young woman with a maid's cap and a white uniform, wearing a green cardigan. Her ankles were thick and she had no bosom or waist, but these may have been suppressed by her uniform. Her complexion was fresh and flawless. She turned out to be from Limerick, sustaining the myth of perfect skin attached to the young women of that city.

Old Biddy, who chewed constantly on, as far as I could see, an empty mouth, negotiated her way into an armchair with worn arms and rents in the seat through which stuffing showed. I sat off a little to one side on a ring-topped wooden chair with a woven rush seat. The young woman—a cross between a nurse and a maid—stood beside Biddy during our interview, her hand on the back of the armchair as if posing for a photographer. During the course of the interview, Biddy farted loudly several times, surrounding us with an aroma of stale cabbages. Each time she did so, the fresh face of the maid/nurse was suffused with a rosy glow. On the front of Biddy's smock or uniform (pale blue from much washing and of a type worn by young girls in boarding schools) were some breadcrumbs, which survived the changing ridges and valleys of her bodice as she shifted in the chair. She wore shoes with eyeholes but no laces, the tongues sticking up in front of her ankles, which were wider than her calves. Above the shoes, worsted lisle stockings—brown in color—had gathered into a concertina of wrinkles. Her shins showed the brown-ringed ABC pattern, the result of close exposure to a lifetime of turf fires.

Several times during our interview she showed a lively interest in her own secretions, inspecting what she managed to retrieve from her ear with the little finger of her left hand, and from her nose with the forefinger of the same. She occasionally dislocated a bit of food from between her teeth, chewing it, or spitting it out from the tip of her tongue, like a smoker an errant flake of tobacco, accompanied by a brisk "th-IP" sound.

"That was a hard time you had up the mountain," I said. She said nothing, but looked at me out of the side of her eye, chewing steadily on her gums. "I hear you were a great cook," I said. No response. "Does anyone come to see you?" I asked her.

"Why would anyone want to see me?" she said.

"Do you get outside at all?" I asked her.

"Outside, inside, it's all the same to me," she said.

"Do you ever hear from Fr. McGreevy?" I said.

"Will you have a bit of sense? How can he visit me when he's dead?" she said.

"Whatever happened to that boy you were so fond of?" I said.

"A right randy fellow he was," she said. "He'd split you in two. Like a wild horse he was."

"I mean the child on the mountain. Young Éamonn, Muiris' son."

"Éamonn an Chnoic. He had more than one," she said.

"You laid out the other one, I hear," I said.

"There's many a one I laid out. Close their eyes. Wash them down, lock their jaw, stuff their arse, and cross their hands."

"This was the one that burned up," I said.

"We'll all burn up if we're not careful," she said. "You'll burn up yourself and let that be a lesson to you."

"Did Fr. McGreevy ever come visit you?"

"Why would he, the little priesteen?" she said. "He's dead now and no great loss. So he's too busy to come see an old woman with nothing in the world to her name."

I'd seen Fr. McGreevy's grave in the graveyard at Portumna in County Galway. I found his death certificate in the local register of births and deaths. Cancer of the stomach. His last years—and there were not too many of those—had been spent as chaplain to the convent in Portumna. He was sixty-four. He had not survived the end of his village by more than two years.

"If he was alive, he'd want to know things were all right with you."

"He was better than some and no worse than most," she said.

"Do you remember that night when everything went up in flames?" I said.

"In flames," she said. "What's your name?"

"Maginn," I said, "William Maginn."

"William Maginn had no britches to wear, he went to the tailor to make him a pair."

"There was a great blaze up there after those cold winters," I said.

"Cold winters," she said. "Do you have a drop for me?"

I was ready for that. I took a Baby Power out of my pocket. Her eyes glommed on to it like a pair of magnets.

"She's not supposed to get any spirits," said the nurse.

"A little drop won't do her any harm," I told her.

"I'll lose my job," she said. "If she has a drop, there'll be no controlling her."

"If you bring me a little cup, there won't be any sign of it," I said. "And a fine girl like you with a good heart wouldn't deny it to her."

"You don't know what she's like," said the nurse.

"Well maybe just one sip, then," I said. "I'll watch her while you get a cup."

"If they smell it on her, they'll blame me," she said.

"They won't smell it," I said.

Biddy's eyes never left the little bottle. The nurse went off for the cup.

"Biddy," I said, holding the bottle where she could feast her eyes on it, "what happened the night of the fire?"

"There was never a fire," she said. "And what they call a fire here wouldn't warm a sparrow."

"That's not what Fr. McGreevy says," I said.

"He never knew anything," she said. "The sky could fall and he wouldn't know it. I turned his wine into water and he never knew it." She began to laugh silently.

"Do you mean the altar wine?" I said.

"What else?" she said. "Do you think there was a pub up there? There was nothing up there. He had a lot of wind, both ends. I could hear him farting through the door at night."

"But he was a good man," I said.

"Better than some and no worse than most," she said again, "but he hadn't much sense."

"What do you mean?" I said.

The girl came back with a Delft cup. I poured half the little bottle into it. Biddy held the cup in both hands and drank it in one gulp. She smacked her lips several times and looked at the bottle. I gave her the rest. She swallowed and chewed at the aftertaste. I had another Baby Power in my other pocket.

"You can go now," she said. "And when you come back bring back another of them." There was a pause while she scraped at a scab on the back of her hand. Then she turned and looked at me directly. "Who sent you?" she said.

"There's nobody sent me, only myself."

"That's a likely story," she said, "but one story is as good as another if the same teller tells it."

"I heard you have a great store of stories," I said, "and that no one told them better."

"Muiris told them as well as I did," she said. "The young lads from Dublin used to talk to him more than to me. But I could have told them things they never heard if they'd treated me right. But who notices a poor old woman?"

"I'm sure you've forgotten them all," I said.

"What I forget and what I remember is none of your business," she said.

"That's true," I said, "but I doubt if there's a story left in you."

"I have stories upon stories," she said. "But there's a place and a time for them and this is not the place."

"There's always time for a story," I said, "for them that can remember one."

"Do you think I'm a fool," she said, "trying to milk a story out of me like you'd milk an old cow?" She turned her head away from me. "Why don't you get yourself back to England where you came from and leave us all in peace."

"If you send me on my way with a story, I'll do what you say."

"What do you do over there, apart from bothering people?" she said.

"I have a magazine I put out," I said.

"A magazine for what?"

"For stories and things, and poetry and the rest."

"What kind of stories?" she said.

"Stories are stories wherever they're told," I said, "and the way you can tell it's a good story is if someone reads it or listens to it."

"If that's your job," she said, "you tell me a story and don't be bothering me. You've no need of stories from what you tell me."

"There's a great pleasure in a good story," I said, "and there was a time when you had the biggest store in the county."

"They're all in my head," she said, "and they're still in there the same as they were when I learned them. But the electric mixed them up."

"Who did you learn them from?" I said.

"You learn them from anyone who has a story," she said. "Other storytellers would come round and they'd have the whole house under their feet. But before a story can be told things must be right."

"What's the best story you have?" I said.

"They're all the best of stories," she said.

"How do you choose which one you're going to tell?" I said.

"It depends," she said.

"Depends on what?" I said. "The weather or the moon or the time of night?"

"Don't make a mockery of me," she said. "There's too many in here that make a mockery of themselves. There's a lot of changelings in here. I'm with a strange bunch surely. Half of them have had their spirits stolen. They must have annoyed the little people. I still see them do things that show they've no sense."

"What things?" I said.

361

"There are so many doors, there's bad luck all over the place," she said. "There's danger everywhere for those that pay no heed."

"She's always talking like that," said the nurse. "She's full of those superstitions. She had terrible cramps in her legs and nothing would do her but to turn her shoes upside down under the bed before she lay down on it. It stopped the cramps! Or so she said."

"That Father!" said Biddy, "he had no sense at all. I'd be churning milk and he'd lean forward and light his pipe from the fire. Muiris had too much sense to do that. Muiris was a good man. He never let Máire Rua out on May Day. She stayed in the house like she should that day."

"Why is that?" I said.

"It's bad luck if a red-headed woman crosses your threshold on the first of May. Everyone knows that. That Father never knew anything. He was always thwarting me. I remember one May Day years ago, Séamus Mór's wife came around for some butter, more fool she, she must have forgotten what day it was, and the bold Father of course said, 'Give it to her, give it to her,' and when I told her what day it was she laughed and went away. I brought her the butter next day. If you ask me, the Father himself was the cause of all our troubles. He had no sense at all of what annoyed them."

Biddy then went on to cite various transgressions that bring bad luck and annoy "the little people"—spirits that must be placated or they will exact vengeance.

"What happened to my story?" I said.

"Since the electric, I can't find half my stories," she said.

"Was that the treatment they brought her up for?" I asked the nurse.

"It might well be," she said, nodding, and went over to a windowsill to sit down. Biddy sat with her eyes closed, her chin on her chest. Down the long room five bare bulbs in the ceiling threw weak pools of light on the floor. It was darker outside. Most of the inmates had blankets over their shoulders and crouched and stirred as if there was no posture that answered their needs. A few walked slowly up and down, dragging their feet, occasionally gaining a tonsure of light when they passed under the naked bulbs. The smell of bodies, Lysol, Jaye's fluid, and a hint of a perfume that attempted to cover it had grown heavier. I turned back to Biddy. She was sitting straight up, her eyes still closed, her chin in the air. Her hands were clasped quietly in front of her. She looked so different I thought something was wrong. She took a big breath that lifted her shoulders. She let it out, put her chin on her chest, raised her head again and began to speak. I hardly recognised her voice. It was strong, almost youthful, and she spoke in Irish. When I closed my eyes, it seemed as if there was a young girl speaking. What she said could be translated roughly this way:

"When a lad that lived in a giant's castle got to be a young man, he began to think of getting a wife, but he didn't know where. He met a *fear-beag-ribeach-rua*. I expect it was a fairy. The *fear-beag-ribeach-rua* said to him, 'What are you looking for?' 'A wife.'

"'There's a Queen that's under a spell in the East world. It's very hard to get to but I'll give you three messengers. Call on these and they'll help you along. A hawk, a hound, and a horse. All you have to say is *Chuige chuige seabhac* and the hawk will appear. *Chuige chuige cú* and the hound will appear, and *chuige chuige capall* and the horse will appear.'

"The boy called on the horse and they went off. They were now at the end of the land and the beginning of the sea. What do you think he did? The castle was on the land beyond the water. He called *chuige chuige sea-*

bhac and the hawk took him on his back and left him at the castle. Around the castle there were so many soldiers. He called *chuige chuige cú* and the hound set at the soldiers. He went into the castle and found the queen sitting there under a spell. 'Get up and come with me,' he said.

The hawk took them both on his back and carried them to their own land. The spell then left her. The *fear-beag-ribeach-rua* said to marry her at once. The wedding lasted a year and a day. I was at it, and I wearing nothing only but stockings of thin milk and paper shoes."

The young voice ended. Her breath seemed to leave her, and she visibly shrank into the familiar old woman, scratching her hair and gobbling with her empty gums until her chin almost met her nose. The nurse on the windowsill was looking down at the middle fingernail of one hand cleaning the nails of the other.

"Why the stockings of milk and paper shoes?"

"It's the way you end a story," she said.

"That's a fine story," I said, hiding my disappointment. "And I'm sure you have a wealth of them."

"That I do," she said, "but they're all mixed up in my head since the electric. I can't remember half of them."

"Well," I said, "there was a story to end all stories up in the mountain with Muiris and Fr. McGreevy and young Éamonn and the rest—Séamus and Oweneen and Thady and the rest."

"Don't forget Tadhg," she said, "and it wasn't a story."

"Well, it's a story now," I said.

"I hear my mother calling," she said. "I've got to go in."

"You're in already," I said.

"I know you," she said. "Your mother was a tinker."

"She's getting tired," said the nurse, coming over. "It's best to leave her now."

"You're a tinker's son as everyone knows," said Biddy.

"I'll get Fr. McGreevy for you now," I said.

"Keep him away from me," she said. "He was the ruination of me."

"What happened at the wake, Biddy?" I said. "Who started the fire, Biddy?" I said. No answer. "Why did you cut open the ram, Biddy?"

"Peter Murray is a fine-looking man," she said, "and I caught my mother casting eyes at him at Mass last Sunday."

"Watch out, Mister," said the nurse, "she's close to making trouble."

"What trouble can she make," I said, "the poor old woman?"

"When I'd go to the outhouse," said Biddy, speaking up unexpectedly, "he'd have pissed all over the place like he was watering flowers."

"Who?" I said.

"Fr. McGreevy," she said. "He must have had a squint in his eye when he passed through the pisshouse door."

"What about the ram, Biddy?" I said. "Why did you cut him open?"

"There was a devil in that ram and we had to let it out," she said.

"What gave you that idea?" I said.

"I knew from the way he looked at me," she said. "There was evil in his eye, and his guts spoke the answer. I knew that ram had a secret. Muiris killed his son from shame."

"How do you know that?" I said.

"It was in the ram's guts," she said. "I laid them out on the floor. There's no blame to Muiris. He's a fine man. But who could tell what Tadhg would become when he was just a thought slithering around in his father's bollocks? Better he'd never been born. Eat your soup or I'll pour it down your neck."

"Don't worry," I said. "I'm drinking it now."

"Himself and the sheep," she said. "He had a bull's balls and a cock as thick as your arm."

"Did you ever see him with the sheep?" I said.

"Sure every one of them was with the sheep. They're men, aren't they? It's their nature. All balls and no brains."

"Did you ever see it?" I said.

"I've been up the pole and down the pole," she said. "Up and down, in and out like a fiddler's elbow. You're a pale poor imitation of a man."

"Watch out," said the nurse again, "or she'll start."

"Fr. McGreevy knew it," said Biddy, "as sure as I'm sitting here. That's why he was hard on me. He knew I knew what the ram's guts told me. Poor Muiris. They'd have hung him like a dog. I wouldn't tell them if they tore me limb from limb. Where are my shoes?"

"She'll go on for hours like this once she gets started," said the nurse. "We have to give her an injection to quiet her down."

"Who took my shoes?" said Biddy.

"You're wearing them," said the nurse. "There's no

good talking to her," she said to me. "She only hears what she wants to hear."

"Who gave me these two left shoes?" said Biddy. She had pulled her skirt back from her feet and was regarding them closely.

"God bless us, she's right," said the nurse. "How did that happen? I'll get you your shoes," she said to Biddy. Biddy leaned back with great satisfaction.

"What did you say your name was, Sonny?"

"Maginn," I said, "William Maginn."

"Fancy that. And what did they put you in here for?"

"I'm visiting you," I said. "And I'm going to see Muiris."

"They hanged him for killing his son," she said.

"Well, I'm going to see him anyway," I said.

"That's good," said Biddy.

"There were two hard winters you had up there," I said.

"Colder than a wart on a witch's tit," she said, "but it'll be colder in the grave."

"They say you're a witch, Biddy," I said.

"Every woman's a witch," she said.

"Why is that?"

"Because every woman wants to ride a man's broom-

stick. When is the middle of something also its beginning and end?" she said.

"That I don't know."

The nurse came back with the shoes, two right shoes
and a normal pair. Biddy put them on the ground and
began to exchange shoes with much muttering. She
ran through several permutations until she got two to
match to her satisfaction. She turned and looked at me.

"I've had my fill of this fellow," she said to the nurse.
"Who is he? He has a face on him like a pig's arse."

"Hush now, Mrs. McGurk," said the nurse. At the
"Mrs. McGurk," it struck me that Biddy must have
mislaid a husband somewhere in her past. But she was
one of those old women with no past, who seem to have
been born exactly in the form which she now pre-
sented.

"Where is your husband, Biddy?" I asked her.

At this, Biddy, who had shown such calm and toler-
ance during our interview, let out a great screech. She
half rose from the chair, held onto an arm, and shook
her fist at me. The force of her drove me back a step.

"You fuckingfucking whitearsed shite-hawk. Don't
be asking me for answers you wouldn't like to hear
with your fat *bolg* [belly] and *boidín* [small penis] that
wouldn't stretch as far as my little finger. Coming

in with your smart ideas to disturb a decent woman minding her own business, you shite-eater, you're not fit to wipe my arse. So get your lily-white bum out of here, this place is not for the likes of you with your smiling and soothing. You have us all distracted. I'd prefer be in here than be out there with the likes of you and your notions. Yiz is all the same, all of yiz. Put a bit of drink in yiz and you'll all be wanting the same thing. Little maneen with your hoity-toity. I'll suck the lot of yiz, that's what I'll do. I'll suck every last one of yiz, suck yiz all. It's all yer good for. I wish I had a tooth in my head and I'd make yer lights and liver jump out of your chest. Fucking fancy fuckin man. Bloody feckin fuckin. May the devil meet you on your way out, for he'll be wanting your black heart. Jaysus fucking Christ, yerself and yer fucking sheep. If a sheep cocked its arse at you all you'd do is look at it. There's a power of waste in making a little fellow like you, with a nose like a sow's tit. May the Lord prevent me from ever seeing sight nor light of you from this day forward—"

"I think you'd better leave her alone now," said the nurse.

MUIRIS

I had no great desire to go back down to Kerry again, but the thought of the old man put away in another asylum wouldn't let me alone. I wasn't sure he'd want to see me or have any of the past dug up. But of all the characters I'd read about, he was the one who most aroused my curiosity. It was now fifteen years after the collapse of the village. He would be well into his seventies. He was down there, completely innocent of the way he was occupying my thoughts, and unaware that I was—I finally decided to go—on my way to see him.

.   .   .

"He's a great gentleman," said the sister, an ample, cherubic woman. "He never gives a bit of trouble. If we had more like him we wouldn't have a job at all. He works a lot in the garden. He's there now. I'll show you the way."

We went around the corner of the red brick wing. Red brick indeed. The building stretched itself across the top of a hill. Approaching on the road you could see it riding along with you for a long moment before it was snatched back. These palaces of the insane are on hilltops all over Ireland. Visitors always ask, "What's the big red brick building on top of the hill?" More often than not it's the insane asylum.

When we turned the corner, we saw several men working in the garden tending peas, cabbages, and turnips. The garden stretched out too, with sticks holding up the peas, and an arbour here and there over a path. It must once have been a flower garden. "We get most of our produce from the garden," the sister said. "The only time we have to go down to the market for vegetables is in winter." I stopped and she stopped with me.

"Do you know anything of what brought him here?" I asked her.

"Of course I do," she said. "Everyone does."

"And do you believe it?"

"Of course not!" she said. "That man wouldn't hurt a fly. He's a strong man with a great good nature. It's

MUIRIS

criminal what happened to him. But the town had to have its pound of flesh."

"I'm surprised to hear you say so," I said.

"Doesn't everybody know the truth?" she said. "It's that they won't admit it."

"Does he speak of it at all?" I asked her.

"Why should he?" she said. "It's all in the past now."

The weak sun didn't warm the air. It was still too early in the morning for it to gather strength.

"I have a cousin who lives over in that town," she said, "and even she felt the town was disgraced. Even though she admitted to me that Muiris was as innocent as a baby."

"Do the other inmates know what brought him here?" I asked her.

"Some of them," she said, "the ones that have some sense left. But most of them are in their own world. We do have some that land here for no reason at all, other than that their families wanted to get rid of them. The world is not a kind place a lot of the time. When some of them get old, the children start fighting about who will get the land. And the old father doesn't want to give it up. There's been a case or two of that."

There were five or six men working in a desultory

way. "He's over there," she said, gesturing towards two a space apart from the others. I recognised Muiris immediately, even though I'd never seen a photograph of him. He was tall with a fine craggy face, wearing that hat the good Father had described, with the brim turned down. The other man was bareheaded. As Muiris turned his face towards us, I could sense the quality in him.

"Does his boy ever come and visit him?" I asked.

"He was here a few times with his aunt when he was about fourteen," said the sister. "Quite the little man he was, with his collar and tie. That aunt of his kept him in close tow. She didn't leave him alone with Muiris for a minute. The boy must be about twenty now. He's studying for the priesthood. The Jesuits."

"Does he ever get out at all to visit—"

"The rules don't allow it," she said. "Sometimes we take a few of them out in a bus for a ride. But they're not welcome at the hotel restaurant down below. One poor fellow made a fuss once, and he spoiled it for the rest. That's the way it is, I'm afraid."

"Is there any way of getting him out and back where he belongs?"

"And where would he go?" she answered. "Back up to

that mountain? How could he make a living up there, even if he were young enough? Anyway there's not a soul up there now."

The man with Muiris stopped work, turned his back to us and wiped his forehead with his sleeve. Muiris gave me a long look and then went back to digging with a spade. The other man got down on his hunkers, thinning turnips, it looked like.

"So what brought you here?" she said. "It's a rare visitor he has. Once a red-headed fellow came who had eyes all round his head. He was no sooner here than he was gone again."

"Why am I here?" I answered her. "I got interested when a friend of mine started telling the story at a pub in London. He was from Listowel and he heard about it when he went back to see his family. He hadn't been back for ten years. When he was telling it some of the English people at the pub started off on the Irish in general."

"Sure they'd believe anything about us, the poor things," said the sister.

"After I read the Father's story, I got curious," I said. "I went to see his housekeeper in Grangegorman. And then I thought I'd come down here and see Muiris myself if I could. Muiris seemed like a good man who got little justice. I thought maybe I could write something about it. Why did they send him here?"

"It's what they do whenever a case like this comes up once in a blue moon. Rather than send them to jail. They persuade the solicitor to plead insanity. It's better than jail. And everyone saves face."

"Except Muiris," I said, "here for the rest of his life."

"Maybe, maybe not," she said. "There may be a way out of it. I'm sure we could get a doctor to certify a 'cure,' whatever that is. But it's the same question as before. Where would he go?"

"He could go to his sister in Cahirciveen," I said.

"Oh, that one!" she said. "She's his sister-in-law and he has no time for her at all. When she was here with young Éamonn, they never exchanged a word. The three of them sat like dummies."

"How does he pass the time?" I asked her.

"He wasn't here always, you know. He was transferred from the criminal asylum after a year. I'm told it was hard on him when he came. He'd sit for hours doing nothing with his head down. They couldn't get him to wear the uniform. Some of the male attendants made jokes you can imagine. But the nurses were fond of him from the start. He got a little bit of money from his land, so he can afford a few things now and then. He even makes a little money doing odd jobs. It's outside the rules of course. But when you have a man here that's as sane as you or I, it's a shame to treat him like the rest of them. He even minds some of the others for us now and then. Things got better for him after I came. I saw at once what he was. He's no more guilty of what they charged him with than I am. I got the whole story, and it's ashamed they should be, these people. But I think he's happy enough."

"Do you think he'll talk to me?"

"I told him you were coming. It depends on who comes. Three or four years ago, the word got out that he had a bushel of stories and the folklore people came around, a man called Delgany, or something like that. He came several times and he spent hours with him in the parlour with this big tape recorder. They spoke Irish. I don't have a word of it myself."

"Does he have any friends here?" I asked her.

"He keeps away from most of the others, except for that fellow you see with him over there. He's harmless, like a child and he does whatever Muiris asks him. I think Muiris is fond of him. He tries to teach him things. Muiris has an understanding of these poor people that surprises me. You'd think he'd known people like that all his life."

"He had a son who was defective," I said.

"I knew that," she said. "What happened to him?"

"He was killed in an accident up the mountain. It's a sad story."

"Indeed," she said, "there are sad stories everywhere you turn. Even the one son he has left. If you ask me, I think the aunt has turned him against Muiris. She told me she was going to make a priest out of him, and I'm told she has. He's good with the books. Well, I'm keeping you from him. He knows he has a visitor. I told him yesterday. He's seen us talking. Why don't you go over and introduce yourself without me in the way? I'm overdue at the chapel as it is."

I walked over to Muiris. He turned his fine head to me as I approached. He was over six feet tall, hardly bent, and the face was surprisingly unlined for a man who must be over seventy.

"Mr. O'Sullivan," I said, holding out my hand, "I've been looking forward to meeting you." His reaction made me step back. He covered his face with both his hands.

"No No No, leave me alone! Leave me alone!" he

shouted, crouching down and rocking back and forth. The other man bent over him.

"It's all right. It's all right," he said. "He means you no harm. Do you see that spade over there?" he said to his companion. "I want you to get it for me."

He turned to me. "Are you looking for Muiris O'Sullivan?"

"I am," I said.

"Well, you're looking at him," he said.

"I beg your pardon," I said. "I'm sorry I upset your friend." The other man brought the spade over to Muiris.

"He'll be all right," he said. "He doesn't like being surprised. Now what is it you want?"

He was looking at me very directly and an answer was needed. He made no concession to my confusion. "I wanted to talk to you," I said. His eyes were shrewd and unforgiving.

"That I know," he said. "What's on your mind?" The other man was looking up at me with eyes so vacant I couldn't understand how I had made such a mistake. Muiris took off the man's hat and patted the bare head at knee level.

"I thought maybe we could talk somewhere," I said.

"Well here we are and this is as good a place as any,"

was the way he answered me. I thought of telling him I was collecting stories. He had two faded blue eyes deep set on either side of a prominent aquiline nose. There was a white stubble on his chin and cheeks. Two large wrinkles ran from his nostrils to bracket his mouth which was full-lipped though the lips were the same color as the face. Two large ears were laid back against his head. He had most of his hair and it was brushed carelessly across a high narrow forehead. "What is it you want?" he said again.

The other man got up and backed away from us. Muiris looked after him, nodding reassuringly. He put the hat on his own head, and saw me look at it. "He likes to wear my hat sometimes," he said. We looked at each other. He wasn't going to help me.

"I was looking for Fr. McGreevy," I said, "but he died a few years ago." Muiris said nothing. "I looked up Mrs. McGurk in Dublin," I said.

"Did you now," he said. I remembered how she was convinced that Muiris had killed his own son.

"She has a great fondness for you," I said. He took a spade that was standing in the clay and took it out and stuck it in again. The other man came over and stuck another spade in beside it.

"Good man," said Muiris. The man backed away again, looking at me with those empty eyes. We both looked after him for a moment, then Muiris turned to me again. "If you're after what I think you're after, you can take your leave this minute."

"I've come over from London," I said.

"I don't care if you've come from Timbuktu," he said.

That sister had more to her than met the eye. No wonder she hadn't come with me. She knew what kind of greeting I'd get.

"Mr. O'Sullivan," I said, "I think you were done a great injustice."

"Do you now," he said. "And what is it you do?"

"I'm a writer," I said.

"I thought as much," he said.

"Could we go somewhere else?" I said. He lifted the spade and dug it into the soil without an answer. Gradually he fell into the rhythm of working. I stood there embarrassed. I turned and looked out over the top of the hedge at the trees. He stopped working and engaged in a complicated movement—one hand cupped the top of the spade, it was then inserted under the opposite armpit as the free arm crossed itself on the other, tilting the body out of balance, as one leg crossed the other below the knee, toe on the ground, a long triangle of space between spade and flank, through which I saw the hands and back of the other man, crouched, weeding. Muiris looked over at the trees.

"There's not much point in you detaining yourself here," he said.

"Well, it's on my own time anyway," I said. "But maybe it's a wrong time to talk. Maybe I could come back again."

"Do as you please," he said. That was our first meeting.

·   ·   ·

When I came upon him the next day, he was talking to the same sister in the entrance hall. He had his hat in his hand and they were laughing. When they both saw me, she came towards me with a smile as he started to walk away.

"Muiris," she said after him, "wouldn't it be a nice thing for you to talk to this poor man that's come to see you again? I have a feeling he'll be here every day until you talk to him. What harm is there in exchanging a word with him?"

Muiris turned and looked at us. I could see his wavering reflection in the polished floor. It looked as if he were standing on water.

"Come on now, Muiris," she said with a smile at me. "If he annoys you, I'll pack him off in double-quick time back to where he came from."

Muiris looked for a moment, then slapped his hat against his thigh and came over slowly without looking at me.

"I'll put you both in the parlour," she said, opening a door. "I'll go and get a cup of tea. Would you like a cup of tea, Mr. Maginn?" she said.

"Well, I suppose it wouldn't do any harm, Sister," I said.

"It's too early for anything stronger," she said.

Muiris and I were left sitting on opposite sides of the polished table. He seemed as comfortable as I was not.

"To tell you the truth," I said, "I don't know what it is I wanted at all."

"Well if you don't—" said Muiris.

We looked at everything but each other. "I read Fr. McGreevy's version of what happened," I said, "It was a terrible time for all of you. It's hard to outlive your own village and to meet with so little understanding." He chucked his head up and down in a dismissive nod. A small red-haired maid brought in the tea-tray, with an elegant teapot, a big jug of milk, and a silver bowl of fine sugar. Muiris saw me looking at her red hair.

"It's a good thing it's not May Day," I said. That got the first rise out of him.

"Or that you're not going to sea," he said. He knew then that I knew about the superstitions surrounding a red-haired woman. If a fisherman sees a red-haired woman on May Day, he should not go to sea.

The sister came bustling in, her hands tucked up the opposite sleeves. "When you've had your tea," she said, "why don't you take a little walk? It's a beautiful day outside."

We walked along a leafy path between two rows of old trees. There were pin-cushions of green moss at the side of the walk and on the roots of the trees, which dipped under and came up like snakes before disappearing again. There was a warm, rather pleasant fetid smell.

"When I was a young lad in Wicklow," I said, "you could hardly stir but there was a superstition to match it. We moved there from Kerry when I was sixteen."

Muiris picked up a branch and poked at whatever took his attention on the path before us, turning over a stone or a cluster of leaves and scribbling them around before he moved on. I waited for him each time.

"I don't know where they come from," he said, "but there must be a reason for them, even when they make no sense. I'm fond of the pipe to this day. If there was butter in the churn, Old Biddy wouldn't let any of us light a pipe from the fire. And she'd scold me if I lit my pipe in the house on May Day—'*Loscadh do chroí ort, a ghadaí na gcaorach.*' You know what that means?"

"I'm not sure," I said.

"It means 'May you have heartburn, you sheep-stealer!'"

He picked up my quick glance at him right away. I'd thought the last word out of his mouth would be about sheep. He stopped and turned over a piece of rotten wood. There was a scattering of wood-lice underneath. Even though it was part of what I wanted to talk to him about, I was embarrassed and changed the subject.

"Do you know the one about the black cat's ear?" I said.

"For curing *tine dhia*? Indeed I do. The cat must have no white spots at all. Rub the blood on the rash. And if there's enough to write the sick person's name, so much the better."

"I think they call it erysipelas," I said.

"There's no shortage of black cats in these matters," he said.

"Old Biddy must have had you all driven to distraction that first winter when you had all those tragedies," I said. He looked at me, then walked on, swiping a bush with his stick. "I remember there was a notion that a dead body couldn't be cried over until it had been washed and laid out."

"I've heard some believe that," he said. "It only makes sense. And if you don't do it, I never heard of a punishment attached to it."

"Did you ever hear that the touch of a dead man's hand would make you invisible?" I said.

"There were times when I could have used that," he said. He didn't smile, so I didn't know whether to laugh or not. We came to a high wall of the kind you see around a Big House. These high walls were often built with famine labor. The path ended in lush untrodden grass. There were nettles and brambles at the foot of the wall. He went over and inspected a blackberry bush, holding the small unripe berry between his first and second fingers. We turned around and headed back. The path we had come was speckled with sunlight. I didn't know what to say next.

We walked on in silence. He stopped and looked up at the ceiling of branches. I felt he was going to say something and he did.

"The one thing I'll never understand is why the women had to die. That was the beginning of all our troubles." He walked on and muttered something in Irish that lay in my ear before my mind made sense of it. It was "no one can ever explain that to me."

"Fr. McGreevy had no explanation of it either," I said.

"If my woman of the house had lived," he said in Irish, "none of this would have happened." We spoke Irish from then until we got back.

"There was a village in India where it happened fifty years ago," I said. "It was in the British Medical Journal. A friend of mine found it for me. The women died and the men got sick but they recovered."

"Did they find the cause of it?" he said.

"That they didn't," I said. "That's why they reported it."

"I don't know what we did wrong that it demanded that the women be sacrificed," he said, "but our punishment went way beyond whatever it might be."

"You were all treated cruelly, surely," I said.

"You'd think we had annoyed the *sí*,"[34] he said.

---

34. The *sí* go back to the island's pagan past. In the country, the "veil" between this world and the world of spirits is tissue thin. When it tears, the two worlds overlap and the spirits become visible. They frequent the

The ceiling of branches thickened and darkened the path. I shivered and smiled, thinking of the roar of traffic outside my office in London.

"You can't argue with the past," said Muiris. "It takes its own way at every turn."

"Most of us go back and think of how it might have gone another way," I said.

"There's no profit in that," he said. "Everyone has a great supply of ifs and buts. What's done is done."

"Maybe if that stone hadn't been thrown at your young lad long ago, you'd all be still up there on the mountain," I said. He looked at me and walked on

---

pre-historic circular earthworks, called *raths*, and one must be careful not to annoy them. Farmers who have ploughed a *rath* in their field have come to a bad end. The *sí* are small, elegant spirits, often travel in hosts, are immaculately dressed, shining with light, speedy as quicksilver, arbitrary in their rules, sometimes generous, always touchy, and dangerous to cross. An example: A woman coming home with a full jug of milk stumbles and falls near a *rath*. She manages not to spill a drop. She sickens and dies. If she had spilled some of the milk, she would have survived. The *sí* didn't like that she hadn't spilled the milk. But who could know that? Spirits with such powers require a prudent study of their etiquette, for unknowing transgressions are harshly dealt with. In the degenerate precincts of popular myth, the *sí* survive as fairies and leprechauns, fodder for Irish gift-shops displaying little thatched cottages, clay *dudeens* [pipes], and *shilelaghs* [blackthorn sticks]. They have the same attitude to us as we do to our beasts—seeing us as slow, uncomprehending, incapable of understanding the transgressions we unconsciously offer. Occasionally they covet an earthly child.

ahead. I caught up with him when he paused to turn over a cluster of wet leaves with his stick.

"They'll be waiting for me inside," he said in English and walked on briskly.

The sister was waiting for us in the parlour. "There's a bit of a chill out there if you've been walking in the woods," she said. There were two glasses and a bottle of Locke's on a tray on the table. "Maybe you need a nip to warm yourselves up." She smiled her smile and left. Muiris and I waited. Eventually he reached out and poured from the bottle with a courtesy as if this was his own house.

"*Sláinte go deo,*" he said.

"*Go n-éiri an t-ádh leat,*" I said. We sipped and drank companionably enough. I didn't know how to break the silence.

What did I want from Muiris? That's what the silence brought to my mind. The answer was—simply to meet him. Was there any mystery he had to reveal? It was clear to me there was not. I had met him and taken his texture, not as well, I'm sure, as he had mine.

"I wanted to meet you," I said, "and I'm glad I did." He nodded his head. "There's nothing I want from you," I said, "but you were a man I wanted to know."

"Is it in London you are?" he said.

391

"Yes," I said.

"And are you going to write about this?" he said.

"No," I said. He nodded again.

"That lawyer I had at the trial—if that's what it was—his mother was an Englishwoman."

"Is that so now?" I said.

"He was an educated man. Maybe that's why he went into all that business about man and the animals in Egypt and Greece," he said.

"The judge stopped things immediately after that," I said.

"And well he did," said Muiris. "If that fellow had kept on he'd have had me in jail still."

"It's a shame you're here at all," I said.

"Maybe it's not a bad thing," he answered me. "I've a roof over my head."

"But you shouldn't be here at all," I said.

"Where would I be if I wasn't here?" he said. I didn't say "With your son and your sister-in-law."

I visited him every day for the rest of the week I was there. I'd come around three o'clock and the sister would have the same tray on the table. We had plenty to talk about. We lowered the bottle to a half-inch at the bottom, and with a mutual courtesy left it there. He

told me a few Fianna stories that I'd heard before, but
he told them well. We talked about the Irish poets,
Ó Rathaille and Ferriter. He was a great admirer of
Ferriter. One day we talked about the *aisling* form,
in which the poet falls asleep and sees the visionary
woman who personifies Ireland. The poets used her to
encode information that their audience could decipher
but which to the English was merely a harmless piece
of versifying. Her message was the one all oppressed
people want to hear: help is coming. The fantasy of salvation through French intervention became a powerful
consolation. We talked about how the poets' description of the woman is always chaste.

"There's only one poem where her bosom is frankly
described." He closed his eyes and quoted, *"A dhá cíoch
ghléigeal mar an sneachta ar fhaill"* [Her two shining
breasts like snow on a height]. "I forget which poem it
is," he said. "They all had the same message—you are
the children of an ancient race, you have suffered, op-
pression will not last forever, help is coming. *How* they
said it is what made the difference. That's where the poetry is," he said.

"She always spoke to the sons about the blood they
could shed for her," I said.

"That she did," he said. "But there wasn't much else to do in those times. Then when she lost her sons, she turned into an old woman."

"An old hag," I said. "But she still had the same message—'The French Are on the Way, said the *Sean-Bhean Bhocht!*' [the destitute old woman]."

"The *Cailleach Bhéara* [the Hag of Beare]," he said.

"Of course to see the Beautiful Lady you had to fall asleep," I said.

"Did you notice," he said, "that they always fell asleep out of doors somewhere, as if they didn't have a place to rest their heads?"

"Always some bank of grass or other where they lay down for a bit of comfort," I said.

"They never had a place of their own, it's true," he said. "It's a nice class of verse," he said, "and often it turned into a competition to see who could do best with the description of the lady." We laughed.

When I came back the next day the tray was on a different part of the table. The bottle was half-full again.

"Well, you're off today," he said.

"I'll get the train up to Dublin and take the boat from Dún Laoghaire for Hollyhead, then the night train to London."

"That's a long journey you'll have," he said.

I wasn't leaving for another two days, but there was no point in telling him what was in my mind. He seemed in a good mood. We always spoke Irish.

"Did you dream of a beautiful woman last night?" he said.

"Not last night," I said. "And yourself?"

"I had a dream all right," he said, "and it's the strangest dream I ever had. It had to do with our conversation yesterday." I said nothing, which I thought was the best way of getting it out of him. "I think that dream was the end of something," he said.

"Is that a good thing?" I said.

"It might well be," he said, "and it shaped itself into words even as I was dreaming it."

"Did you write it down?" I said.

"Of course not!" he said. "It's a poor story-teller that can't remember a story. When I woke up in the pitch dark I didn't know what to make of it."

If I said the wrong thing I knew I'd never hear it. It was amazing that he would even mention one of his dreams to me. He must have mellowed a lot since he'd left the mountain.

"Sometimes I wonder if our dreams belong to us at all," I said.

"I think this one belonged to me," he said.

I had to find a word that would give him the excuse to tell me. I couldn't find it.

Leaning back in his chair, one arm resting on the table, he looked out the window with his thoughts far away. "You know the whole story as much as anyone does," he said. "We'll see what you make of this. That's if you want to hear it."

"I'd take it as a compliment if you would share it with me," I said.

He smiled and shook his head, raised his hand from the table and leaned his forehead into it, covering his eyes. He spoke in a low even voice, every word was clear, and there was a slight intonation as if he were reciting a poem. I translate it with the minimum of interference, for in translating from the Irish, there are dozens of clichés in the English language lying around and eager for employment.

"I had fallen asleep in my room and had a dream in which I found myself on a grassy bank by a river under a flowering tree and fell asleep again. In this second sleep I was visited by a vision. She fixed her eyes on mine, with a meaning that tantalised me, for those large eyes, unblinking and steady, asked me a question I could not fathom. I was eager to respond with an answer that would remove the yearning from her eyes, for yearning it was, or as close to it as I could understand.

"Her long white lashes were perfectly arrayed top and bottom, each row turned to a slight curl at the end. Her forehead was noble and broad and around her head her curls were tightly coiled, evenly dispersed, neither wiry nor too soft. Each separate curl seemed to emit its own radiance. Her dark lips were somewhat hidden but enough was visible to convey an impression of gravity and calm. Her nostrils were perfectly shaped and curled neatly above her lip. Her ears were firm and alert, and seemed to ask a question that matched her gaze. Her breast was rich and full, the golden curls thick and springy. She spoke no word, but as she began to withdraw from me, her eyes were infused with a great sadness.

"Before she vanished, she removed her gaze and re-leased in me a storm of emotions. She paused once, her golden fleece rippling with light, and looked back at me. She continued to withdraw until she was lost in a golden haze, as if her spirit had become an emanation which contained all our sufferings and all our hopes for redemption. My heart was destroyed with memories. I knew she wanted me to right the wrongs, to free her and her kind from the calumny of those who saw her and her flock as degraded creatures. When I awoke a trace of the golden glow lingered in the room until the walls became visible and advanced on me so swiftly I thought I was in a prison, I wept for her and for myself. And then I seemed to awaken again in this place. I lay awake and thought of our conversation of yesterday. It wasn't long until a great peace descended on me."

After his voice stopped, I didn't know where to look or what to say. I was touched that he'd trusted me this much, for we never spoke of the mountain. That was the price of his friendship, for friendship it was. Now he had given me something that brought the priest's story back as vividly to me as if I had been there myself. My thoughts were racing, confused between cynicism and awe. For some reason I felt devious and unhappy with myself. He had lost his village, his family, his freedom, his world, and a vision had come to him as it had come to the poets. I had learned enough from him to say what my first thought was.

"I don't know whether to laugh or to cry."

"I felt that way myself at the time," he said.

"There was no word of the French bringing help," I said.

"No there wasn't," he said.

"Do you think she might have been sent in some way to ease the memory of the hardship?"

"Maybe," he said, "but I knew who she was."

"And who might that be?" I said.

"It was the little lamb grown up."

"Your son's lamb?" I said.

"That's what came to me," he said, "and that's the way it settles." I thought of Fr. McGreevy's story of the daft boy stopping the Mass with his *Lamb of God, Lamb of God*. There was a long silence.

"What happened to that lamb?" I said.

"They took it and killed it and examined it," he said.

What came out of my mouth surprised me. "An innocent lamb?" I said. The shadow of what had happened on the mountain was falling across the room. But Muiris spoke of brightness.

"I never saw a light like that in the world, a gold light like you might see sometimes at evening, but much, much brighter. It spread everywhere like the fleece was giving out light."

"Well, now," I said, "you're as good as any of the poets!"

"And better!" he said with a smile. I smiled back and for a second it entered my head that he had made it all up for my benefit. I'd played a few tricks like that myself. As he continued to look at me with his small shrewd eyes, we seemed to step sideways out of ourselves and look back at the two of us sitting at the table talking of a sheep *aisling*. The laughter came out of us at exactly the same time.

The door flew open and the sister looked in, with the smile of someone too late for a joke.

"What are you two laughing at?" she said.

"Nothing, Sister," we both said in English. "Nothing at all."

EPILOGUE

I climbed the mountain that Fr. McGreevy had so often climbed, up past the boggy wetland and the purple rocks. The paths—once you left the side road —were overgrown with brambles, rushes, blackberry bushes, and nettles with white spots on them. How a man as old as our Father was able to go up and down the mountain like a goat was a mystery, especially when I started to sweat half-way up and I only half his age. I refused the view until I got to the hump on this side of the graveyard and the village. It was a clear, breezy day, with a chill when the sun went behind a cloud, of which there were a few piling up in baroque curves. The town below with its two spires was sharp with details that twitched as the wind plucked curtains of air across it, or the twitch may have been in my inconstant stare. Beyond the town, the land, scooped as if by a great tilted spoon, spilled out to the strand and the sea with its uneven fingernail of white foam at the shore where the low cliffs didn't hide it. The wind as always was coming around the shoulders of the mountains to the right, stacking themselves in a row to the end of the peninsula. Occasional gusts blurred my eyes, but the smell of fresh air with a bit of salt in it was the kind of elixir I'd often dreamed about when stuck in my office in London.

I turned, climbed over the ridge. The graveyard looked as if it had been abandoned for a hundred years; tilted headstones pointed to the same heaven. I stumbled over a nest of broken glass around waxy artificial flowers. I searched for Máire Rua's grave, and found it after I pulled away handfuls of grass obscuring her name. There was a sprinkling of white pebbles hidden in the grass. Looking up from the graveyard across a little stream, the houses and cottages hunkered down, haphazard, like animals grazing, thatches gaping here and there like old fur. Nothing is sadder than abandoned thatch. I went into the second cabin up, and the stillness was like a sepulchre. You couldn't see much in the faint light coming through the tiny windows in the thick wall. Whose cottage it was I had no idea. I could tell Fr. McGreevy's house easily enough. It was larger

than the others with a slate roof that was fairly intact.
About twenty yards up the hill from it was a burned-
out hulk, its roofless walls half-tumbled and uneven.
I stood in the doorway looking at the charred inner
walls. I had that strange feeling you have in a doorway
that divides the outside from an inside that is abandoned and open to the sky. Weeds and nettles up to my
waist flourished inside as if it were a hothouse. I walked
against the wind up to the largest building, with a slate
roof and a narrow gothic window in the gable. The
altar looked like a heavy piece of abandoned luggage.
There were a few benches, one overturned. I stepped
on a piece of wet paper and spread it with the help of my
other foot: "—a mortal sin not to hear Mass on Sunday
or holiday of obligation if the omission—"

There are people who can feel the atmosphere of a
place, and we all like to think we can. The burned-out
cottage and the church should have been alive with
presences, but not a whisper came through to me, even
as I imagined what had transpired. Outside again, perhaps because a cloud had covered the sun, the village
looked darker and more desolate, though the sun was
still shining higher up on the mountain. The dead village, with its lost memories, reached back to similar
desolations, to depopulated townships and failed lives

that at such moments seem to fill a reservoir of national regret, a resentment that only remembers itself and the oppressions that bind the island to its past.

When I reached the ridge of the graveyard again, islands of shadow paced themselves across the fields below. Where the rim of the sea disappeared under the cliffs, tiny explosions of white occasionally bloomed and faded. The sunlight came back on a gradient as the cloud passed. Leaning against the rising wind, watching the racing shadows below, I had a notion the whole island was getting under way, forging out into the hazy pastures of the Atlantic, into the past, bearing its cargo of deserted villages and broken hopes, its hatreds and lost chances, its graves of heroes and traitors. Down past the town, the eye sought out the missing horizon where sea and sky melted into a seamless sphere, then tilted up beyond the puffs of clouds to the Mary-blue heavens. Above, a lark was bellowing, its song falling like fragments of toy ladders, lifting itself higher on jets of air, pausing and rising buoyantly to a height where its song did not reach me, and its dot was lost in the spots and floaters within my eye as I gazed at the void.

404

ACKNOWLEDGMENTS

I am much indebted to Dorothy Walker, who offered several useful geographical and sacerdotal suggestions; to Caoimhín Mac Giolla Léith, who polished to a fine finish the Irish language beaten into me at Loughlinstown National School; to Anthony Cronin, for retrieving the names of BBC announcers during World War II; to Christopher Cahill, who published a part of this novel in his magazine, The Recorder. *Thomas Kinsella's* An Dúnaire: Poems of the Dispossessed *has been indispensable. I am indebted to Ruth Greenstein for her close reading of the manuscript. I am deeply indebted to my agent, Maia Gregory, who had a passion for this novel. My debt to Barbara Novak, because of its magnitude, will always remain unpaid in full.*

ABOUT THE AUTHOR

*Brian O'Doherty is well known in the world of
visual arts, about which he has written extensively.
He lives in New York with his wife, Barbara Novak.*